Rebecca

Back to the Beginning

Volume 5

A novel by

Stephen M Davis

Author Stephen M Davis was born in East London in 1957.

He was educated at Woodbridge High School, Woodford, Essex and St John Cass Royal School of Art, East London. He started writing seriously in 2009 after retiring from Royal Mail.

First Published 2022

Typeset Stephen M Davis

Cover Design Stephen M Davis

Published by DMS Literary Publications

Author's website stephenmdavis.co.uk

Setting – modern-day – 1827 – and beyond

For 41-year-old Rebecca, life was running in a positive, straightforward direction. She had two beautiful daughters and a wonderful marriage.

Ever since the first time she entered the summerhouse, climbed the old spiral staircase, and ended up back in 1853, she had learned to accept the mysterious directions her life could and would follow. Now though, life was stable, and importantly there were no impending twists afoot. In fact, she felt she'd fulfilled her life's destiny.

So, when she entered the secret garden, hoping to see Meredith one last time, she wasn't expecting any new twists or a change of direction.

Nothing she'd experienced in the past could have prepared her for what was about to happen. Her heart, mind, and spirit were about to face their biggest test yet. Every belief she held close was about to cascade into chaos, including where she truly belonged.

Inexplicably, she will find herself at the centre of the British Suffrage movement in 1827, forty years prior to this group making headway in Parliament.

This though is just the first step on a path that will lead her to a mystical, world within a world.

ALTHOUGH THIS IS THE 5TH VOLUME IN A SERIES, IT CAN BE READ AS A STAND-ALONE NOVEL

Contents

Introduction

So, in the previous novels, I offered a synopsis of what went before. As you are here on volume 5, I am guessing you've read 1 to 4. Therefore, rather than fill the pages with stuff you already know, how about we get straight to it?

As a side note, I'm often asked if all the events are purely fiction. This question is difficult to answer simply. When writing Rebecca's story, I have learned to listen to an inner voice buried somewhere in my subconscious. Often, I think we are going left, but invariably we end up going right. Remember, Rebecca first came to me via a dream, a dream that was so clear it was as if I'd just watched a film.

The thing is, as her story has progressed, her voice has gotten louder. Odd, I know. Spare a thought for a 60-odd-year-old guy writing from the perspective of a young woman. Make no mistake, I believe, somehow, I am telling Rebecca's story, which is a surreal emotion. It has been suggested in a very positive way, the emotive thoughts, reactions, and indeed dialogue reflect the voice of a young woman.

Interestingly, one of the very few negative reviews I received for Volume 1 suggested it was as if the book had been written by a 16-year-old girl. Hmm, pretty amazing if you ask me when you consider I was 59 at the time.

So, getting back to the fiction or fact aspect. Here's an example. I'd just completed what I believed to be a completely fictional chapter about a made-up Queen Matilda. Something in my subconscious suggested I looked up the period around 1123 on the internet. I wanted to know about that era in history and so on. Lo and behold, there she was, Matilda, Queen of England, in the year 1123. How can that be, I asked myself several times? It is bizarre how this happens and as yet, I don't have a rational explanation, but then who needs rationality with

Rebecca. I should add that this has happened with many of the events throughout all volumes. You see, I allow Rebecca to lead me. I really thought we were done and dusted after volume 3. Think again. She gets twitchy and shouts, loud. So, here we are heading down another crazy road.

Finally, and hopefully shedding some light, how would I describe the proceedings in these books? Historical events that have been fictionalised with an artistic licence. I should say, some stories are completely fictional, well I think they are, maybe I haven't researched them enough, yet.

Chapter 1 - Awakening

Rebecca woke from a dream like no other dream she'd ever experienced. To compound her dumbfounded emotions, she truly felt she'd lived every second of the most surreal sequence of events. She laid there for a few moments and with her eyes closed, tried to recall the details. For some reason though, even though it had seemed so tangible and real, the more she thought about the events, the further away they drifted. Opening her eyes and feeling quite odd, she was a tad surprised to see the room in total darkness. Wondering if it was the middle of the night, she scrabbled around for her phone to check the time. As she stretched her hand out for the bedside table, she nearly fell out of bed. Bizarrely, the table was missing. Now questioning what was going on, she eased her legs out of bed and lowered her feet to the floor. As her feet settled on an ice-cold, hard floor, shivers of curiosity run amok with her already jumbled thoughts.

It wasn't the cold floor that caused the shiver, it was the missing carpet, the one that was fitted only two weeks before. Climbing out of bed, she felt as if she wasn't in her room, which caused the oddest emotion. Now at a complete loss what to think, she lifted her feet back up on the bed and tried to regain some rational thinking.

Getting out of bed and making her way towards the window, she tripped on a hard object that really shouldn't be in the middle of her bedroom. She bent down, rubbed her toe, and continued towards the window. Well, as if her emotions weren't scrambled enough already, the window wasn't where it should be.

With her hand leaning against a hard, odd feeling wall, she stood there for a moment and as she did, the strange dream reared its head again in her thoughts. She shook her head, and felt along the wall, trying to locate the curtains. *This room is too big*, she thought. Now things were getting silly and again, she wondered where she was and what was going on. Once more, trying to get her bearings, she turned and as she did, felt a heavy material rub against her arm. Somewhere in the depth of her subconscious, and unlike the strange feeling wall covering, this material most definitely felt familiar. She pursed her lips and reached out. The instant her hand touched the material a distant and weirdly familiar memory nudged at her thoughts.

Gripping the heavy velvet-like material, she pulled it back allowing a little light in. Turning, she instantly knew she was in her bedroom in her parent's house, instead of the summerhouse, where she'd gone to bed the night before. As she pulled the curtain open a little more, she could see it was her old room for sure. Unusually though, it smelt peculiar. It wasn't a bad smell, just unfamiliar. To scramble her emotions, the bed was not only different, it was in the wrong place, and her dresser was missing. The only thing she recognised was the old full-length mirror that was there when they moved in. The thing was, she was adamant she'd gone to bed in the summerhouse and this was messing with her thoughts and emotions.

Aside from the curtains, the mirror was the only recognisable, tangible thing in the room. She touched the edge of it, trying to give herself a little reassurance, and as she did, caught site of herself in the mirror. In a flash, every detail of her dream thudded into her consciousness. Looking at her reflection in the mirror and seeing herself as a 15-year-old girl, she recalled every word Meredith had said to her. Her memory was now so clear, it was as if she'd spoken to Meredith only moments earlier. She sat on the bed and went through Meredith's words over and again.

"Fear not, my beautiful Daughter. Your journey in that other life is now complete. You are home where you belong.

You are once more fifteen and your journey is about to follow a new set of adventures. It is time for you to truly follow your destiny and fill your heart with all the love you deserve."

She stood up and glanced at herself in the mirror, still shocked to see herself once more as a fifteen-year-old girl. She then looked out of the window wondering what may lay ahead. Seeing the old summerhouse down by the lake created the strangest emotions, but mysteriously, she felt calm. She stood closer to the window and stared out as memories of Duncan playing with Gabrielle and Faith down by the lake flowed through her thoughts. In an odd way, part of her was sad, but once more any feelings of detachment were missing. Yeah, that memory was of her beloved husband and dear daughters, but Meredith's words were now once more telling her she had seen that life through the eyes of another. Considering Etienne and how she'd felt so unemotional after returning home, even though she'd spent thirty years with him and had two children offered her tangible comfort. Sad as it would be to most onlookers, she knew in her heart that Gab and Faith were not her girls even though it had felt that way when she was with them. Although this thought should have cascaded tears of emotion through her consciousness, there was nothing, other than a fond memory.

Just as she was considering her inexplicably detached feelings, she heard Meredith's voice.

'Rebecca dear-heart, are you awake? I heard your movement.'

She turned from the window to see Meredith standing in the doorway. The instant she heard and saw Meredith speak, she realised how her heart should feel. She just knew this was her real mother. It was an odd indefinable feeling that was just there. Over the years, she often heard people speak of their unconditional love. Just being near this woman, in this environment, Rebecca now understood that emotion. 'Hello, Mother,' she said, but as she did, felt a strange feeling deep in her subconsciousness. It wasn't anything she could put her finger on, just a weird sentiment.

'Goodness me, the emotion on your face tells so many stories. I suspect you have realised what is happening, where you are and how this all came to be.'

'When I first woke, I was lost in the remnants of a dream, or so it felt. I now realise that dream was reality. I've stumbled through a thousand thoughts and emotions since waking.' She glanced in the mirror and smiled. 'Here I am, back where I belong.' She then chuckled, but this was just hiding that strange feeling in the depths of her mind. 'Unless you have another surprise awaiting me. Actually, I know I am home. I can just feel it through every sense in my body. My heart, my conscious and unconscious emotion and thoughts tell me I am home.' Just these few words caused a reflective memory of how she'd felt every time she'd been with Meredith. 'You know, that day all those years ago when you stood up to Millicent, I knew then you were reacting the way a mother would do.'

Meredith held her hand up, smiled the way she always does, and said, 'That incident my dear was just five days ago. Since we have moved back into the manor house and Millicent in return has taken up residence in the servant's quarters. All thanks to you and your timely intervention, I should add. I knew you were my girl and would love to have told you. I knew though that you had many missions ahead of you. Although this has taken many years in your time, for me, it has been a brief moment.'

Rebecca took in every word Meredith said but was unable to focus on anything other than Millicent. Briefly, she tried to get a grip of the way Meredith was speaking to her, almost as if she was trying to convince her, rather than comfort her. Quickly though, her focus went back to Millicent. 'Servant's quarters, do you mean the summer house down by the lake?'

Grinning, she nodded. 'Yes, the summer house.'

Suddenly alarm bells started reverberating in Rebecca's head as she recalled the approaching shooting accident. 'Meredith, I must tell you of an impending incident involving Millicent.'

Narrow eyed, Meredith held her palm up in a delightfully familiar way. 'Come down for some morning refreshment and tell me of your incident.'

On the way downstairs, Rebecca considered what she should say. She knew whatever she said was likely to change history forever. She'd come across this before and had always worried what might happen in the future if she did change anything, even slightly. Fortunately, in all incidents, the fallout was positive. This though meant saving an unsavoury character and who knows what may happen. That was if she could save Millicent, after all the woman must have been at rock bottom to even consider suicide.

As she entered the kitchen, everything was just as it should be, just as she remembered it, peculiarly though, not as she recalled it from her time with Elizabeth in 2007. This weird sensation made her feel really quite odd and a little disordered. Extraordinarily, where Elizabeth's clock was, was instead an ornate barometer. The thing was, she knew this barometer well, but for the life of her, couldn't remember what Elizabeth's clock looked like. She blew out through her pursed lips, and as she did, Meredith placed a glass of milk on the table in front of her.

'Now, tell me of your incident, Darling-Heart. Then we must arrange some suitable day clothing for you. We cannot have you sitting around all day in your bed ware, however, befuddled you are. All at sea, your eyes floating with a glazed expression. To be expected, no doubt.' She then touched Rebecca gently on the arm.

This caused an outpouring of suppressed emotions. Teary-eyed, Rebecca stood and turned to Meredith with open arms. There were no words, none were needed. Mysteriously, the

12

peculiar sentiments she'd had rumbling around had now dissipated. The thing though was why she'd had this sudden change of emotions, however distant they were. Had she consciously dispelled that remote, distant thought, or was it Meredith's considered approach that had comforted her to the point where her inner thoughts had cast them aside? *Hmm*, she thought, *tis what it is.*

Meredith appeared to look into Rebecca's heart, held her arms out and cuddled her. She whispered, 'I have missed you even though you have been away for but a brief moment. For you, it has been years. Take every breath, and know you are home now.'

'Thank you, Meredith, I mean Mother.'

Chapter 2 – Millicent

With her sentiments settled a little, Rebecca sat at the kitchen table. Surreal like, distant feelings and emotions towards Elizabeth, James, Tommy, Duncan and the two girls were becoming increasingly faded. Although this should have upset her, the absence of any emotions once more helped compose her disposition. She looked at Meredith and inside, she knew she was where she belonged. The odd thing that was now rumbling through her thoughts was how she could feel so distant from Elizabeth, the person she'd called mother for so long. If her inner subconscious could override her conscious feelings that easily, what else could they do.

'You appear less at sea. I suggest you take your time, step gently, and share your thoughts. Much awaits you, for now, feel my love.'

These last few words again made her recall the way this woman had defended her. Although in her previous life, it was 25-years ago, for some strange reason her recollections were fresh. 'Mother, how long ago was I here when we had the dispute with Millicent?'

Narrow eyed, Meredith, clearly thinking, said, 'well, in all you have been gone five days from my life, this life, our life. Although, you returned two days ago as the future girl. It was then we had our little chapter with Millicent.'

Two days, Rebecca thought, trying to recall when Millicent took her life. As much as she racked her brain, she realised she didn't actually have a date for her death, only her funeral. *Enough speculating*, she thought. 'Earlier, you mentioned Millicent now lives in the summerhouse. Have you seen her recently?'

Unusually narrow-eyed, Meredith held her hand up in a questioning manner. 'You keep referring to Millicent with an anxious tone.'

'Well, Millicent is in danger and I need to know if you have seen her recently.'

Appearing a little surprised, Meredith shook her head. 'The last time I saw her was the day she left the main house, which was two days since. It was soon after you returned to the future. I must say, Madam, your use of words, tone and candour has changed. I suspect this is because of your time in the future. Either way, it is of no importance.' She then seemed to consider her own words. 'The time you have been gone is merely a few days. I suspect for you, it has been considerably longer, hence your change in style. How long do you believe you were gone?'

'I was forty-one years old, had two daughters, and a delightful husband.' She shook her head. 'I will tell you on the way to the summerhouse. We need to check on Millicent. I know we had our fractious moments, but she is in danger.' *Right, I need to tell her*, she thought. 'I discovered in my future life that Millicent took her own life. Initially, you were blamed for her murder. It was only because I found a suicide note and was able to bring it back to your time that resulted in your name being cleared.'

'Oh, crumbs, that is not what I expected at all. Let us hurry. An ill-fated doomed wench, she is, however...'

As Rebecca got up to head outside, she suddenly realised she still had on a white lace nightdress. Although in her time with Elizabeth this may have been ok to be seen in nightwear, in this era, well. Just as she was about to speak, Meredith pointed to the corner.

'More suitable clothing, Madam. Not what you are used to, but hey, this is now and that was then. Your shoes are by the front door.'

15

When Rebecca slipped off her nightie, she was a little shocked to see she was also wearing underwear from this time. 'How did I get changed,' she mumbled.

Grinning, Meredith said, 'as with all your journeys, you return to your own time in the same clothing you left in.'

Rebecca immediately thought, *all your journeys*, but she had to focus and reckoned she had an eternity to have her questions answered. Standing by the front door, she beckoned Meredith. 'Come along, time is not on our side.' This brought a wry grin to her face, knowing time actually was on her side. This settled her a little, but at the same time stimulated the most unsavoury thought. *What if Millicent is dead already, do I try to find a way back to save her, or do I accept this sad demise was her destiny.* Without realising, Meredith had passed her and was now outside beckoning her.

'Come along, Missy. You appear adrift once more. Deep in thought, I suspect.'

'I was considering Millicent's fate and if we should intervene.'

'I understand your conundrum. As always, you will find an answer, and it will be the right answer. As always, follow your intuition.'

Rebecca could see from Meredith's expression she was also feeling uncomfortable. On the way towards the summerhouse, few words were spoken. Following a well-trodden path, everything seemed so very familiar. She drifted off into her thoughts, considering her mood. It was as if she'd never been away, and she wasn't sure if this was because she'd travelled here so many times from the future, or because it was her true home. Without realising, she was standing behind Meredith at the front door to the summerhouse.

Meredith banged on the door a couple of times to no avail. 'Most odd, no answer.' She then produced a very familiar key from a small bag and unlocked the front door.

'I know that key. It opened the summerhouse for me the very first day my journey started.' Then recalling Meredith's earlier comment, she thought, *was that the first time I journeyed through time?* 'Obviously not,' she uttered.

With pursed lips and narrow-eyed, Meredith said, 'your journey started long before that day, my lovely.' She then opened the door and called, 'Millicent, are you there?' There was no response. She then turned and beckoned Rebecca inside.

Bizarrely, for Rebecca, the inside of the summerhouse appeared different to how she remembered it from her previous visits. Beyond the door at the end of the hallway was a kitchen, instead of the spiral staircase. Mysteriously though, it was as if she had two memories because this layout was both recognisable and unrecognisable. It caused a weird unbalanced emotion. She considered her thoughts momentarily, then turned to Meredith. 'I must say, Meredith, this is going to take a lot of getting used to. It is as if I have two memories, one from the future and one from my life with you. It is all rather unsettling.'

'In time, I suspect your memories of the future will fade.' She then called for Millicent again, and still, there was no answer. After searching top to bottom, she turned to Rebecca. 'Either we are too late, or she is outside.'

'Before we look outside, I need to check something. You see, Millicent left a suicide note in the bureau in this room,' she said, pointing.

'I know of no bureau.'

'The tall cabinet,' she said entering the room. Wide-eyed, she stood just staring at a small table in the corner where the bureau was. 'This is most strange. In nineteen-eleven, I found a suicide note written by Millicent and it was in a bureau. You may know it as a tallboy affair, and it was in this corner,' she said, again pointing.

Narrow eyed, Meredith said, 'I am a little confused. You mentioned this note earlier and I questioned its validity. You should understand that Millicent is unschooled. Barring scribbling her name, she has few words at her disposal.'

Rebecca stood with her mouth open, unsure what to say.

'You seem all at sea once more. Share your thoughts.'

'The suicide letter from Millicent ultimately saved you from being charged with her murder. So, who wrote the letter and when was it hidden in the bureau, a bureau that apparently doesn't exist?' Now with her thoughts going in circles, she tried to focus. 'We need to act quickly, because if we don't and we cannot prove she took her own life, who knows what might happen.' She thought for a moment. 'Let's check outside.' She knew only too well that if Millicent was found shot and there was no suicide note, Meredith would be charged with her murder once more. Even though she was focused, she couldn't see how this would pan out favourably. For a brief moment, she wondered if George had perhaps written the note to save Meredith. Then put a bureau in this room, with the hope the note would be found. That though didn't make sense, because he would have found a way to point someone in that direction. The fact that she found it in nineteen-eleven just didn't stack up with that notion. 'So what?' she uttered.

Meredith looked at her quizzically, so Rebecca briefly explained her thought process and the idea that George wrote the note.

'That, sadly, does not hold water.'

'I agree. Not only do we have the missing cabinet, bureau or whatever you call it, but we also have a suicide note written by an illiterate individual. Even if George wrote it to defend you, it would have still been found, or there would be no point in him writing it.' She pursed her lips, 'unless there is something else, or someone else involved.'

'By that you mean?'

18

'Well, just guessing here, maybe there was a third party. A disgruntled lover of Millicent, perhaps. I'm clutching at straws, but I have no other answer, for now at least.'

'Even if there was a third party, how does that explain the suicide note? Why would they write it and hide it in a tallboy that doesn't exist? The only rational explanation is Millicent did write the note and hid it in a tallboy in the main house. That tallboy was then moved to the summerhouse.'

A little taken aback by this new information, she asked, 'Is there a tallboy…'

'Before she could finish, Meredith nodded. 'In the library.'

Library, she thought and shook her head not knowing of a library. 'Are you sure Milicent cannot write?'

Meredith shook her head ever so slightly. 'According to George.' She then narrowed her eyes in an unfamiliar questioning way.

'Well, that is the only reasonable explanation, other than…' She then stopped dead in her tracks.

'Other than?' Meredith exclaimed with her palm raised in a deliberately questioning manner.

Rebecca thought for a moment about how to relay an idea that kept rearing its head in her thoughts. 'So, go with me for a moment. Suppose, just suppose George and Millicent had a falling out because he'd banished her to the summerhouse. She then pulled a gun on him and in the ensuing scuffle, she was shot. As a result, George tried to conceal what had happened by writing the note.' She narrowed her eyes a little. 'So why then didn't he point the police to the note when they came for you. Or, just tell the truth in the first place.' Once more her thoughts started going in circles, moving from one idea to the next. She realised she was referring to events that hadn't happened yet and this might be too confusing for Meredith. 'So, what if George, in a dark moment murdered Millicent?

Then covered his own tracks with the note. I must stress, I am talking of future events, something that may never occur if we can prevent it ever happening.'

'Why though, would he not draw their attention to that note when the police came for me?' Meredith said, clearly showing she was aware they were talking about something that may never occur.

Just then, an emotional bomb went off in Rebecca's head. 'Okay, supposing he wrote the note, hid it, then in his anguish took his own life. That is how the note remained hidden for years. Because it is in your future and I never came back after our meeting, not to this time, neither of us would know if he did take his own life.' Just saying this nudged at her memory. 'Hang on a moment, I did travel back in eighteen-fifty-six, and then also two years later. It was for your daughter's proposed wedding, then her actual wedding. It was my sister, I guess. Either way, I do not recall George being there.'

Meredith shook her head. 'You do not have a sister.'

That hit Rebecca like a clap of thunder, realising the girl getting married must have been her, hence why she couldn't be seen by anyone other than Meredith. 'I am guessing, even though you know of my time travel, you have no knowledge of future events.'

'Well, your assumption is correct. You see, it is my future and as yet, a story untold. The future you saw and lived in, could and will change. It is the same for my potential future. For example, if your thoughts of George's possible suicide are right, we could still change his path. Everyone's destiny is a proposed direction, but not fixed.'

Considering Meredith's words, Rebecca narrowed her eyes a little and thought deeply. Relating this to her own journey, she looked up and nodded. 'During my journeys both into the past and future, I have often faced delicate scenarios whereby my actions could potentially affect the equilibrium of time. I recall one incident when I had to take a medicine back to the twelfth century to save an individual's life. A medicine that would not be discovered for another seven hundred years. In the end, I decided I had no choice and as it turned out, the medicine worked and importantly, went unnoticed.' She then paused to think briefly. 'Since then, I have always followed my intuition, which has served me well so far. The thing is, we could end up saving either Millicent and or George and that could change everything for everyone. Yours and my future could and will most likely take a completely different route. George and Millicent's future will obviously be, well, they'd both be alive. That's if George commits suicide, which we don't yet know. Everything could go in a negative or positive direction. This is something we need to consider carefully, although I can't see there is a right or wrong answer. One thing for sure is we cannot act with sentiment. It must be a pragmatic decision.'

'It is a future not yet told. You are in this world, like others who lived previously and shared your calling, with one purpose, to protect and interject, if need be. Ultimately, to maintain a balanced path for us all.' Unusually, Meredith then hesitated for a moment. 'Consider this, perhaps all you witnessed with Millicent's sad demise was no more than time taking an alternate path. From the future, you observed a path that ended with her suicide, perhaps George's death and ultimately, me being imprisoned. Maybe, just maybe, you have seen this all and changed the outcome with an element of positivity, whereby you saved me from imprisonment. This then subsequently allowed you to continue your own quest in the future without hurdles from the past.' She then nodded with an assured positivity. 'Now you are back in your own world, you have seen a possible route with both a negative and positive conclusion. I would suggest, if the door opens for you to stop Millicent's demise, then it is meant to be so.'

'That makes complete sense, and maybe this is why I always feel confident following my gut,' she said and nodded several times.

21

'So, here is a thought for you to consider. Just perhaps Millicent's suicide was an alternate existence and only came about because you were living in the future. The subsequent suicide note was written by one of your kind travelling from the future. Put in place to iron out any time wrinkles and thus allowing you to continue your quest. This would suggest you are meant to save Millicent.'

'That is a practical notion and makes a lot of sense to an otherwise complex scenario. Throughout the years I spent in the future, I witnessed many events that were cursorily affected by people that are not from my time. I was aware their interactions were to keep my path smooth.' Rebecca then considered her own words for a moment. 'So, if as you suggest someone from the future wrote the note that would be completely logical. You see, you were always there for me whenever I stumbled, almost like a guardian angel. Had you been imprisoned you may not have been there for me. The thing is, especially in the early days, I needed to know you were there if I tripped or stumbled. It gave me the confidence to go forward without fear. So, in essence, the suicide note was a temporary fix. Now I am back here where I belong, I can stop Millicent's death. For me now, this is no longer a conundrum, it is a must.'

Meredith nodded and taking Rebecca's hand, said, 'we must go outside and find Millicent. Because, if your notion is even remotely true, we need to re-set the hands of time and keep an even keel. Let us go out and look now.'

They headed outside, calling as they went. The further they walked without a response, the louder they called. After around ten minutes, and now in the wood near where Rebecca first found the key, she heard a whimpering.

Holding her hand up, Rebecca said, 'I think I heard someone crying faintly. Come on, follow me. My intuition is sending me to an area of the woods I know.' Inside, she was thinking, well it would be. As she turned the corner and could see the sun shining through the trees in an area she knew as the Spry Wood, she could see Millicent sitting on the bench by the old oak. She turned to Meredith and pointed.

'Yes, I see her,' she whispered.

'I do not know why I think this, but I feel I need to speak to Millicent alone. It is just my intuition leading me and over the years, I have learnt to trust such feelings.'

Squeezing Rebecca's arm gently, she said, 'go, I will hold back here.'

As Rebecca made her way over, Millicent looked up, her anguish all too clear. Once again, she wondered how saving this sad individual might change the present and perhaps even alter the lives of those one-hundred and fifty years from now. Mysteriously though, she knew it wasn't her future, just a world she'd seen. Although she should have been bothered by the potential outcome of her intervention, she wasn't troubled. Thinking about the way she felt, she realised between speaking with Meredith and analysing her own emotions, she was now certain Millicent's suicide was a point in history that may not, or should not exist. As for Millicent's survival affecting the here and now, she knew they could cross that bridge if it ever appeared to be heading down a negative path. Feeling comfortable with her choices, she sat next to Millicent. 'I am sure I am the last person you want to see right now. I promise you I am here to help you.'

Teary-eyed, Millicent looked up. Her weary, fraught expression all too evident. She then looked down briefly and as she again looked up there was a melancholy remoteness surrounding this woman. To Rebecca, it was as if this woman's soul was lifeless. 'I feel hopeless and lost. I do not see how you could help me. It was your words that led me along this path.' She then looked down and let out a quiet but anguished whimper. Without looking up, she said, 'you see, I know I deserve this path. I selfishly acted with greed and no regard for anyone but myself.'

23

'Your heartfelt words show you acknowledge your misguided actions. This alone suggests you deserve an alternate future. One where you will find happiness. We all take the wrong path. It is how we respond once we know.'

Still, with an expression of loneliness, she looked up and forced a shallow smile. 'I appreciate your words. However, no amount of forgiveness will change my destiny. I feel doomed towards a damned existence, and cannot face going back to the penniless world I once lived in.' Again, she looked down and whimpered quietly.

Reaching out and touching Millicent gently on the arm, Rebecca said, 'together we can find a better life for you.' She then turned and beckoned Meredith towards them.

Meredith came over, sat, and put her arm around Millicent. 'I heard your words and understand your troubles, Millicent. Fear not, we will find a solution. All is not lost, even though you feel condemned and predestined to a sad existence.'

Millicent looked up, and once more forced a smile. Still, though, her despair showed. 'I do not see how I can live here, even if I was to work for you. I do not know what I could do. The only thing I am good at is being horrid.'

Meredith again reached out to Millicent. 'When you were young, your father ran a fruit and vegetable yard in town before he sadly lost his life to that tragic accident. As a girl still in your youth and not having a mother, you were pushed down a road of ill-repute. You had no choice. At no stage were you to blame. You were a victim of circumstance. I knew and respected your father. He was a good man and within you, his way exists. From the age of six, right up to his death when you were fourteen, you worked in his yard. I suggest you could reopen his outlet. After all, you still own his yard, it will just need a little fixing up. This farm can supply you with all the fruit and vegetables you require.'

Appearing a little more animated, but still anxious, Millicent asked, 'How will I pay for the supplies, I have no money?'

'No need to concern yourself with money. In time, when you are on your feet and your business is running well, you can pay us back gradually.'

Nodding, and smiling, Rebecca said, 'I can help you get the old yard ship-shape and help you with the customers.' Nodding and now grinning, she added, 'I would love to do this with you. A new start for us both.'

Millicent appeared to think for a moment. She then squeezed Rebecca's hand. 'You would do this for me even after all I did and said?'

'Loathing, hatred and holding a grudge is a cowardly way, and all involved carry the pain for all time. Forgiveness is the only way. Together, we can work for a better life for us all.' Rebecca then thought for a moment. 'I recall someone once saying, "to give with both hands is a good way. However, to do this, you must give for no reason other than to give. If you expect something in return, you are giving for yourself alone. Give with an open heart and only for the benefit of the receiver." Those words meant so much to me and I live my life this way. I want to help you, for no other reason than I can. Significantly, your actions, as Meredith said, were through no fault of your own, you were a victim of circumstance. If anything, most put in your position would have just withered. You stood up and fought, and therefore created a better existence for yourself. You learnt quickly that nothing is free. So, the road you took was clear and understandable.' Rebecca then touched Millicent's hand.

'Still no excuse for my behaviour.'

'I agree with Rebecca, the route you took was the only one you could. Now, we move on and put those sad days behind us. It will be a new start for us all.'

Chapter 3 – New start

The three chatted for a while longer. As the sun started to lower, Rebecca shivered and said, 'I love the autumn, but boy does the temperature drop when the sun starts to close her eyes.'

'Yes indeed, we best get in doors,' Meredith said, standing up.

Rebecca rose from the bench and noticed Millicent still sitting. Without a thought, she held her hand out. 'New start for us, come on, come with us.'

'Yes, come along,' Meredith said, 'we have a room you can stay in, Millicent. Let's let bygones be exactly that, bygones. A new start, and a new day. We have a long day tomorrow fixing up your yard.'

Appearing hesitant and clearly uncertain, Millicent stood up.

Aware of her uncertainty, Rebecca took her hand and followed Meredith back towards the main house.

When they arrived back, George met them at the front door. With his hands up in a questioning manner and frowning with a distinct air of suspicion, he glanced between all three. He then turned to Meredith and as he was about to speak, Meredith held her hand up.

'No questions George. I will explain all later this evening during supper.' She then turned to Millicent. 'Come along, Millicent, let me show you to your room. We can run you a nice warm bath and arrange some suitable clothing.'

Millicent looked down at her bedraggled hessian dress, then at her grubby hands. She glanced at Rebecca, then back towards Meredith, who was now standing in the hallway beckoning her. She ushered past George outwardly averting her eyes and followed Meredith up the grand staircase.

Seeing this staircase caused the most bizarre sensation in Rebecca's thoughts. She knew these stairs well but wasn't sure if she was remembering them from her time in the future or the few times she'd travelled back to this era. The paintings were the same and in the same position. Even the carpet tread was just as she knew it. Now standing at the bottom of the stairs, something nudged her to turn and look back. Glancing towards the front door, she took a sharp intake of breath. She made her way back for a closer look. Sure enough, the delightful painting of Meredith was still there. Opposite though, instead of the painting of Millicent, there was a painting of another woman. She joined Meredith on the stairs. 'Where is the painting of Millicent, and who is the woman in the painting opposite you?' she asked, wondering how she hadn't noticed when she came in and glanced at both paintings.

With slightly tightened lips, Meredith shook her head somewhat. She glanced back towards the paintings and frowned. 'I know of no Millicent painting. The other painting is of your beloved great aunt Rebekha.'

'You mean the one who died in the Americas?'

Again frowning, Meredith shook her head. 'Rebekha is not dead. She is, however, due to leave for the Americas fairly soon. I do not understand why you would suggest otherwise. You were there when she left.' She then hesitated, clearly deep in thought. 'Is it reasonable to assume your recollections are from your time in the future, and you are recalling events yet to happen?'

Rebecca looked at Meredith and it was as if both had a bolt of realisation. Inside, she suddenly grasped she was within an entirely alternate reality. What she believed she knew as a time traveller and this world were different. This reality check also helped her understand that although some things were similar or slightly different, many aspects were significantly alternate.

27

Considering this and what she'd just said made her frown, knowing she had to keep her pages blank and as best she could keep her emotive thoughts and loose comments under wraps. It was okay with Meredith because she would understand and accept her comments, no matter how insensitive they may appear. George and Millicent though would question her emotional mindset. She glanced toward Meredith aware this woman needed answers about her comment regarding her beloved aunt. 'Umm, you need an explanation.'

As perceptive as always, Meredith nodded with a hint of a frown. 'We can talk about this later after we have organised Millicent.' She then turned to Millicent who was appearing befuddled. 'Come along, Millicent,' she said climbing the staircase, 'and you also, Madam.'

As Rebecca followed the pair upstairs, she found herself involuntarily glancing around searching for familiar aspects. This in itself caused an odd stir of sentiments.

After they'd showed Millicent to her room, organised a bath and alternate clothing, they headed down for supper with George. Once they'd finished their food, they chatted for a while. Meredith explained the situation to George almost as a fait accompli. She indicated they should head down to the old yard and see what needed to happen to make it a workable setting. George didn't say a lot, but Rebecca could see he had several questions.

Appearing to pick up on this, Meredith said, 'George, I will explain all to you tomorrow. Just be assured what we do, is done with considered reasoning.' She then suggested an early night.

The following morning Rebecca woke early. With her 21st-century head-on, she headed over to take a shower in her ensuite. Two steps and she quickly realised there was no ensuite in the 1850s, let alone a shower. This reality bump was a rather abrupt awakening, which in an odd way brought an inward grin. As if she was in any doubt, she realised she had to let go of her recollections from the future and live in this world as the 15-year-old daughter of Meredith. Although her memories had started to fade a little, she knew she was still impulsively thinking and acting like a 40-year-old woman. Thinking about this as she headed downstairs, she struggled to see how she could get back into the head of a 15-year-old and do so without the 40-year-old woman taking over. Significantly though, she was all too aware of the impact of her actually being fifteen but speaking and acting like a grown woman. She also knew how this would be received by those around her in the 19th-century. She could recall her grandparents in the 21st century, and also her mother, Elizabeth often suggesting she was a second-timer. Initially, she'd struggled to comprehend this, but when she spoke to Elizabeth about the notion, her mother had proposed in spite of often dreaming of fairies and such like, she also thought and behaved in a way beyond her years. *Hmm*, she thought, *perhaps I just need to be aware of what I say, how I behave, and importantly, my response to others and their reaction towards my behaviour.*

Entering the kitchen, she was a little surprised to see three women busying themselves preparing food. One of the women, an elderly full-bodied lady turned toward Rebecca.

'Madam, can I help you with something?'

'Errr, I was looking for Meredith.' She felt like she could kick herself for erring.

'Meredith will be in the breakfast room, Madam,' the lady responded with the hint of a frown.

Rebecca turned thinking, breakfast room, what breakfast room. As she did, she could hear Meredith talking. She was standing opposite the room she knew as her father's study, albeit, her memory was from 150-years in the future. As she headed towards Meredith, she found herself laughing inwardly, knowing she was on a long road of discovery. The way Meredith greeted her she suspected this woman wanted an

29

explanation for her comment about Aunt Rebekha. For sure Meredith had smiled the way she always did, but there was a hint of anxiety within her countenance. Looking around, she asked, 'are we alone?'

Meredith nodded. For a moment we are.'

'I struggled to sleep last night. I kept thinking about what I said regarding your aunt and how you must have felt. I know from my time in the future how important this woman is to you.' She then thought for a moment. 'I nearly got up in the middle of the night to come and see you and offer up an explanation.'

'I was troubled by your comment. I did, however, find solace knowing my aunt is still with us. So, in essence, your knowledge from the future may help her avoid any potential fate.'

'This was my thought also.' Rebecca then explained exactly what happened. All the way through, there was this nagging thought. As far as she was aware, Aunt Rebekha travelled to the Americas in 1827 or so, yet here they were in 1853. Suddenly a bizarre thought occurred to her. She'd learnt from her time in the future that there were many parallel existences. She'd never really completely understood how it worked but was very aware that her action in the past would alter the future. 'What year are we in Meredith?'

'It is eighteen-twenty-seven.'

Even though Rebecca had considered this might be the case, she wasn't prepared for the endless questions this posed. In the world she knew, George hadn't met Meredith for another 20-years. Millicent would have been a young child. She shook her head aware she had no choice other than to accept things as they were. Perhaps in time, she may understand how this all knits together. For now, though, her focus had to be on Aunt Rebekha and try to intervene with her transit to America. 'When is your aunt due to travel to the Americas?'

Narrow eyed, nonetheless receptive, Meredith said, 'in six weeks.'

With her attention all over the place, Rebecca knew she had to focus her thoughts. She blew gently through her pursed lips. 'Once we have sorted Millicent, we need to speak about your aunt and ultimately, stop her transit to the Americas.' She could see Meredith had questions. 'For now, your aunt is safe. If she travels, her soul will flounder and be lost. This will result in her sorrowful demise.'

With obvious concern still apparent, Meredith nodded.

'I can see your concern. Your aunt is safe for now. I know this for sure from my time in the future.' No sooner than she'd finished speaking, an alarm rang in her head. She suddenly realised she might not know for sure. When Meredith had told her it was 1827, this notion scrambled her thoughts completely. Having visited Meredith from the future many times, the one thing that remained consistent was the year 1853. So, if she could be so wrong about the year, she could be wrong about Aunt Rebekha.

'How can you be so sure, Rebecca?'

'I was just considering exactly that myself. Where is your aunt now?'

'She has just been moved to an asylum near Liverpool. She is there awaiting transportation to the Americas.'

Searching her recollections of this woman, at no point was she interned in an asylum prior to her move to America. If she'd had doubts, she now knew for sure her memories from the future should be disregarded. 'Okay, we need to refocus our attention. Millicent can wait for a couple of days. We need to travel today and bring your aunt back here.' She then thought for a moment. 'I am quickly realising everything I thought I knew from the future is more than likely wrong. I was certain it was eighteen-fifty-three, and clearly, I was mistaken. So, if I could be wrong about that, well… I'd suggest we need to act swiftly. An asylum is no place for a sensitive soul such as your aunt.'

'I can speak with George now. He can arrange for a carriage to take us to my aunt this morn. On the way, we pass by her step-father's home and can inform him what we plan.' Meredith then looked down briefly. She then looked up with an exacting expression. 'Oh, my word, I have just had a stark realisation. The home her step-father occupies was owned by Aunt Rebekha's dear mother before her sad death. To suggest Rebekha's mother lost her life in unusual circumstances would be an understatement.'

'Crumbs, that is disconcerting, to say the least.' Hearing this, Rebecca immediately started speculating. She wondered if it was possible to alter Rebekha's life, and perhaps prevent her mother's sad demise. She looked down reckoning it would happen if it was meant to, but only if she was still able to move freely through time.

'I will speak with George now in the breakfast room. Will you please speak with Millicent and explain we have an urgent appointment? She is in her bedroom, I believe.' Meredith then headed off to chat with George.

Chapter 4 – Aunt Rebekha

After Rebecca had spoken with Millicent, without telling her any details, she headed downstairs. Waiting for her in the hallway was Meredith.

'The carriage awaits us. With good ground, we should arrive at the asylum by two post meridiem.'

Rebecca shook her head, thinking post meridiem indeed, realising Meredith was referring to the afternoon. She followed Meredith to the carriage, and they headed up the long drive. As the carriage rumbled along the gravel track, memories from her time in the future flooded her thoughts. For some curious reason, even though her recollections had faded quickly, this felt oh so familiar. That was until they arrived at the huge gothic style gated entrance. In the future, it was barely standing, appearing as if it had been neglected for several hundred years. Yet here it was apparently new. She couldn't help wondering how it had become so run down in 150 or so years.

'What are you thinking, my dear?'

'Just about this entrance gate. In the future, it is barely standing. I cannot imagine how it became so run down,' she said, knowing it showed considerably more than 150-years of decay, more like 500 years.

'George just recently commissioned the rebuild. It has been the entrance, we believe, for nine-hundred years and was becoming precariously unsteady.'

Things were just not adding up in Rebecca's head. She was no expert, but there was no way this gate had become so dilapidated by 2007. If she'd been in any doubt, she knew she had to dismiss any recollections she had from the future. For sure, the house was the same, mostly, Meredith, George and

Millicent appeared to be the same people. Everything else, including the year, was like some kind of alternate existence. 'It is odd, Meredith.'

'What is odd, my dear Rebecca?'

'So many things are different, yet some aspects and people are familiar.' As she said this, she realised there will be memories from the future and they will undoubtedly cloud her perspective. The here and now was her actual reality and any recollections from the 21st century should be dismissed. She nodded, thinking that was the alternate existence, not this. 'I think the penny has just dropped. In the future, I travelled to the nineteen-forties and was married with two children. Then suddenly, I was back in what I thought was my life, with Elizabeth, James and so on. I struggled initially with having no emotional detachment even though I'd spent thirty years in the nineteen-forties era. It happened in the blink of an eye, and any physical or emotional memories I had quickly became distant and almost dream like. Here, it's different. Although I feel no emotional loss for my family in the future, my physical memories are strong.' She paused, aware that Meredith appeared to be deep in thought.

'Carry on, please,' she said, looking up as if she'd read her thoughts… again.

'I found myself thinking of this life as an alternate existence. Hello, I've just had a reality check. It would seem my time in the future is a corresponding existence that was part of my journey. The here and now is my true reality. The pages for tomorrow's book have yet to be written.'

Meredith offered a wry grin. 'You have also brought back your emotive terminology. Hello, indeed. On a serious note, I am happy and accepting of your choice of language because I know the full story. Other's however, may frown. In this era, if you don't meet a certain criterion, folk are quick to judge and indeed label individuals as different. To be different is a good thing, but you don't want that label in this time, especially if

34

you are female.' She lowered her head a little. 'My beloved Aunt Rebekha acquired that very label.'

Meredith's words, although considered, went against all of Rebecca's beliefs. She shook her head defiantly. 'Well people's bigoted, prejudiced opinions need to change and quickly. We need to start with people's opinion of your aunt.' She breathed heavily through her nose. 'Do not worry, Meredith, I will be mindful of my language, but…' she sighed, 'in the early nineteen-hundreds women are allowed to vote on parliament. They most certainly are not expected to stand in the corner and speak when spoken to.' She could feel herself getting angry and wondered if this was because of her life in the future where things were mostly equal, or if this was her natural demeanour.'

Once more, as if Meredith could read her thoughts, she said, 'I have always admired your feisty, intrepid spirit, which you have shown from the day you could offer an opinion. Seriously though, women allowed to vote on parliament. That will never happen.'

'Mother, I can assure you this is a fact.' She then once more thought about the future being an alternate existence, one that wasn't reality. *Hmm*, she thought, *I wonder if we could bring that vote forward a hundred years.* 'In the late 19th-century, there was a female movement known as the women's suffrage. Even though they faced discrimination and condemnation from men, they eventually changed the UK parliament's opinion, leading to votes for women in the early 20th-century. It just occurred to me my understanding is from my time in the future and may not actually happen.' This was another jolt to her consciousness making her aware her memory reflected a life that may never exist.

'It is mother now,' she said and chuckled. 'Sadly, in this era, women, as you said, speak when spoken to.'

'Yes, I understand this.' In her thoughts, she felt determined to change things now. 'First thing we need to do is bring your

35

aunt home. Then we can talk more about life for women now.'
A memory stirred from the future of a teacher referencing this
period in women's history. 'In years to come, people look
upon this era as the female dark ages.'

'Well, bringing my aunt home may not be as easy as you
think. She was locked up by her stepfather. It is unlikely those
who work at the asylum will allow us to take her home without
his permission.' She then seemed to think for a moment.
'Female dark ages they are. I have a voice, but it has not
always been like that, as well you know. It was only you
coming to me as a future girl that made me realise, I was living
here without a voice.'

Meredith referring to her as a future girl caused an odd
reaction. She now found herself wondering if there could be
two of her. That didn't make sense though, because she'd
know. Considering this, it again made her ask about her life
here. She realised Meredith was watching her and decided to
get back to the subject of Rebekah. 'So, if I understand you
correctly because we are women, we need his approval.'

'In essence, yes, because her stepfather has jurisdiction. Her
power of attorney lies with him. Even if her mother was still
alive, his say is the only one that counts.'

With pursed lips, Rebecca let out a heavy sign. 'How can
we get around this?'

'I suspect all we can do is visit her with reassurance and
offer her some emotional comfort. Both George and I have
spoken to Jonathon, the stepfather a number of times. We
offered our home as a permanent solace for Aunt Rebekha. He
was belligerent in his refusal. We engaged our lawyer and he
said we had no legal grounds to alter the outcome.'

'Well, we need to do something.' Inside she was wondering
if she could find a door back and alter the past, thereby
changing the here and now. Or perhaps, they could simply help
her escape. But that wouldn't work because she would have to

remain in hiding. Then an idea occurred to her. 'I am guessing Jonathon's main quarry was to acquire the estate of Rebekha's mother for himself. It seems from what you say, he values estate before people. Is there any way George and yourself could offer some kind of financial incentive?'

'We have trod that road, to no avail, His demands were beyond us. To think, George saved his life just two short years previous.'

'Saved his life. Tell me more.' Immediately, Rebecca started thinking this may be a doorway for her to alter events.

'Well, George was on a fox hunt with Jonathon, when Jonathon's horse threw him. They were at Scafell Pike, high up. Jonathon was clinging to a thin branch. George dismounted and pulled him to safety.' Meredith then narrowed her eyes. 'I believe I know what you are considering. I too wondered many times if and when you returned to me perhaps you could intervene in the past and alter the outcome. Over the next two years, Jonathon outwardly despoiled everything and everyone who stood in his path. He was a changed man and had become selfish, negative, and destructively greed bound. I lost my great-aunt to a curiously strange death. Next, he dismissed all the housekeepers, many of whom had been with the family for generations. Then came selling off parts of the estate. Finally, he had my dear aunt gaoled within this horrid asylum.' She narrowed her gaze and looked deeply into Rebecca's eyes.

Rebecca was now at a loss what to think. Should they still visit Rebekha, or should they return home so she can visit the summerhouse in hope of finding a way back? 'What is the time?'

'Pulling a beautiful watch from her bag, Meredith flipped the case open. 'It is thirty past noon. What are you thinking?'

'Mostly, my doorway back is the old summerhouse or servant's quarters, I should say.' She then thought for a

37

moment. 'I think we should still visit your aunt and offer her some reassurance. Then, if I can… well, let's see how things work out.'

Meredith narrowed her eyes. 'Yes indeed, let us see.'

The remainder of the journey passed quickly and soon they arrived outside a huge dark grey building. To Rebecca, it looked more like a prison than a hospital. She knew though in this era such buildings were more like a prison. The inmates, mostly deemed lunatics through a lack of understanding were here for life. Her memories from 21st-century historians would suggest the care of those inmates was meagre, their lives sad and often short.

They headed up to the main door and were met by a stout, hostile looking woman.

'Why are you here?' she asked with what Rebecca considered a confrontational tone.

Meredith stepped forward, placing her feet firmly in front of the woman. Looking her in the eye, she said with an equally curt tone, 'we are here to visit with Rebekha Merchant.'

'Are you family?' the woman asked, stepping back a little.

'Yes.'

'Both of you?'

'Yes,' Rebecca said in an abrupt tone. 'Any more questions?'

'Wait,' she said and returned through the huge windowless black door.

They had been waiting for around 15-minutes, when Meredith turned to Rebecca and said, 'I am not waiting any longer, I am going to find out what is going on.'

As she did, an elderly, wispy looking man wearing a long brown lightweight coat appeared at the door. Without any words, he beckoned them towards him.

As they followed him through the door, the first thing that hit Rebecca was this horrid smell. It was a bizarre combination of vinegar and mentholated spirit. Then as quickly, the horrid stench was overtaken by saddened cries and whimpering. They followed the man down a long dark, shadowy corridor. He then stopped outside a large door that appeared to be made from iron or something similar. If Rebecca had considered this place a prison, this door exaggerated that disposition. With no words, the man opened the door.

As he did, a stench of ammonia filled the air. Inside the darkened room, they could see 4 beds squeezed in side by side. All four occupants appeared female and alarmingly, all 4 were strapped to their bed with what appeared some kind of leather binding.

Frowning, Meredith pushed the man to one side and entered the room. She turned and growled, 'bring the senior doctor to me now.' She then led Rebecca towards a bed at the far side.

Rebecca had only seen Aunt Rebekha a couple of times and she'd always had a happy disposition, often singing. The woman that lay in front of them was an almost lifeless, sorrowful looking soul. As Meredith leaned over and touched her cheek gently, this shadow of a woman flicked her eyes and offered a lifeless smile.

She beckoned Meredith towards her and whispered, 'Help me.'

Meredith, still stroking her cheek, whispered, 'I am going to speak with the head physician now. We will come back shortly.' She then beckoned Rebecca into the corridor. 'We cannot leave her here like this. However, I do not see how we can do anything else.' She then looked around. 'I fail to see a route for us to help her escape.' She shook her head. 'I suspect our only option is to assure her and then try once more to speak with Jonathon. The money he wanted was beyond our financial means. Perhaps though, we could offer him some alternative.'

As she finished speaking, the elderly doctor returned. Once more, without speaking, he beckoned them to follow him. The two followed him further along the corridor, and up two dimly lit stair flights. He then stopped outside a large white door and knocked once.

'Come.'

He opened the door and ushered Meredith and Rebecca inside.

Sitting behind a large oak desk was a stern-looking man, dressed in a tartan suit that Rebecca recognised. This immediately triggered an idea in her head.

Meredith stood in front of his desk and said, 'my aunt, Rebekha Merchant, needs to come home with us. This place is not right for her and I suspect she will perish quickly if left strapped to her bed.'

'Your aunt you say. She was interned by her stepfather, who deemed her a lunatic. We assessed her. Her ramblings of years past and years yet to arrive showed us her stepfather's assessment was correct.'

After around 10 minutes of fruitless back and forth between him and Meredith. Rebecca said, 'McCray tartan, I believe.'

The man turned to Rebecca, and pouting his lips a little, he said, 'You knowing of my tartan is rare this far south. Please tell me how you know of my clan.'

'I have friends and family from Perth and in particular the Priory. You will know of the Hewison clan.'

Instantly, his whole demeanour changed. Smiling, he said, 'I am married to Isabell Hewison.'

'Well, it would seem we have common ground. So, with that in mind, let us see if we can sort this situation out with my great aunt.'

He nodded. 'It is most irregular, however. Her stepfather, who has her power of attorney, assured us he would not return for Rebekha.' He then seemed to think for a moment. 'If you would like to offer a small donation, I can quickly arrange for Rebekha to travel home with you today.'

Rebecca glanced toward Meredith.

'I carry no money with me. However, I have this time-piece, and its value is substantial.' She then handed him her beautiful watch.

'He nodded. 'This donation,' he said, emphasising the word, 'will be greatly appreciated by the trust. 'Can I offer you tea while I arrange for Miss Merchant to be readied?'

Meredith stood up. 'No tea, thank you, we will wait outside in our carriage.'

On the way outside, Rebecca whispered to Meredith, 'I was not happy you handing over your lovely watch. If it was down to me, I would have just punched him in the face and taken your aunt.' She then thought for a moment. 'I can tell you now, that clan were a bunch of wideboys.'

'Not to concern yourself. That watch was a cheap copy. I have the real one locked up and only wear it during special occasions.' She then looked at Rebecca in an odd way. 'I assume you know of his clan from one of your journeys.'

'Your assumption is correct, but that is another story, for another volume.'

Chapter 5 – Welcome Home

After around an hour, two men wheeled Rebekha out in a push-chair affair. Meredith and Rebecca helped the almost lifeless body of Rebekha into the carriage.

'We are taking you home,' Meredith said, gently touching her aunt's hand.

She offered a listless smile and slumped back in her seat.

Rebecca glanced at Meredith, tightened her lips, and raised her eyebrows. Inwardly, she was very concerned for this poor soul's wellbeing.

'We will feed you well, my dear aunt, nurse you with love and bring some joy back to your life.' She then also raised her eyebrows. 'I am not sure if she is sleeping or slumbering under the weight of misused remedies.'

Not much was said as they made their homeward journey. Most of the time, Rebecca stared aimlessly out of the window, to the point where she hadn't noticed darkness fall. When they arrived home, George met them at the door. Between George, one of the carriage men, and some help from Rebecca and Meredith they took Rebekha to a first-floor room.

On the way up the stairs, Rebecca suddenly realised George was moving freely and without the aid of a walking stick. When she'd met him previously, he was burdened with a leg injury. She glanced down at the floor for a second now certain whatever she knew from the future was unlikely to exist in this reality. Entering a room that was used by her future brother, Tommy, briefly brought back a memory of him continually kicking his ball at her. The combination of George without a stick and memories of Tommy jolted at her inner thoughts. Strangely, her recollections of Tommy although remote were fond and lovingly tactile. This in turn got her wondering if any of the people she knew in the future would actually exist. Clearly, what she thought she knew about the world she was in now was abstractedly dissimilar with the exception of Meredith. Then hearing Rebekha's hollow whimper refocussed her mind back to the present. Over the next hour, she and Meredith bathed and redressed Rebekha as best they could. Meredith then pulled the covers over Rebekha and kissed her forehead.

As Meredith closed the door behind her, she turned to Rebecca. 'I am not at all optimistic. If we are able to bring spirit back to my aunt's world, the journey will be lengthy. Best we get some sleep now,' she said and kissed Rebecca on the cheek.

In a bizarre way, the way Meredith had kissed her on the cheek was a reminder that this woman saw her as her young daughter. Inside, Rebecca still felt like a woman. As she lay in bed, her thoughts were a little mixed. On one hand, she felt very concerned for Rebekha's wellbeing. This concern though was increasingly overtaken by thoughts about her life here with Meredith. The instant she'd woken that first morning and saw Meredith, she felt this was her rightful home and her real mother. Very quickly, memories of her time in the 21st-century had virtually evaporated and alongside this, she'd felt no emotional loss for Duncan or her two beloved girls, Faith and Gabri. Of late, accounts of these people had come to mind more than she'd expected. Although she felt tired, her mind was too active to consider sleep. As it was so warm outside, she decided to go and sit on her balcony. There was a full moon tonight and she knew it was due to slip from sight over the lake. This was something she'd done often in the future and sitting there watching the same moon, set over the same lake exaggerated her already rambling thoughts.

All of a sudden, she heard Meredith calling her. With pins and needles in her arm and a tense painful neck, she realised she'd fallen asleep in the iron balcony chair. As she dragged herself to her feet, she reckoned she had to get some cushions for these chairs.

'Why are you out here so early,' Meredith asked narrowing her eyes.

Stretching her arm and neck, Rebecca said, 'I came out to watch the full moon and fell asleep. Ooops.' She then followed Meredith into the corridor. 'How is Rebekha?'

'I am just going to check now. Will you join me?'

Rebecca followed Meredith along to Rebekha's room.

Rebekha was sitting up in bed sipping some tea the maid had brought up for her. She turned toward Meredith and Rebecca and offered a sorrowful smile. After a couple of minutes, her eyelids started to flicker and it was clear she needed some more sleep.

On the way downstairs, Meredith suggested she was still extremely concerned for Rebekha.

'Yes, I agree. She is very unwell and...' She then squeezed Meredith's hand.

The two sat with George in the breakfast room. Rebecca had some porridge. Curiously, this nudged at an almost inaccessible recollection, although focussing her thoughts made this memory less elusive. Staring at her bowl, she could visualise sitting with Duncan and her two daughters eating breakfast. After some weak, unnecessarily sweet tea, she turned to Meredith. 'I think I'll go for a walk outside.' She needed some time alone to consider her emotions.

'Our physician is coming over this morning to check on Rebekha. She is so very weak and I am concerned she may not recover.' She then looked down briefly, clearly thinking. 'It is a nice morning, so go for a meander and hopefully by the time you get back, we may have better news.' She then gave

Rebecca an odd sideways glance, almost as if she was once more looking into Rebecca's thoughts.

Although Rebecca felt she should stay and wait to hear the doctor's prognosis, she also needed some time on her own. On the way down the path, her thoughts were all over the place. They were jumping between this route being vaguely familiar, Meredith's sideways glance, fragile memories of her future family, and her desperate concerns for Rebekha. With all that had happened over the last couple of days, she felt like she was in some kind of limbo. She was relaxed and comfortable around Meredith, but everything else seemed almost surreal. As she neared the summerhouse, her thoughts returned to Rebekha. Even though she didn't want to openly admit it, she felt deeply concerned for this poor soul. This morning, she'd hoped to see signs of recovery. Instead, she seemed weaker. Several times since they'd brought Rebekha back, she'd wondered if somehow, she could alter this woman's destiny. The second she thought this, the smell of Christmas cake filled her nostrils. Instantly, she knew she was on the verge of travelling somewhere in time if she hadn't already.

She stood there for a few seconds and decided to head back and hear the doctor's prognosis.

As she made her way back towards the main house, she could see several people milling about outside. In addition, there were two black carriages. Drawing closer, she could see Meredith stood beside one of the carriages that were carrying a coffin. Seeing Meredith weeping into a hanky, Rebecca reckoned she'd perhaps jumped forward in time and was witnessing Rebekha's funeral. Now hindered by a deep sadness, she needed to make sure what was going on. Moving towards Meredith, she passed several people, none of which looked in her direction. Somewhere deep in her memory, she recalled this scenario before. To compound this, Meredith looked straight past her and beckoned George towards her. Rebecca knew there and then she was here as an observer only.

Rebecca listened as Meredith spoke to George. "If only we'd brought Rebekha back sooner, she may have had a chance to survive."

That was all Rebecca needed to hear. Stricken with grief, she turned and hurried back towards the summerhouse.

Chapter 6 – A New Journey

Hurrying down the well-trodden path, for some reason, it seemed curiously different from when she was here just moments earlier. She stood briefly, trying to get her bearings. Glancing back towards the main house, there was no sign of the people or carriages. She raised her eyebrows, and although a little surprised, felt safe in the knowledge she'd probably moved to another time period. For the last couple of days, most of her recollections from the future, including her movement through time had been a vague memory. Now though, they were abruptly fresh in her consciousness. The only question in her head was deciding if she should head towards the main house, or continue in the direction of the summerhouse. As she stood there pondering her thoughts, something was telling her to wait.

In a state of conscious oblivion, she gazed towards the lake without actually focussing on anything. Abruptly, the sound of several dogs barking jolted her like an alarm clock. Turning, she could see several red-jacketed horsemen surrounded by many beagle-like dogs. Getting closer to the main house, the yelping dogs, men shouting and a badly played bugle created such a horrid sound, she put her fingers in her ears. Still, with her ears covered, she headed closer trying to work out what was going on, although she had a sneaky suspicion this might be the hunt where George saved Jonathon. Outwardly invisible once more, she stood behind a picket fence watching the toing and froing. Looking around, she tightened her lips, thinking, no women. No sooner this thought came to her, she felt a hand on her shoulder. Without turning, she knew it was Meredith. 'Good day, Meredith.'

'It seems you are up to your old tricks once more.'

Weird, vivid memories of her time with Meredith in the future cascaded through her mind. Although this unbalanced her thoughts a little, she clearly recalled the many times when Meredith was the only one who could see her. She stood there, as she had many times before, wondering if Meredith was also in this bizarre void with her, as some kind of guardian angel. 'I have this odd question, Meredith. Are you with me in this other dimension?' She thought for a moment. 'Or are you simply the only one, out of all these people, who sees me?'

The way Meredith squinted, Rebecca wasn't sure if it was because it was so sunny, or the question had thrown her a little. 'I have many memories, as it seems you do also, of our times together in this situation. Although I am relaxed with my thoughts, I seem to know things I should not. By example, I know briefly, I was aware of your presence at my dear aunt's funeral where you were, as now, unseen by all except myself. The strange issue is that scenario is in two years from now. I know not why I have memories from the future, I do though.'

'How does this make you feel? Because, for me, although the situation we find ourselves in is at best outlandish, I still feel calm and relaxed.'

'I feel similar to you.' She then seemed to think for a moment. 'I have information in my thoughts and I know not why. I am aware you are here to alter today's events in some way. Although my thoughts are fragmented, I nevertheless know it may affect my aunt Rebekha's existence. I am also aware the solution to your task may involve today's hunt. These few fragments are all I have at my recall. Although, I do also have a snippet suggesting there may be an incident that involves George and Jonathon. I should be alarmed by this but I am not.' She then shook her head, almost as if she was coming to terms with having information about something that was yet to happen.

The moment Rebecca had seen the horsemen and dogs, she'd had a good idea why she was here and Meredith mentioning George and Jonathon confirmed her beliefs. 'I also know why I am here today, although my understanding is clear.

There will be an accident today with Rebekha's step-father, Jonathon. Your dear husband, George will save Jonathon after he falls from his horse. I understand the incident will occur somewhere around Scafell Pike. Someway, I need to travel with them and make an attempt to alter the outcome.' She then looked around. 'My only question is how will I get there. I can ride a horse well, so could follow the hunt. However, if I am invisible to all except you, I do not see how this could work. My horse would appear to be without a rider.' She then thought for a moment. 'Perhaps you could join the hunt and I could ride with you on your horse.'

Meredith shook her head. 'A hunt is no place for women, so that option is not available to us. We could, however, leave shortly and arrive at Scafell before the hunt.'

Rebecca shook her head, thinking about what Meredith had just said. 'Hmm, no place for women indeed. These aspects of society need to change, and soon.' Inside she was thinking, I'm not waiting until 1918 to have a voice.

'The position of women infuriates me also. For now, though, we must head to Scafell. Wait around the back of the main house and I will meet you there.'

Rebecca headed around the back. As she did, she was aware although invisible to everyone except Meredith, the beagles seemed to be aware of her. Somewhere in her memory was this knowledge that dogs would often react to something in a bizarre way, almost as if they were seeing something their owners couldn't. Moments later, and before she had time to consider the dogs any further, Meredith arrived on horseback.

'All the horses are with the hunt, except this old lady. She is, however, more than capable of carrying us both. Climb up behind me. We should reach the Pike within the hour. The hunt will not be far behind.'

Somewhere in Rebecca's thoughts, she had a vision of where today's incident would occur. Although the image was vague, there was a distinguishing tree close by and she felt sure she would know the right place once there. She climbed up behind Meredith, wondering why or how she had this vision of where the incident would occur. Thinking about this, it was the first time she'd experienced this kind of scenario, and now found herself wondering if she had somehow made the vision up in her imagination, or if it had somehow come to her in an odd, yet tangible way. *Oh well*, she thought, *find out soon enough.*

Meredith led the horse around the old walled garden and down a track that headed beyond the wood. Once out of the wood, they passed a pine forest that was instantly familiar to Rebecca, although she didn't know why. Since the day she'd woken in this new life, situations, events, and areas such as this pine forest kept nudging at her inner thoughts. It created the strangest emotions. It was as if she had two memories. One from the future, which kept coming and going. The other, recollections of this existence she was now living. Many times, she'd inwardly questioned if this was her real-life or if she was here from a future life. The one overriding aspect was she felt at home in the here and now. She often reassured herself that in time, all would become clear and if nothing else, having both memories could work in her favour.

With the sun high in the sky and a gentle southerly breeze, they started up a long track toward what Rebecca considered a small mountain. Initially, they meandered their way past many oaks, ash, and elm, intermingled with vast areas of bracken and bramble. These soon turned to pine trees and, in the distance, where the trees thinned, she could see a huge yew tree beside a number of large boulders. As they drew closer and she could see the boulders covered in lichen and moss, she knew this was the area. 'We are here,' Rebecca said, nudging Meredith gently.

Meredith led the horse around the back of the rocks and as they dismounted, Rebecca heard the faint bellows of a bugle, quickly followed by dogs barking. 'Right, by the sound of it, they will be here soon. I need to check the lie of the land. For some strange reason, I have a clear image in my head of where Jonathon falls from his horse. I can even see within my thoughts a small shrub he clings to when he falls. This gives George time to rescue him.' In her thoughts, Rebecca was in no doubt about what she needed to do. Remove that shrub and any nearby shrubs. In her inner thoughts, she'd made her mind up that if destiny wanted this callous, selfish man to survive, it would intervene. Knowing the dubious nature of his wife's death and the subsequent treatment of Rebekha, she felt her conscience would remain intact. Stay here, I will be back shortly.' She then headed around the front and the image in her mind's eye was right in front of her. Gingerly, she knelt on the rock edge, leaned forward, and pulled at the shrub with all her strength. Although she could move it a little, there was no way she could pull it from its roots. Then an idea popped into her head. She headed back to Meredith. 'Have you got a rope I can use?'

'Yes, I have this,' she said, pulling a sturdy looking rope from a saddle bag. 'We always carry such things in case of an emergency.'

'Well, this is an emergency,' Rebecca said, taking the rope. 'Will you bring the horse around the front. I need both rope and the horse to help pull the shrub from the ground. We should hurry because the hunt is close.' She then quickly made her way to the cliff edge and climbed down towards the shrub.

'Be careful, Rebecca. It is a long way down.'

'Thank you. I am just fine,' she said, glancing back. She then tied the rope firmly around the base of the shrub, turned and handed Meredith the other end. Before she had a chance to say anything, Meredith tied the rope around the saddle and geed the horse forward. With one forward movement, the shrub pulled free. Rebecca then looked around to see if there was anything else Jonathon could cling to. Confident, she joined Meredith behind the rocks.

'May I enquire how you feel? Affectively, you are sending Jonathon to certain death.'

'My conscience is clear. If his path is to survive, he will. Knowing of his nature, both his wife and step-daughter will be better without him.'

Meredith narrowed her eyes. 'You know much about this man. I suspect you have gained this insight from the future. I must agree though, he is a despicable excuse for a man. Both my aunt and her mother were always smiling before he entered the marital agreement. Even that agreement, between both fathers, was dubious. George and I talked about this matter often. Although, frustratingly it was never our place to intervene.'

'Intervene is exactly the right word. Throughout all of my journeys, I have been presented with many conundrums such as this. I now trust my instinct to show me a clear road. We are maintaining a just and reasonable equilibrium here.'

'They will be here soon and we need to take the track down the other side of the hill and avoid being seen,' Meredith said, pointing.

Rebecca was hoping to wait around and see what happens. As she was considering this, once more Meredith seemed to read her thoughts.

'We will find out later if your plan was successful. We must be scarce. If we are seen, I am not sure we could offer an acceptable reason for our presence here.'

'That makes sense and it is something I hadn't considered.' Inwardly she was thinking, yeah, compounded because of the male attitude towards females.

They headed down the other side of the Pike and when they entered some dense tree cover, they dismounted.

'We can watch from here. If the situation pans out as you suspect, we will have plenty of time to be home before they return.

The two stood and watched as horse after horse passed the rocky outcrop. Rebecca turned to Meredith with a quizzical look on her face.

'Worry not, George and Jonathon will be towards the back.'

No sooner she'd finished speaking they heard a lot of shouting. Exactly in the spot where Rebecca foretold, there were several men, standing and looking over the edge. Among the din of raised voices, Rebecca was certain she heard someone shout, "he has gone." She turned to Meredith. 'Although I cannot see too well, from what I heard it would seem something just occurred.'

'I heard that also. It would be reasonable to assume he has fallen. To my mind, there is no way he could survive that fall. I am no expert, but that drop must be a furlong.'

The use of the word furlong caused a weird reaction in Rebecca's head. She knew this word well, but half of her brain remembered it as a horse racing term from her time in the future. Whereas, her thoughts from this life knew it as a farm measurement. She shook her head as she got back on the horse with Meredith.

'I know an alternative route home and we should be back before the hunt.'

They passed the opposite side of the lake and through an area of shrubland Rebecca hadn't seen before. They then travelled through a small wooded area, again new to Rebecca. On the way, they went past a handful of small cottages that seemed distantly familiar. Before she had time to consider this vague memory, they arrived at the manor. Meredith suggested, as it was still warm, they sit out back in the walled garden. The idea of the walled garden, combined with the small cottages caused a rush of distant, but mysteriously tactile emotions.

Meredith pointed to a wooden gate in the wall adjacent to the kitchen. 'Go sit and relax and I will arrange with the cook for some tea and cakes.'

Rebecca opened the wooden gate and entered the walled garden. Sitting at an elaborate looking white metal table, her thoughts filled with two intense, but vague memories. Considering her emotions and all that had happened today, something deep in her thoughts was stirring. Her recollections of travelling from one era to another were vague at best. Nonetheless, there was a weird notion, if today's mission had been successful, she would move back to 1827. Here she was though, still in 1825. She considered this for a moment and suspected either there was more for her to do, or, somehow, Jonathon had survived.

Chapter 7 - Back

Just as she was trying to unravel her thoughts, she heard an extraordinarily familiar voice singing. Moments later, she was joined by Meredith and Rebekha. She was fairly certain she was back in 1827, and it would appear her intervention had achieved the right outcome. Even if Jonathon had survived, it mattered not, because here was Rebekha once more singing, showing her delightful, youthful character. Enhancing this delightful scene was Meredith's joyfully radiant expression. The last time she'd seen Meredith, her appearance showed an inner fatigue and her sadness was all too evident. She'd had no issue intervening with the hunt, but even if she had, this scene was all the reassurance she'd ever need. Over the years, Rebecca had faced a number of conundrums, which could result in an unsavoury outcome. She'd taken mental solace knowing the persons affected negatively were clearly unscrupulous, corrupt, or deceitful characters, often all three. Repeatedly, she'd assured herself the adverse outcomes were part and parcel of her journey. This scenario with Jonathon was no different.

As Meredith and Rebekha joined her at the table, the way Rebekha looked at her was a little peculiar. It was as if she knew her, but wasn't sure.

Outwardly appearing to pick up on this, Meredith said, 'look how grown up my daughter has become. To think it is just two short years since you were last in her company. While you were away with your dear mother in Scotland, Rebecca's hair has turned blonde, I suspect because of the glorious summers we have experienced.' Meredith touched Rebekha's hand gently, 'she is almost unrecognisable to me.' Meredith then leant over to Rebecca and whispered, 'I have an understanding in my thoughts and know not why. I am aware you intervened two years past and this led to you, Rebekha and I sitting happily at this table.'

From what Meredith had said, Rebecca was able to work out the lie of the land to some degree. Although she was curious why Rebekha had been in Scotland for 2 years, she knew that could wait for later. More curiously, she was wondering what colour her hair was previously. In an odd way, this added to her tentative uncertainties that this was her actual life. Every time this notion had drifted to the back of her thoughts, something like this occurred. It created a weird sensation because she felt so comfortable with Meredith. Something though wouldn't allow her to settle.

Just as she was considering her emotions, an elderly, delightfully friendly cook placed an elaborate silver cake stand on the table. She was quickly followed by a younger female who Rebecca considered to be in her early teens. She placed an equally elaborate tea set on the table.

Rebecca touched the young girl on the arm. 'May I ask, how old are you?'

With an almost nervous frown, the girl, kind of curtsied. 'Ma'am, I be eleven years this coming September.'

Rebecca shook her head, glanced at Meredith and then back at the girl. 'Do you work here with your parents or relatives? Also, may I ask your name?'

Now with tightened lips, the girl glanced back and forth between the cook, Meredith, and Rebecca. Meredith touched the young girl on the arm and nodded.

'My name is Jane.' She then hesitated and again glanced around. 'My uncle sold me into this household as part of my development. That is my understanding and therefore, I am accepting of my situation.'

'Sold you,' Rebecca exclaimed, 'sold you to whom?' In the back of her thoughts, Rebecca wondered about this girl's circumstances. Clearly, she was educated to some degree, and this was evident in the way she put her words together.

'Again, the young girl curtsied. 'My uncle sold me into this household to work in the kitchen. As I emphasised, to help facilitate my development.'

Infuriated by this concept, which seemed to be clearly acceptable, she needed to know more. 'Do you get paid money?' She then noticed Meredith frowning. 'Meredith, are you alright with me asking Jane these questions?'

Meredith nodded. 'Ask all you want. I can assure you, Jane is paid for her service, alongside this, she receives board and keep.'

Jane curtsied towards Meredith. 'Ma'am, I do not get any monies, just my food.'

Meredith shook her head and glanced at the cook. 'I was of the understanding all our staff are paid an appropriate wage. They also receive their food and a good bed.'

'Ma'am, your assumption is correct. Jane only joined us two days since.' She then hesitated and appeared a little uneasy. 'I assumed she was paid, fed, and slept in the junior maid quarters by the lake.'

Jane was shaking her head. 'I know not of the maid quarters.'

Meredith was now frowning. 'Where do you sleep?'

'In the woods, Ma'am. I have made a camp from branches.'

Meredith, Rebecca, and the cook all exclaimed simultaneously, "In the woods?"

'Yes, Ma'am. My uncle receives my wages, plus some extra for me not taking a bed.'

Meredith stood up. 'Call the Housemaid and the Butler please,' she said, turning to the cook.'

She nodded and headed indoors. Moments later, a tall, rather brusque looking man appeared, closely followed by an elegant woman, dressed in a delightful, although well-worn white dress.

'Who brought Jane into our service? Meredith asked with a stern, questioning look on her face.

Just as the woman was about to answer, the man quietened her with a curt glare, while holding a finger to his mouth. 'Be quiet, woman. It is not your place to speak or answer such questions.'

Rebecca then stood up and said firmly, 'so, with that understanding, it is not my place to speak either. I assume your view is based solely on us being female. I have never heard anything so illogically absurd.'

The man turned towards Rebecca. It was obvious her comments had hit a nerve even though he was trying to force a smile. He then seemed to be considering his response.

Before he could answer, Rebecca held her hand up. 'Do not frown at me with your weak shallow smile. In this house, women are equal. If you find this unacceptable, I would suggest this is not the right occupation for you. To my mind, I would propose alternative employment elsewhere that may suit your churlish, chauvinist mindset.'

Appearing flummoxed, the man turned towards Meredith, appearing arrogantly curt.

Infuriated by his distasteful expression, Rebecca said, 'and you can wipe that look off your face. Clearly, you have low regard for women, and it would appear your prejudiced opinion is exaggerated towards me because I am young.'

'Rebecca is right in all she says. In this household, women are equal, irrespective of their position or age, accept it or leave.'

Ma'am, with respect, she,' he said pointing at Rebecca, 'is a child.'

Seeing Meredith with a resolute, focussed look on her face triggered a distant memory. Rebecca could vaguely recall watching Meredith challenge Millicent in a similar way. The more she thought about this, the clearer the image became. She could now remember Millicent's hostile challenge and Meredith promptly stepping in.

Standing up and stepping close to the butler, Meredith stated, 'right Mr Smythe, answer one question. Did you bring Jane into this household and if so, did you make arrangements with her uncle regarding her employment conditions?'

Showing clear surprise and somewhat sheepishly, he nodded. 'I did make all arrangements.' In spite of his verbally passive change in direction, he couldn't hide his contempt, even towards Meredith.

Meredith turned to the elegant woman. 'Excuse me, April, I do not know your surname and from where you hail. Please inform me so I can address you correctly.'

The woman offered a delightful smile befitting of her natural beauty. 'I am from Dunbar, Ma'am. My name is April McCall.'

'Well, Ms MaCall. You are now head of this house. Please arrange for Jane to be paid her rightful wage, and she has somewhere to sleep. Of most importance, please make sure her uncle no longer receives any money.' She then turned towards the butler. 'Mr. Smythe, you have until Friday to find alternative employment. In addition, when you speak with me, or any other female, correctly, you should address them by their name, informally or otherwise.'

Frowning. He glanced towards April, and then peering at Meredith sideways, he said, 'you cannot put a woman in charge.'

'We, the family of this house, decide who is the head of household duties. We pay you to follow your duties and no more. It is clear you have acted in an amoral way with regard to Jane. That amoral demeanour has been exasperated by your view towards household hierarchy and in particular towards women. If you have low reverence towards women in general, it would be reasonable to assume you have this opinion towards myself, my aunt, and my daughter.'

'I have been in this employment for eleven years.'

'Therefore, you should be grateful we have not been made aware of your unprincipled character before this day. Now, leave us and make your arrangements.'

He stood there clearly flustered, his irritation obvious.

Apparently picking up on this, Meredith flicked the back of her hand dismissively. 'Leave us now, Mr Smythe.' She then turned her back on him. 'So, Jane, please tell me about your circumstances, where you are from and your full name.' Turning to April, she said, 'please arrange Jane's accommodation. Thank you.' Turning back to Jane, she pointed toward an empty seat.

This appeared to unbalance Jane a little and clearly aware of this, Meredith said, 'please take a seat, Jane.'

Hesitantly, Jane perched on the edge of the seat, clearly unsure. 'I was born on a farm nearby and lived there with my mother and father until they died.' She hesitated. 'My name is Austin.'

'Austin, as in Drewry Farm?' Meredith asked.

Nodding, and appearing a little more comfortable, she said, 'Yes, Ma'am.'

'I recall your parents dying in what was described in the local paper as a "strange barn fire." I remember reading about it with interest.'

'I was only young, and do not know what happened. One day, my ma and pa were there, and the next day my uncle moved in. Four days later, I was moved into a barn. And then after a woman moved into the main house, I was sent here two days ago.'

Frowning, Meredith said, 'please, Jane, sit a little more comfortably and tell me about your uncle.'

The girl sat back in the chair a little. 'I was told he was my uncle, but I did not know him. Prior to this event, I recall meeting my mother's sister who was introduced as my aunt Cassandra. I met no other aunts or uncles. Often, she visited us and we also took the long journey to her home. Other than that, I do not recall any other relatives.'

Hearing the name Austin, stimulated a distant, but clear memory about a famous author in the mid-1800s. Rebecca looked at her and thought *it can't be, can it?* Hearing Jane say her aunt's name was Cassandra energised her recollection. She was sure Jane had been raised by her aunt after the death of her parents. As she looked at this child, she was as sure as she could be. Everything was right for her to be the Jane Austin she knew as an author, just here in front of her as a child. Her age, name, hometown, and circumstances surrounding her upbringing by her parental Aunt Cassandra all pointed in this direction. Bizarrely, she could actually remember reading her books in the 21st century. These books had had a significant impact on Rebecca, albeit 180 years in the future. Austin's plots often explored the dependence of women on marriage in their pursuit of positive social standing and economic security. For Rebecca, it was clear Austin wasn't just alluding to and commenting on these social circumstances, she was passively critical. Between the lines, Austin would often, inertly, suggest the balance of power was unfair. Rebecca leant over and whispered, 'Meredith, can I talk to you quietly please?'

Meredith nodded. 'Excuse me, Jane, Rebekha, I need to speak with Rebecca briefly.' She then led Rebecca to one side.

Rebecca told Meredith all about Jane, suggesting they should contact her Aunt Cassandra as soon as possible. Inside, although she was aware her memories from the future were perhaps sometimes an alternate existence, she felt it was essential they offered this path to Jane. She'd known from the moment this girl joined them that she had a hearty character and presence. Even the way she thoughtfully constructed her sentences was precisely considered.

'You seem so sure about Jane. I presume you are going on recollections from the future.'

'Exactly that. As I said, everything is right. Even if my memories are from future events that never actually occur, we need to offer Jane a chance.' As these words were coming out, a strange thought echoed around in her mind. 'Run with me on this one. It just occurred to me that Jane's future as an author is dependent on us. Perhaps, just maybe, this is all part of my journey, to effectively keep time going in the right direction.'

'I am not sure I follow.'

'Maybe my memory from the future actually depends on our intervention now. Just say we do not offer Jane an alternate existence, she may never put pen to paper.' She then thought for a moment, seeing Meredith looking a little vague. 'So, my memory from the future is of a famous author named Jane Austin. I actually read all six of her books. Often it has occurred to me that some of my memories from the future might never exist. With that in mind, perhaps our actions now will ultimately determine future events. Importantly, thinking about this notion, we know this is true because my actions around the hunt resulted in Rebekha being here with us now. Had Jane not brought out the tea today we may never have become aware of her predicament and she may never have had the chance to become an author. Worse still, she would have perished sleeping in the woods come winter.' Although for some time, Rebecca had gained an ever-increasing understanding of her role in time, today's events magnified her belief that her destiny was to maintain time's equilibrium.

'I follow, although I am not sure I fully comprehend your notion.' She shook her head. 'As you suggested, let us run with this.' Meredith then joined the others at the table.

'Jane, do you know of the whereabouts of your aunt Cassandra?'

With narrowed eyes, Jane said, 'my aunt resides in Winchester. For some reason, I recall her address. She lives in a house named "The Bookend." Thirty-eight West Lane Field. I do not know why I know, I do, however.'

'Before the death of your parents, what job did your father do?' Rebecca asked, still searching to ratify her assumptions.

'He worked in wool manufacturing.'

That was all Rebecca needed to be sure. She turned to Meredith. 'This is who I said it was.'

Jane, sat glancing between Meredith and Rebecca.

'I am so sorry to speak of you in that way, Jane. Both Meredith and I were discussing your situation just a moment ago and I said I believed your father was involved with the manufacture of wool. It would seem I was correct,' she said glancing at Meredith, then smiling towards Jane.

Rebekha leaned forward and touched Jane on the hand. 'I have not offered many words this day. I like to observe. Jane, in years to come, you have much in front of you. Your future will be literarily fluent and your words will inspire others. Many will clearly hear your voice. Allow your intuition to flow freely.'

Hearing Rebekha speak in this way brought home a stark realisation for Rebecca. She could recall speaking about her journeys through time in the 21st century. Even then, her words were met by some with raised eyebrows. However, people in this era are considerably less accepting and she could see how some may perceive Rebekha's foresight. Those fearful of her words would be all too quick to label her and without a doubt that is how she ended up in that horrid asylum. Rebecca had always felt free-speaking females such as Rebekha had been condemned. Male-dominated societies just hadn't accepted women as equals. She could recall learning that until 1982 publicans in Great Britain could refuse to serve women. This had got her thinking and the more research she'd done, the greater her annoyance had grown. Although she'd learnt this in a future life, for some reason, her recollections on this subject were clear. She felt sure, many females that were labelled witches in the 13th, 14th and 15th centuries were probably no different from her, or indeed Rebekha. For all-time, free-spirited women who saw the world differently and spoke of their visions with verve, mostly faced criticism. Waking up in 1827, Rebecca knew only too well she had to be careful what she said in certain company. *This needs to change*, she thought. 'I believe Rebekha's words are insightful. Jane, you show a naturally robust understanding of the English language. Like my great aunt suggested, you could and should use this to aid your journey through life.'

'Ma'am, I love to write. I have not done so of late.'

Narrow eyed, but having a good idea why, Rebecca asked, 'Jane, why is this?'

'Ma'am, I have no pen or parchment.'

Meredith touched Rebecca's hand. 'Many mock Rebekha when she shows such inner wisdom, so it is nice to hear you approve, Rebecca.' She then went to the door and asked April to fetch her a quill, paper, and the family seal. 'Oh, and please bring extra paper. 'Jane, once I have written my letter, you can keep the quill and extra parchment. Feel free to write as much as you desire.'

Grinning, Jane said, 'thank you, Ma'am.'

Moments later, April appeared. 'Ma'am, as you requested,' she said, placing a fancy looking quill, an ink pot, a candle, the seal and to Rebecca's mind, some rather fancy looking parchment. Inexplicably, although all these items were instantly recognisable to part of her brain, the other side was thinking, *what a rigmarole*. She then watched as Meredith wrote a letter with beautiful handwriting, and placed the letter between folded paper. She then lit the candle, gently heated some red wax-like material, and sealed the envelope. Once more, the two sides of Rebecca's memory pulled in opposite directions.

'April, please have this letter sent quickly to Hampshire in our carriage. Advise the coachmen they should wait once in Hampshire until Miss Cassandra is ready to travel back here. I expect her to return here at her convenience.' Turning to the others, she said, 'I have explained the situation to Jane's aunt by way of my correspondence, and requested her pleasure. Jane, knowing of your circumstances, I would like you to stay as our guest until your aunt arrives.' Again, she went to the door. 'April, please take Jane to bedroom seven. Offer her a warm bath. After, dress her in some of Rebecca's old clothing.'

Appearing somewhat taken aback, April nodded.

Picking up on this, Meredith said, 'Jane was placed in our service incorrectly by an unscrupulous relative. Her parents, I have learnt, were of the landed gentry. As such, we should afford her the same status.'

April smiled and beckoned Jane to follow her.

As Jane got up from her seat, she turned to Meredith. 'Thank you, Ma'am.'

'Please call us all by our Christian names. You are one of us now, Jane.'

Rebekha said, 'Meredith, this is why you are my favourite niece.' She then got up and headed towards the walled garden, singing as she went.

Seeing Rebekha this way invigorated the scraps of a delightful, yet sadly distant memory for Rebecca. As she was trying to grasp the vague accounts that were just out of reach, Meredith spoke and brought her back with a jolt. Inexplicably, it was as if she was dreaming and had just been woken.

Meredith gently tapped Rebecca on the arm. 'Tomorrow, we must see to Millicent. George has already commissioned work on her father's old yard and that is complete.' She then seemed to think for a moment. 'It is peculiar having two memories. Thoughts in my head are a little mixed. One recollection is of Millicent, you and I speaking of her situation and arranging a room here. The alternate memory is of George, Millicent and I arranging her room in the servant's quarters. Matter not, in the morro we can help with her onward journey.'

Inwardly Rebecca realised that although her intervention with Jonathon and the hunt had altered much, it hadn't interfered with Millicent's destiny. What it had done though, was to create an alternate route for Millicent. This notion got her to wonder how Millicent would respond to her, or indeed if she knows her at all. Perhaps, because of her intervention in 1825 Millicent's path has altered completely. *Perhaps she only knows me as the daughter of this house, and not the protagonist who travelled back from 2007*, she thought. She shook her head thinking, *maybe her life's path has changed completely*. 'Meredith, have you checked on Millicent? You see, I also have two memories, albeit, mine are one-hundred and eighty years apart. My recollection from the future has Millicent in a complex situation whereby she is prepared to take her own life. Any memories from this life are very jumbled, confused mostly, I suspect, by my intervention two years previous to today.'

Meredith smiled and gently touched Rebecca's hand. 'I have checked and she is fine. I know of her vulnerability and nothing you have done has altered this.' She then seemed to consider her next words. 'I have thought much about the position we both find ourselves in. For you, your conflicting

66

memories are from markedly different eras. This has been complicated further by your intervention two years previously. An intervention that has apparently altered the here and now, albeit, only slightly. Mine, on the other hand, is from a world I know, and a world I do not know. It is as if these alternate recollections just appear in my thoughts. Sometimes when we dream, we wake suddenly and the dream feels oh so real, however peculiar the circumstances might be. It is like this with my alternate memory, except, unlike a dream, it stays with me as factual.'

The two chatted for a while longer until it started turning a little chilly.

'Best we go inside.'

'Yes, I think I may go to bed early. I am exhausted.'

'I am not at all surprised after all you have experienced in just three short days.'

'Yes indeed, three days covering one-hundred and eighty-plus years of memories all jumbled in together.'

As Rebecca lay in bed that evening, although so much had happened today, her inner thoughts focussed on how her intervention with Jonathon had changed so many lives. The more she thought about this, a notion started to become clear in her head. Suddenly, a light went on in her head. In the past, although she was aware her intervention altered both the time she was in and the future, she'd always accepted each door that opened as a new journey or adventure. She was now wondering, especially after today's events with Jane, if her route was somehow mapped out by a higher authority, maybe Ethernal or someone like him. The situation now, with Millicent not committing suicide and instead re-opening her father's old yard. Also, Rebekha being here, happy and any notion of her going to America has been completely dispelled. Plus, Jane's destiny and path changing to her rightful path are all things that were supposed to happen. What she'd just realised was without her intervention with Jonathon, none of this would have occurred. *Maybe that's it,* she thought, *my job is to keep time going in the right direction.* She considered this a little longer and now found herself wondering if every decision she ever made in the past altered history for good. *If so, perhaps that is my destiny, to maintain the equilibrium of time. What if though I make the wrong choice and the results are negative? Nah, enough thinking, I'd just go back and keep changing it until I got it right.*

Chapter 8 – Where do I belong?

The following morning, Rebecca woke feeling weary. Not for the first time, she decided to have a shower and then slumped back in bed realising her only option was running a bath. 'I'm gonna rig something up,' she mumbled, reckoning all she needed was the end from a garden watering vessel and some rubber hose. Running the bath once more made her wonder if she was better suited to her life in the future.

After her bath, and getting dressed with what felt like fifteen undergarments again made her compare the two lives she'd experienced.

She headed downstairs thinking about this, although seeing Millicent at the breakfast table refocussed her thoughts. The way Millicent looked up and half smiled, made Rebecca question this woman's thoughts.

'Morning, Millicent. How are you this fine morning?'

With the corner of her lip twitching, Millicent grumbled, 'like ya care.' She then looked away.

Rebecca raised her eyebrows. Thinking about Millicent's reaction and comment would suggest the conversation the two of them had had a couple of days ago never actually occurred. Although somewhere deep in her thoughts, she was ready for their relationship to perhaps alter, she had never considered her intervention with Jonathon would have deleted their chat from time. *Oh well*, she thought and sipped her tea. To her mind, all that mattered was Millicent was here, and her path had been altered for the better.

Moments later, Meredith and George joined them at the table and Millicent's reaction was completely different.

Rebecca actually felt a little uncomfortable and was unsure what to think or say. In fact, the more she thought about today's impending events, the more she was trying to think how she could duck out somehow.

Meredith turned to Rebecca. 'George and I are going to take Millicent to the yard and get her sorted. I thought because you were so tired last night, you might like a relaxing day pottering about here. Aunt Rebekha has gone for a walk over to the lodge on the far side of the lake. I suggested it was perhaps too far to walk, but she was insistent.'

Rebecca shook her head, not knowing what to think. Did this woman read my thoughts again, she wondered? To compound her sentiments, she was thinking that is half a day's walk at best. 'That will be nice. I could do with a day doing nothing. I agree about walking to the lodge. That must be a four-hour walk on a good day.' For some odd reason, she once more had a distant memory from the future of this lodge, and although she knew it was on the other side of the lake, there was nothing else. Just then, George and Millicent, who had been talking headed off. One thing that occurred to her, was the way Millicent was speaking to George. When Millicent addressed her, it was with a heavy, almost indolent accent, yet speaking to George, her words were concise and clear. She wasn't at all sure what to make of this, however, there was a question that had been nagging at her thoughts. 'Meredith, can I ask you a question?'

'Yes, my dear, ask what you wish.'

'You mentioned my hair colour the other day when you were talking to Rebekha. Actually, I have two questions. What colour was my hair before Rebekha went to Scotland, and why did she go there and where did she stay.'

Meredith lent her head slightly to one side. 'I saw your reaction when I said that and wondered when you would ask. Your hair before your time in the future was dark brown. When you came back to me, your hair was this beautiful blonde colour. Strange at best. Anyways, the last time Rebekha saw you was just before the hunting incident with Jonathon, so she only ever knew you with brown hair.' She then nodded. 'So, Rebekha went to stay at a convent in Perthshire, all of her own choice.'

'Where is Perthshire?' Rebecca asked as another distant memory rumbled through her thoughts. In fact, this memory was so vague, she didn't even know why she was asking, just felt the need to know.'

'She stayed at the Matilda Monastery within the grounds of Perth Priory. You seem keenly interested. May I enquire why?'

'I don't know, I just need to know. I think it may have something to do with an incident from my life in the future.'

Meredith seemed to think for a moment. 'I suspect there will be many questions like this. I believe, in time, your life from the future will fade and you'll face fewer conflicting memories.'

'I hope so. Right now, I sometimes feel as if I am in some kind of limbo.'

'Limbo, how so?'

'Well, sometimes my recollections are distant. More so of late, they are clear and vivid. What is confusing is that both my memories from this life and my future life are on par. Both existences seem real and feel tangible. There are times though, as, with Perth, my memories from the future are distant, and almost dream like. As you alluded to yesterday. What is most confusing is I constantly find myself analysing things as if I were a woman in her forties, but at the same time, feel fifteen.'

'That must be exhausting.'

Rebecca nodded. 'Very.'

'Right, I am going to head off with George and Millicent. I hope you have a good day. Try not to think too much and just allow your thoughts to relax. Maybe go for a walk in the Spry Wood. Always your favourite place.'

Rebecca narrowed her eyes certain she'd given this wood its name 180 years into the future. 'How long has it been called the Spry Wood?'

Meredith smiled, 'ever since you gave it that name when you were about five or six years old.'

Hearing this made her wonder if she'd named it the Spry Wood in the future because there was a subliminal memory from this life lurking in her subconscious. The more she thought about this, the more convinced she was that it must have been this way around. There was no other explanation. *So maybe this is my true life*, she thought.

After everyone had left, she had a brief chat with Jane. Now sitting there on her own, she decided to go for a walk in the Spry Wood. Her brief conversation with Meredith had left her with unanswered questions. She thought walking in the wood might just trigger a memory and give her some answers.

As she made her way into the woods, she found herself involuntarily walking with purpose. Her consciousness had no memory of this wood, oddly though, she seemed to know where she was going, as if she was being led by a distant inner thought. She paused for a moment, searching her brain for some kind of recollection. There was nothing other than an inner light leading her. Once more, she found herself confused, wondering if this was her real life, just she was missing any conscious memories, almost as if she had amnesia.

It had been dreary and overcast when she initially entered the woods, and rain looked a certainty. As she turned and entered a curiously familiar part of the wood, she was a tad surprised to see bright sunshine. She looked back up the path she'd walked and bizarrely it looked dingy with no sign of sunshine. She stood there for a few seconds looking back and forth. On the far side of the wood, she could see a wooden bench. The sunlight filtered through the trees and nestled invitingly around this bench. *A good place to gather my thoughts.*

She took one step forward and felt the most bizarre sensation. The ground below her foot was spongy to the point of being springy. She looked down and couldn't believe what she was seeing. Where there had been straw-like grass just a second ago, instead, the ground was covered in a kind of moss, which had an array of tiny pink, yellow and red flowers. She glanced around and this moss covered the ground as far as she could see in any direction. It was as if she'd stepped into some sort of dream. Why she thought this, she didn't know, but there was this strange notion in her head that this is where the fairies, pixies and elves must live. In the most peculiar way, it felt as if she'd stepped into the middle of a fantasy story. She headed over to the bench and sat down, feeling rather odd, but very relaxed, almost to the point of being enchanted.

As she sat there trying to work out what was going on, she heard youthful female voices. Narrowing her eyes, and listening, it sounded as if the voices were getting closer.

Seconds later, two young girls walked into the wood.

'Mummy, there you are,' the smaller of the two girls said, 'we've been looking for you all morning.'

With her emotions dancing, Rebecca smiled at the girls unsure what to say. She glanced down for a second trying to gather her thoughts and noticed she was wearing some kind of dark blue, tight-fitting material on her legs. To her mind, the material was that of a farmer's dungarees. It was obvious something really bizarre was going on but she just couldn't get any grip. Realising her hair was short and the way her skin felt strangely different made her question what was actually happening. Over the years, both in the future and to some degree in this life, she'd experienced many strange scenarios.

Nothing though had ever come close to making her feel like this. It really was as if she was in a dream, but awake.

The older girl sat next to her, touched her arm, and brought her back to the here and now. Then Rebecca felt the most peculiar sensation, and without actually moving, she was standing up. She shook her head trying to focus her thoughts. She was now looking at an older version of herself sitting, talking to the girl. It was as if she was there, but not. At a complete loss what to think, she tried to listen to what her older self was saying to the girl. Mysteriously, the words were muffled to the point where she was unable to hear what she was saying.

As much as her thoughts were all over the place, she felt unusually calm. From behind her, she heard a clear, peculiarly familiar male voice.

'Worry not, it is I, your watcher, Ethernal.'

She turned, but there was no one there. Still feeling calm, she mumbled, 'what is going on?'

'You have faced a conundrum over the last few days. Unsure if your world is here with Meredith, or in the future with your daughters.'

'Daughters,' she exclaimed. She closed her eyes, ransacking her mind, trying to recall anything that would give her answers. She had no recollection of daughters, and any memories of a future life seemed profoundly distant and vague. All she had was snippets of another life. It was as if her conscious brain knew she'd had some sort of life in the future, but there was nothing tangible. What she did have at the front of her thoughts, was a somewhat distant, but fascinatingly reassuring memory of this male who was speaking to her. It really was as if her mind was a blank canvas. She couldn't even remember how she got here, or where she'd come from. It was the most bizarrely unsettling notion, but mysteriously, she felt peaceful.

'Your accounts of a distant life many years from now are fading quickly. I have brought you here today to offer a glimpse of a life you will live in the future. The female you see in front of you is you in another world many years into the future. The young females are your daughters. You now have a choice to make.'

'Choice?' Rebecca asked, turning once more.

'A choice indeed. You can stay here in eighteen-twenty-seven if you so decide. Alternatively, you can choose to re-join your family in the future. If you decide to stay here, any recollections of your future life will disappear. You will continue to venture along the corridors of time and follow your life's destiny. If, however, you decide to go back to that future world. Your journey through time will be over and you will have no memory of this world. Indeed, you and those around you will have no knowledge of your ability to open doors into the past, or indeed future.'

'Err, I need time to clear my head.'

'I understand this.'

'Where do I belong, here or there?' she asked pointing.

'That is your choice alone. If you stay, you start afresh. Your next journey through time will come as a complete surprise to you and those around you. You may find your path met with scepticism. So, be mindful of your words, and with whom you speak. Your only solace will be Rebekha. Not even Meredith will know of your ability. She will, as your mother, be accepting of your words.'

'So, she is my mother?'

'You must decide that.'

Rebecca stood there for a few seconds watching herself with the girls. 'If I stay here, will the girls have a mother?'

'They will. Although the woman in front of you is a mirror image, she is who she is and is where she belongs. For many days, you walked in her shoes.'

These words cleared Rebecca's focus. 'I know what…' Before she had a chance to finish, she was once more sitting on the bench, alone. She rubbed her eyes, feeling a little at sea. Shaking her head, it was as if something had just happened to her, but there were just the odd fragments of a conversation in her thoughts. She sat there, again rubbing her eyes, and reckoned she must have nodded off and been dreaming. It was weird though, because normally her dreams were relatively clear, at least for a short while.

She shrugged her shoulders and decided to head back indoors and continue working on a project she'd been going through with her great aunt Rebekha.

As she made her way through the wood and down towards the servant's quarters, she again felt a tad uneasy. She knew she'd been working on something with Rebekha, but right now, didn't have a clue what it was. *How very peculiar*, she thought.

Fleetingly, she had the odd snippet of something happening and as quickly it was gone from her mind. She was now feeling really rather odd and stood for a moment trying to gather her thoughts. Right now, it was as if her brain was empty. She couldn't even recall what had happened this morning, or how she got to the woods. Mysteriously though, although this should have unsettled her, she was actually feeling rather focussed. There was this peculiar sensation telling her she was on a mission of sorts.

Chapter 9 – Starting over

Arriving at the back of the manor, she could see Rebekha sitting at the garden table. She headed over, sat down, and said, 'Good afternoon, Aunt.'

Rebekha narrowed her eyes a little. 'Are you feeling alright, Rebecca? You appear a little disordered.' She then lent forward and squeezed Rebecca's hand. 'I believe I know the journey you have been on and what occurred.'

Rebecca sat back in her chair unsure what she meant. 'Yes, my thoughts are a little muddled. I went to the Spry Wood for a walk, fell asleep, and woke suddenly with the remnants of a peculiar dream. It was most strange because my dreams are often clear. Today, not so.' She then realised Rebekah was supposed to be out all day on a long walk. 'I thought you'd gone on a walk to the lodge across the lake?'

'I did, but halfway, something was telling me to head back. As always, I followed my intuition. It would seem I was needed here to speak with you.' She then seemed to consider her next words. 'When you went for a walk to the Spry Wood, you were not dreaming.' Again, she squeezed Rebecca's hand. 'I will impart some information with you now. Initially, you may find my words confusing. Know I have your wellbeing at heart and allow your intuition to lead you as mine does me. You have been on many journeys through your life of which you will have no recollection. It may appear hard to comprehend at first, but inside you will have enough predisposition and character to settle your confusion.'

As much as her words should have sent Rebecca's mind into a spin, she felt strangely calm. Rebekah's aim was with good intent. She felt comforted and reassured, knowing for sure this woman had her well-being at heart. With a need to know more, she said, 'please continue, Aunt.'

'My dear Rebecca, you have a unique ability. What I am about to say, to most, will sound and be unfathomable. Many folks would dismiss my words as ludicrous through no fault of their own. Society dictates an uncompromising opinion towards far-reaching voices and in particular, those who are female. As a result, many travel their life blinkered towards the likes of us. You, however, have a free agenda.' She then paused for a moment, clearly thinking. 'Rebecca; you have a unique gift that allows you to journey seamlessly through the pages of time. Sometimes, that ability will take you to another century. Although you have no recollection now, you have ventured along this path many times. On every journey you took, you faced complicated and multifaceted decisions. Always though, you followed your intuition and thereby maintained the equilibrium of time. Often, your destiny required you to alter past events. Every choice you made was the right one and this allowed time to continue along a smooth path. You see, without your intervention, time could and would take a negative direction.' She then looked at Rebecca as if she was looking into her soul. 'You appear settled.'

Nodding, wide-eyed, and particularly excited, Rebecca said, 'I am with you, please tell me more.'

'So, while in the woods, you were offered two options. One was to live in the twenty-first century with a family you would see as your own. Taking this option would result in you losing all knowledge of your time movements, your experiences, and you would lose your ability as a time-fixer. The other option was to stay here. Like the first option, you would lose any recollections of your time journeys. However, you would feel you are with your real mother, dear Meredith, and of course, myself, your guiding light. Importantly, you would still hold onto the gift of movement and therefore, still be able to follow your life's destiny.'

Rebecca thought for a moment. 'Presumably, I chose to stay here with you. You said I would lose any recollections. Mostly, I have, although...' She then thought for a moment. 'There are tiny shards of light, enough to suggest I know of the world you speak. Perhaps that is why I am so relaxed. I am actually excited to see what tomorrow brings.'

'That is good. I was once able to travel through time. When I was young, I faced a conundrum and was unable to choose the correct path. This resulted in a malevolent female continuing her life in the fifteenth century. The outcome of her survival would have a hugely negative impact some five hundred years later. Because I could not forward her demise, I lost my ability to walk the corridors of time. My ability then passed to you. You are stronger than me and were able to complete your mission. Although this resulted in the untimely death of that evil female, you knew it was the right choice. You have the ability to make a judgement, knowing even if the outcome for one or more may be negative. Ultimately, you are preventing an adverse outcome that would outweigh the present situation you find yourself in. I was never able to make that judgement. Of interest to you, although Ethernal suggested you would start with a clean memory slate, you have a strength none of us has seen before. Therefore, you may still hold some memories.'

Still feeling comfortable with Rebekha's words, part of her brain was a little misty. She wasn't sure if this was because of excitement, what her aunt had said, or just simply comprehending this most inexplicable information. Inexplicably though, although her aunt's story was outlandishly magical, she knew it was real. 'For some reason, I am reading from the same page as you. I accept all you say as true. My intuition, consciousness and subconsciousness tell me so. I sat with you today with no knowledge of my ability to travel through time. For all that, there were snippets rumbling around, almost a make-believe notion that I had seen incidents beyond my years. Your words have brought that notion to the front of my consciousness and the more we speak, the greater these distant memories become.'

'This is your strength. Through time, there have been many who share your ability. They are, and forever will be the time-fixers. All with one destiny, maintain a balance and keep ours and future lives on an even keel. I believe, as do others I have spoken with, you are the strongest since the first Rebekha some four-thousand years since.'

This brought a vivid, but distant memory to the front of Rebecca's brain. For some strange reason, her mind's eye was seeing a beautiful woman surrounded by huge sand dunes. 'I know this person, but I do not know why.'

'You will often see fragments, but they should be out of reach. Although, I suspect with you, unlike others who have been in this position, your memoirs may not be completely out of reach. You now face many new pages. On your way back to me, you were possibly aware of a scheme we were following together. I suspect, although you were conscious of this path, the details may have been beyond you. This is because you are starting over, starting afresh.'

'What was the scheme, may I ask?' Incredibly though, although Rebecca asked, there was something telling her she knew the answer. She couldn't grasp the details though.

'In the future, during our journeys, you, and I both witnessed many changes in society. One of these changes gave a voice to women. Our detailed memories of these changes were vague. Nonetheless, what little recollection we had was enough to invigorate us sufficiently to plan a scheme and try to affect these changes now.'

Nodding, Rebecca said, 'I know this.' She didn't know why she knew, because there was no recollection of having this conversation with Rebekah. Nonetheless, something was telling her she knew of their plan. 'It is most odd because although I feel like I am starting on a blank canvass, so to speak, there is something telling me this female movement is very important to me.' Rebecca thought for a moment. 'Inside, I feel resolutely empowered by this concept. In fact, the more I think about this, the more invigorated I am. It is most strange though because part of my brain says this is how it is in today's society. Whereas something in my subconscious wants to fight this level of disparity. It is as if I have two alternate emotional reactions.'

'I feel exactly the same. I have within me a clear and detailed recollection from the future. I was just a child when I travelled into the future and witnessed an event and the details have stayed with me. I know that in eighteen-sixty-six a group of women will organise a petition that demanded the same political rights for women. They presented this petition to two MPs who supported this ideal. That bill was defeated, but only just with seventy-three MPs voting in favour. This subsequently led to many female groups forming across the country. Frustratingly, it took these groups until eighteen-ninety-seven to join together. This, I suspect, is because the national press either did not support such movements or did not consider the story newsworthy. As a result, each group was oblivious that the neighbouring city or town had a similar movement.' She then once again seemed to be thinking deeply. 'When I lost my ability to move in time, it would seem I did not lose touch with my recollections.'

Rebecca thought about this for a moment. Although her memories prior to today were sketchy at best, she knew somewhere inside, this had always been important to her. 'So, our mission is to start this movement now, forty years ahead of time. I must stress it is imperative the individual groups speak to each other. Although my memory is devoid of any movements in time, I do have snippets of information. It is most odd, because my common sense tells me the idea of travelling to another day, let alone a year, or century is ludicrous. My intuition tells me it is true. I have a peculiar notion telling me to look to the future to find solutions that will aid our movement.'

'I am sure you will find answers either in the future or past. We must tread lightly when speaking of this with others. Even your dear mother will raise her eyebrows, she will nonetheless support us, as she always has. She is an advocate for our outspoken, and what is to most folk an outlandish notion, however, even she will struggle with this idea. With that in mind, we must be prudent when considering sharing this with dear Meredith. There may be a time when either of us feels she may be receptive. For now, at least, we must travel this road alone.'

'I understand that. For me, the only questions are where and how my journeys start?' Although Rebecca was comfortable with the idea of jumping from one year to the next, not knowing how it would happen or what to expect was a little unsettling.

'Worry not. As in the past, you will follow your intuition. You may initially hold your breath briefly, wondering what is going on. You will quickly settle though.'

These words helped ease the little apprehension she was feeling and once more she found herself excited by the concept. As she sat there considering her feelings, a tiny shard from a remote memory said she should head to the summerhouse. 'Rebekha, do you know of a summerhouse?'

Rebekha smiled. 'I suspect the summerhouse you ask of is the building we know as the servant's quarters. I have often thought it would be a fabulous summerhouse.'

Inwardly, her emotions were a little jumbled. For sure, these glimpses of memory were invigorating her imagination. There was, however, a tiny element of trepidation. 'Do you know how this all works?' Seeing Rebekha narrow her eyes a little, she thought about this question and reckoned she needed to ask it in a different way. 'When I travel through time, how does it happen? Will I feel anything and, is there any danger?'

'I can only speak from my own recollections. When I moved to another era it was seamless. One minute I was here and the next I was somewhere else. I never felt anything, it just happened. I recall the first time I was around twelve years old. Although my emotions were a tad jumpy, I felt calm. Something inside me said it was alright and I was safe.' She narrowed her eyes a little. 'As for danger, I am not sure I can answer that. For me, the only danger was from the situations I found myself in. I knew to keep my wits about me and was always able to make the right choices. I suspect it will be similar for you. Know this, you have travelled these roads before and always came back safely. Because you have no conscious recollections, your trepidations are understandable. Worry not. Your intrepid nature and vibrant intuition will lead you.'

The two sat around chatting for a while. Sometime in the afternoon, Meredith joined them.

'Hello, my two-favourite people. How are you both?'

'Hello, Mother,' Rebecca said. Instantly, this triggered an odd emotional feeling. She considered this for a moment but couldn't find a reason for her reaction. In a bizarre way, it was as if she wanted to call her Meredith, rather than mother. As the three sat there chatting, she kept feeling the need to speak with her mother about her conversation with Rebekha. She did though, realise she had to be prudent. The only idea she couldn't shake was wondering how she would be with Meredith once she'd actually jumped through time.

After a while, Meredith said, 'it is time for supper. Shall we join George inside?'

Chapter 10 – A New Chapter

The following morning, Rebecca lay in bed with a thousand thoughts running around in her head. She'd had a fairly restless night and was feeling weary. Mysteriously though, there was something telling her to get up and go for a walk. As she was running the bath, an idea popped into her head. She turned the bath tap off, slipped her clothes on, and headed downstairs. Entering the morning room, she said, 'Morning, Mother. I have this idea. I want to make bathing easier.'

Clearly curious, Meredith pouted her lips a little. 'What do you mean, you want to make bathing easier?'

'Well, it strikes me running a bath is a bit of a fuss. So, I had the idea of connecting a hose to the tap. Then connecting the top of a watering can, and… well, it will be easier if I show you.'

Meredith lifted her head a little and half grinned. 'You and your ideas. If you go to the walled garden, I think you will find the gardener is there now and he may be able to help you.'

Rebecca headed outside. Around ten minutes later she returned with a length of hose and the sprinkler from a watering can. 'Mother, I was thinking, I need a lightweight waterproof sheet or something similar. Perhaps the kind you might have placed on my bed when I was a baby.'

'I know what you mean. You go upstairs and I will see April for the sheet you need. I will see you in the bathroom shortly. Curiosity, the cat, and all that, as you often say.'

As Rebecca headed upstairs, her mother's comment about curiosity rang a distant bell in the recesses of her mind. As she entered her bathroom, this notion was soon forgotten as she started trying to attach the hose. 'Well, that was easier than I thought,' she mumbled.

'What was easier? Also, here is the sheet you asked for.'

'Thank you, Mother.' After a bit of fluffing around, she managed to attach the sheet to a balustrade that ran around the ceiling above the bath. She then turned to Meredith. 'This is my idea,' she said turning the tap on a little and running her hand under the sprinkler. 'Perfect.'

With her palms lifted, Meredith asked, 'so how does this work?' She then seemed to think for a moment. 'Actually, I can see how this might work. So, where did this notion come from?'

'I have no idea. It just came to me while watching the tap run, slowly, I might add.' She then explained her idea in a little more detail, referring to it as a shower. Using this term caused an odd emotion, but she was too focused to consider this feeling. 'Ok, Mother, I am going to give it a try.'

'I will leave you to it then.' Meredith shook her head and chuckled.

After a bit of messing around, Rebecca realised her idea needed work. In particular, with the hose attached to the hot tap resulted in the water either being too hot or just trickling out slowly. Nonetheless, she managed to get herself clean.

She headed downstairs and explained the hot and cold scenario to Meredith.

'Well, if you speak with the gardener, I am sure he will have the parts you need. I must say, while you were… taking a shower… I realised what a grand idea you have come up with. A waterfall in our bathroom, whatever next.'

'Well, I feel invigorated and fancy going for a long walk. Maybe I will speak to the gardener later.' Although she wanted to finish off sorting the shower, something was pulling her and she couldn't quite put her finger on whatever it was. It was the most peculiar sensation and seemed to be overriding her every thought. Rebekha had said to her to follow her intuition and she was going to do just that. It had been an odd morning, what with the shower idea popping into her head, ostensibly from nowhere and now this. 'Hmm, we'll see,' she mumbled.

As she headed outside, she could hear Rebekha singing and following her voice, found her in the walled garden.

'Morning, my lovely,' Rebekha said.

'Morning, Auntie. I heard you singing and thought I would come in and see how you are before I go for a walk.'

'I am very cheerful today. The sun is shining, the bees buzzing and the flowers smell beautiful. Where are you going to walk?'

'Not too sure as yet.'

'Follow your intuition and who knows where it may lead you.'

Rebecca stood there for a moment gazing aimlessly down towards the lake. She was considering that word again, intuition. She felt a tiny bit of apprehension, but for some reason though, it was a positive apprehension. *If there is such a thing* she thought. 'Right, I will do just that, follow my gut and see where it takes me.'

'It has always served you well in the past. Embrace what today brings.'

Rebecca, trying not to force anything, got up and ambled towards the lake. Mysteriously, there was nothing leading her, other than her feet. She continued down the path, brushing her hands through the long wispy grass, forcing her mind to wander aimlessly. As she arrived by the lake edge, she stood there enjoying the warmth of the midday sun. As hard as she tried to clear her thoughts, she kept wondering what may lay ahead of her. It was a weird sensation because her conscious thoughts were telling her to clear her mind and just let something happen. Once more, her subconscious brain kept nudging her, and having never experienced anything like this before, she wasn't at all sure what to expect.

The longer she stood there, the more uncertain she felt. Then, just as she was considering heading back to speak with Rebekha, she could smell a delightfully familiar odour coming from the servant's quarters. Taking a deep breath through her nose, she couldn't put her finger on the smell, so decided to head over and investigate. The closer she got, the stronger the aroma was. She knew she knew this smell well, but just couldn't put her finger on it. Then as she approached the front door, something seemed different. Whatever it was, it had unbalanced her emotions, making her feel a bizarre mixture of apprehension and excitement. She stood at the front door trying to regain some kind of composure, at a loss for what to think. Reckoning the smell was perhaps one of the maids cooking, she decided to investigate inside.

As she opened the front door, there was a whoosh of warm air that filled her nostrils. Instantly, she knew it was the smell of Christmas cake, which unbalanced her a little more, wondering why someone would be baking a Christmas cake in June. As she stood by the door, she could hear some rather distinguished voices coming from the room on her left. *That's not any of our maids speaking*, she thought.

Heading along the corridor, she was feeling most peculiar. She stood with her hand on the doorknob listening. Shaking her head, she couldn't believe what she was hearing. It was as if there were many male and female voices all speaking at the same time. To compound this, there was a lot of jeering, booing, and shouting. Fascinatingly though, every voice, to her mind, sounded as if they were from the aristocracy.

With her heart racing, she gripped the handle and took several deep breaths trying to settle her nerves. Even though she was a little uncertain, her gut was shouting at her to open the blinking door. Involuntarily, she closed her eyes and stood for a second. Mysteriously, the door felt heavy and would barely move. She opened her eyes, leaned against the door with her shoulder and eased it open. *What the heck*, she thought, as her senses were overwhelmed by a din of noise, and the sight of over a hundred paper waving men, all hollering, and jeering.

Then a female voice said, 'Miss, you are not permitted to enter Parliament.'

Before she had a chance to focus, a tall, eccentrically beautiful woman closed the huge oak door in front of her. As she turned, it was obvious she was no longer in the servant's quarters. *How can this be* she thought, looking around and seeing she was now standing in a grand hallway, with high ceilings, and huge male portraits covering every wall.

Whatever had just happened should have heightened Rebecca's anxiety levels. Instead, she was feeling curiously exhilarated and mostly relaxed. The woman who'd just spoken to her, possibly in her sixties, looked so very familiar, so much so, it caused a rather peculiar sensation. Before she had time to consider this, the woman touched her on the shoulder.

'Females are not permitted to enter Parliament.' The way this woman was looking, to the point of scrutinising Rebecca, was rather irregular. 'I feel as if I know you.'

'You, I also,' Rebecca said, ransacking her brain.

The woman narrowed her eyes. 'It is most strange though, the young girl in my thoughts is from a memory many years past.' Again, scrutinising Rebecca, she said, 'The girl I remember though, had brown hair.'

With her pulse now racing, she took a couple of deep breaths. 'I believe I became a little lost and somehow stumbled into this building. May I ask where we are?' The woman had said parliament, but to her mind, it couldn't be the parliament in London.

'With pouted lips, the woman said, 'I fail to see how you stumbled into this building. Especially as you are female. Mostly, this is a male domain and security is strict.' The woman again narrowed her eyes. 'Are you here with your mother?'

'No, I am alone,' Rebecca said, thinking *where are we.*

'Matter not, you are here. This is the Houses of Parliament, Westminster.'

With her subconscious and conscious brain now going in circles, Rebecca's head was full of questions. *First things first,* she thought. 'You suggested this is a male-dominated environment. May I ask why you are here?'

'We are here with a drafted amendment to the Second Reform Bill. If passed, this would give women the same political rights as men.'

Hearing these words stimulated Rebecca to no end. 'Well, it is about time,' she stated, waving her hands profoundly, not knowing why she felt so adamant. Nevertheless, she did. With tiny glimpses of a distant memory drifting in and out of her thoughts, and with an invigorated passion, she asked, 'what year are we in?'

The woman again narrowed her eyes, this time though, it was in a different way. 'It is eighteen-sixty-seven, but surely you know this, unless.' Again, she pursed her lips and looked Rebecca up and down in an inquisitive way. Extraordinarily though, there was a friendliness about her. 'Your passion for equality for women is evident and a match for mine. I agree it has taken too long for us to arrive at this point.' The woman once more looked Rebecca up and down. 'I feel I know you, although I know not why.'

Even though Rebecca found herself in the most bizarre situation, she felt relaxed, with her thoughts recalling Rebekha's words. In particular, she'd spoken of moving from one year to the next. Clearly this was where she found herself now. Not only had she moved seamlessly forty years into the future, one minute she was at home, the next she was here in London. The more she looked at this woman, the less she was able to place her. Then the woman growled under her breath and pulled a terse face after a man brushed past, almost unbalancing her. This jogged a distant memory in Rebecca's brain. 'May I please ask your name?'

Shaking her head and waving her hand flippantly in the direction of the man, she turned to Rebecca and smiled. 'My name is Millicent Fawcett. May I enquire yours?'

It can't be, can it, Rebecca thought as her distant memory became a little clearer. 'Were you once Millicent Black. Oh, and my name is Rebecca Hewison.'

The woman, with her mouth, open a little just stared at Rebecca. She then started blinking continuously with her eyes flitting from side to side. 'How can this be?'

'I too am all at sea. I am not at all sure what has happened to me today.'

Shaking her head and appearing rather anxious, she said, 'I knew a Rebecca Hewison who was identical to you, excepting your blonde locks.' Appearing as if she couldn't believe what she was saying, she uttered, 'that was forty years past though. You are her though, are you not?' She then touched Rebecca on the arm. 'I was Millicent Black, once, many years ago, although I suspect you know this.'

Rebecca gripped the woman's hand. 'I am not sure I understand what just happened. One moment I was standing in the hallway of the servant's quarters, the next I was here.'

Millicent's eyes flickered briefly. Looking directly at Rebecca, she said, 'I have a distant but clear recollection. I recall overhearing a conversation between your mother and you.' She shook her head. 'The words are now clear in my head. You told your mother, Meredith, you had travelled from the future. Of course, I dismissed this ludicrous notion. Then a

90

couple of days later, you returned and convinced me my life was worth living. The rest, as they say, is history. Yet, here you are once more. I wonder what role you will play in my life today.'

'I too now find myself wondering why we are here together.' She thought for a second. 'I believe perhaps it is something to do with the reform bill. I have many scrambled memories rushing through my thoughts. Some are distant, some profound. I know your bill will be defeated today by one-hundred and ninety-six to seventy-three. For some reason, I also know it will take another fifty years before you are successful. I suggest neither you nor I will be here to witness this. I also am aware that today's defeat will be followed by the birth of the London Woman's Suffrage, and subsequently, many groups will form nationally. These groups will form independently as a result of newspaper articles referencing today's defeat. Frustratingly, it will be a further forty years before you form as one national movement.'

'Perhaps this is why we have been brought together. With your knowledge, we can make sure we ladies come together as one movement.'

Seconds later, a man walked up to Millicent.

'This is my husband, Henry. Henry, this is an old friend, Rebecca Hewison.'

'I am delighted to meet you, Rebecca.' He then turned to Millicent and held both her hands. 'Sadly, our bill was defeated One-hundred-ninety-six to seventy-three.'

'Well, that is closer than I expected. At least, aside from you, and our dear friend MP John Stuart, we have a further seventy-one advocates.'

'Sorry to leave you with this news, however, I must return.'

Millicent turned to Rebecca. 'Although I never doubted your story of time movement, you knew the outcome, including the exact numbers. For a breath, I found myself wondering if you had overheard the result. I dismissed this because you are the feisty young lady I remember. My only question is still the same. Why have we been brought together today?'

'To my mind, it is so I impart my knowledge and after today's defeat, you lead a nationwide group to work together, rather than fragmented groups.' As she was speaking, an idea came to her. 'A notion just occurred to me. Perhaps, when I return to eighteen-twenty-seven, which I believe I will, I should speak with you then. That way, you can start this movement forty years earlier. Then maybe, just maybe, you will see success in your lifetime.'

'Your first thought is reasonable and effective. The second…' She then looked down. 'How will you convince me in eighteen-twenty-seven to start this movement? I was in my fortieth year before I even considered this path.'

Rebecca thought for a moment. 'You answered that question just a moment ago. The conversation you overheard between my mother and me would be a starting point. If your name is on the reform bill, perhaps I could take a copy back with me and show you.'

'My name is indeed on the reform bill. However, it shows as Fawcett and not Black.'

'Well, at least we have a starting point. Clearly, you have the tenacity for women's rights within you. Perhaps the combination of your tenacity, beliefs and my involvement will be enough to start you on your mission forty years ahead of schedule.' I was told by my great aunt Rebekha that my life's destiny is to maintain the balance of time. She said, my intervention in the past would lead to a better outcome in the future. Perhaps, this will work in reverse. Whereby, my involvement now, in the future, and subsequent interjection in my time creates a positive outcome for all women.'

92

Nodding, Millicent said, 'it is all we have to work with.' She then handed Rebecca the bill of reform.

Chapter 11 – Woman's Suffrage

No sooner than she'd taken the paper, Millicent started to fade from Rebecca's vision. Unsettled and unsure of what was happening, she held her hand out towards Millicent, but as she did, she was gone. Taking a deep breath and trying to compose herself, she realised she was once more gripping the doorknob to the small room in the servant's quarters. Weirdly, she felt as if she had just woken from a bizarre dream. Looking down and seeing the bill of reform in her hand, told her this had been no dream. She now had the most peculiar impression filling her thoughts. Somewhere deep in her mind was a distant notion she'd been down this road before.

Although her emotions were somewhat scrambled, she felt really quite relaxed. Considering her feelings, she once more reflected on Rebekha's words. Peering at the reform bill, she knew she now faced a complicated journey and it started with convincing Millicent of her journey. If nothing else, she needed the advocacy of this woman. *Right, one step at a time*, she thought, and after one more glance around, headed back to the main house.

Arriving indoors, she called out, 'Mother, where are you?'

Seconds later, Rebekha and Meredith both appeared from the drawing-room.

'Hello, Rebecca. I have just been speaking with your mother. I told her of your ability and suggested she should allow herself sufficient insight to embrace your stories as truthful. I said that in time, she would see all the evidence she needed.'

Grinning, Rebecca said, 'I have evidence here, Mother' and handed Meredith the bill of reform.

Taking the paper, and with Rebekha peering over her shoulder, Meredith said, 'oh my goodness. Wherever did you find this? Clearly it is real, but how can this be? It is dated eighteen-sixty-seven.'

Rebekha pointed to the paper. 'Meredith, I said she would show you the evidence. With prudence, please look at two of those names. Millicent Fawcett, and Henry Fawcett.'

Meredith narrowed her eyes. 'It cannot be. Can it?'

'It is our Millicent. She marries Henry,' Rebecca said, excitedly, not having a clue who Henry was in this time and why both Meredith and Rebekah would know of him.

Meredith narrowed her eyes a little. She then turned to Rebekha. 'Remind me of what you said just two days past. I need to hear it again because as we stand, my emotions are profoundly confused.'

Smiling, Rebekha said, 'I told you Millicent was dating Henry Fawcett and they seemed blissfully happy. Indeed, Millicent blossomed since her meeting with this gentleman and is unrecognisable.'

'I thought that was what you said and just needed to hear it again.' She then turned to Rebecca. 'Well, it seems it is true and you are able to ramble through the pages of time. I am not sure I will ever understand or indeed comprehend how this can be. However, it is the truth. I always knew, like your great aunt that you were positively different from others. I say positive because although many may receive your opinions with a negative response, to me, you are both blessed.'

Delighted by her mother's words of assurance, Rebecca said. 'Well, I have a mission in front of me. It starts with me speaking with Millicent. I need to convince her of my ability to move through time, and all being well this paper with her signature will help to convince her. Then, hopefully, I can help her start her movement now, rather than wait forty years. It is clear, Millicent has it within her to be an advocate for women's equality. The only obstacle will be her accepting my help. Also, thinking about everything, does she have the tenacity to become a female activist now, or does this come later in her life.'

'I have always believed, once given the right opportunity, every individual can blossom. It would seem this is the case with Millicent. We offered her an alternate route, which led to her meeting with Henry. Had we not opened these doors for her, well...' She then seemed to think for a moment. 'It is a battle you face. There are few advocates for the equality of women in today's society. However, it would appear that Henry may be one of those. I know of his family and they are well respected. He also is of good schooling. I recall reading a newspaper article referencing his work as head boy at a well-respected school in Liverpool.'

Rebecca held her hand out to Meredith. 'Thank you, Mother, for accepting my story. I appreciate how difficult it must be for you. The concept of moving through time is at best a fictional story for the likes of Jules Verne.'

Meredith narrowed her eyes. 'Who, may I ask, is this Jules Verne you speak of?'

Rebecca shook her head, not having a clue who Jules Verne was or where his name came from. The way his name just popped into her head made her feel rather odd. Then just as puzzlingly, a vague spark ignited in her thoughts telling her he was a writer... born in 1828. This threw her completely. Although often over the recent days, sparks of memories had appeared in her head, there had been nothing like this. Not only did she have a name she also knew he was an author. To muddle her thoughts completely, this person wouldn't be born for another year. Trying to work out how she could explain this to Meredith, she sat there staring aimlessly.

'You look lost, Rebecca,' Meredith said, with a mixture of curiosity and empathy.

'Umm, I am not sure what to say. His name just appeared in my head. Perhaps he is someone I heard of. I am not altogether sure.'

Rebekha chuckled. 'I would suggest you possess a fragment of memory from another time, maybe in another life. I know this name from my limited time in the future. He is a writer of fiction and will not be born until the year next, eighteen-twenty-eight.' She again chuckled. 'It tells me you have had many experiences in time and for whatever reason, now keep only shards of fragmented recollections.'

Meredith raised her eyebrows. 'I am not sure I will ever understand what you ladies share. I am not at all sure I want to comprehend either.' She then raised her eyebrows. 'However, I do accept you are both equally unique. Additionally, I trust your words absolutely and appreciate you both share an equal path and journey. To that point, perhaps you can visit Millicent together. Your joint words will, as they have with me, be more convincing.'

Rebecca nodded, glanced towards Rebekha, and asked, 'would you consider joining me on my quest?'

'I would delight in this opportunity. I have only had brief interludes with Millicent. We share common ground. Like me, often, she has been misunderstood. She lacked guidance as a child and as such, often followed damaged paths and subsequently acted defensively, to conceal her mistaken choices. I saw within her, easily hidden from many, a virtuous soul. On the few occasions we spoke, Millicent often referenced society's inequity between men and women. Therefore, it comes as no surprise to learn where her future life may lead her.'

'Sadly, my occasions with Millicent have been complicated and fraught with tension. This was due to us both choosing the wrong options. For me, I chose to shy away and accept what I believed to be my situation as a fait accompli. For Millicent, she was misguided into an unvirtuous scenario.' Meredith narrowed her eyes a little. 'I must accept the part I played in this by holding my tongue when George and I drifted down conflicting roads. I will say, I was always aware of Millicent's tenacity. It comes as no surprise to me as Rebekha suggested, Millicent's destiny is profound.' Again, she paused before holding Rebecca's hand. 'To think we convinced her only five days past to follow an alternative route to the suicide pathway she had in mind.'

For some reason, Rebecca was struggling with Meredith's words, having no memory of this interaction with Millicent. This wasn't the first time Rebecca's lack of memory had left her in no man's land. Often, she'd have snippets of distant recollections, but the lack of immediate memory was leaving her increasingly frustrated. Just as she was about to say something, Rebekha held her hand.

'I can see from your eyes, you have no recollection of this incident with Millicent, Rebecca. I recall when I lost my ability to travel, I also superficially lost my immediate memory. In time, I gained fresh memories. I did, however, retain clear accounts of my journeys through time. I suspect, in time, your frustration will ease.'

'It is very frustrating. I was offered two choices, stay here, or stay in the twenty-first century. It was suggested I would lose all memory of either life once I chose my path. I never realised I would completely start afresh.' Rebecca then thought for a moment. 'As frustrating as it is, I do still get glimpses from the past, or future, which shine a clear light.' Rebecca considered her own words and for the first time recognised she was actually starting afresh. 'I accept my situation and must focus on tomorrow.'

'It would seem we have the opportunity to also offer Millicent a fresh start. just as you have, Rebecca. I took each day as if |I were opening the pages of a new book.'

Meredith, pouting a little, looked back and forth. 'Starting afresh.' She then glanced between the two of them, shook her head and said, 'I am not sure I fully comprehend the situation you both find yourself in. It matters not. I trust in you both. I am actually excited to see if together, you can alter society's standpoint towards females.'

Although Rebecca's thoughts were a little jumbled, she had a mission and Meredith's words enabled her to focus. 'Right, I presume we will find Millicent at her yard. Rebekha, would you like to come along with me now? Or should I go alone the first time?'

'I would delight in this venture. It is a long time since I left our grounds.'

The three chatted for a little longer, having realised it was too late in the day.

'A fresh start in the morning,' Meredith suggested.

The family had a delightful evening meal. It was their last with Jane as her aunt was taking her to Winchester the following morning. Often, during the meal, Rebecca felt she wanted to say something to Jane. Every time a thought entered her head, it vanished just as quick. Then just as she was heading off to bed, she turned to Jane. 'I am not sure why I feel the need to say this to you, but I do nonetheless. Please write often. You have many stories to be told.'

Jane narrowed her eyes in a way beyond her years. 'Rebecca, I will. I love to write. Thank you for all you have done for me. My life was sad and lonely until you spoke to me. I will never forget you.'

As Rebecca headed up to bed, she had no memory of speaking with Jane previously. She shook her head, now accepting her thoughts had only brief glimpses of past events. Unusually, although frustrating, she was comfortable with this scenario. She lay in bed considering what may have led her to this day and what tomorrow may bring. She mumbled to herself, 'starting afresh.'

Chapter 12 – A New Page

Rebecca woke the following morning feeling excited by what today would bring. Before heading downstairs, she had another attempt at taking a shower, which after some adjustments was a little better. Feeling pleased with herself, she joined Meredith, George, and Rebekha in the breakfast room.

'You are looking pleased with yourself, Rebecca.'

Yeah, I am,' she said and grinned, 'my shower, or waterfall, as you call it, worked much better today, Mother.'

'I suspected so, going by your wet hair,' Meredith said and raised her eyebrows towards George, grinning.

Narrow eyed, and glancing from the side of his eyes, George asked, 'waterfall. Could someone explain, please? Also, Rebecca, it is yes, not yeah.'

'I know, Father, sorry. Anyways, I rigged up a way to run the water via a hose so it comes out like a shower. Lot less rigmarole than waiting two days for the bath to run.'

'Hmm, indeed. Well, I must leave you, ladies, as I have a meeting in Liverpool today. I should be back for supper.' He then turned to Rebecca. 'I have organised a new copper tank and then your bath time might reduce from two days to one.' He then walked off chuckling.

Replacing the copper tank triggered a significant impact on Rebecca's thoughts. It most certainly rang an alarm, but for the life of her, she didn't know why. 'Have a nice day, Father.'

Rebekha looked at her and said, 'I can see your mood has changed, Rebecca. May I ask why?'

'Yes, I noticed that also.'

'I am not altogether sure. When George, I mean Father, said he was replacing the boiler, it triggered an alarm deep in my thoughts.'

'What is a boiler?' Meredith asked, with that all too familiar inquiring look on her face.

At a complete loss what to say, Rebecca shook her head. 'Err, I really am not sure. I guess it just sounds right.' She then noticed Rebekha smiling and nodding.

'A boiler is a term used for a copper tank way into the future.' Her face then took on a serious appearance. 'In a future existence, you witnessed your surrogate mother lose her life after a boiler exploded.' She held her hand up to stop Rebecca from speaking. 'Fear not, you were able to travel back in time, and convince your proxy father to replace the old boiler, which subsequently saved your mother's life.'

Nodding, Rebecca said, 'That'll be it then. For some reason, as you were telling me the story, I knew the outcome. I do not know why, but hey, I did.' She then nodded again. 'This is going to take some getting used to.'

'You can say that again,' Meredith said, wide-eyed.

After breakfast, they all decided to head into town and meet up with Millicent. Because George had taken the second carriage, while Jane's Aunt Cassandra was using the first, the ladies travelled on horseback. This suited Rebecca, allowing her some time to consider how she would deal with these remote recollections altering her perspective. On route, she found herself recognising some buildings along the way. The strange thing was they felt like old memories. Then, on the outskirts of town, she saw a book shop which instantly triggered a powerful reaction somewhere deep in her thoughts. 'Meredith, may I ask, have you ever used that book shop?'

'I believe George may have, although I do not actually recall it being here. Perhaps it is new, although looking at the wear and tear, perhaps not.'

102

'I need to pop inside, if only briefly. Can we stop for a couple of minutes?' Then as Meredith and Rebekha dismounted, she turned and said, 'I feel the need to go in alone. Sorry, I am just following my intuition.'

Meredith lifted her hand, 'go, follow your lead.'

'Yes, Rebecca, follow your intuition. It has always led you along the correct paths.' She then touched Rebecca's hand, and whispered, 'go find some answers.'

This comment had an odd, yet profound bearing on Rebecca, even though she knew precisely what her aunt meant. She stared up at the old tatty sign above the shop, but it didn't ring any bells. She wasn't at all sure what she was expecting or looking for, but her inquisitive need was becoming stronger. With her lips pursed, she breathed deeply through her nose and pushed the door open.

'Hello, Rebecca,' a gentle-looking, grey wispy haired, elderly man said, his elbow perched on a huge old book.

Rebecca shook her head. 'I know you and you clearly know me. I do not know why though.' Again, she shook her head.

'Opening the huge leather-bound, very old and delicate looking book, he pointed to a page and beckoning Rebecca forward, said, 'our paths are destined to cross often. We have met before and will meet again.'

Rebecca leant over his shoulder, but the page was blank. She held her hand up in a questioning manner.

'Whenever your foresight dims somewhat or you become a little misplaced, my job is to light a candle for you. This page is blank and will remain so until you accept your route wholly. You are confused by the next steps you should take, thinking this way or that way. This is because you turned a new page, as we have in this book and you are starting over. Throughout the coming days, weeks and months, your decision making will become second nature. I am here to assure you that you have guiding lights who will forever be there to catch you. You are the strongest of our time-keepers and many souls follow your every step. Some closely, some not so. Your beloved Rebekha is there to hold your hand, physically. There are others, like me and Ethernal who will appear when you hesitate. Always trust your intuition. It will serve you well, as it has for eternity.'

Although she was feeling really rather calm and inspired, one word jumped out at Rebecca. 'Eternity, you said for eternity.'

He nodded and again pointed at the book. 'This is the forever book. Many pages have been filled by others like you. You too have also filled many pages. This book will stay open for eternity. There is no limit where you can go either forward into a world yet born and back to where it all started in Mesopotamia. So, the answer to your question is within you. You may choose on any day to close your page and bring an end to your time with those like me.'

Rebecca shook her head, unable to believe how comforting this man was and how reassured she felt. Her common sense, on the other hand, was almost choking, and she was aware of this. She was, as she always had been, very capable of ignoring any ugly practical decisions or verdicts that would stop her from seeing what others miss. 'I am still unable to focus on today. I do not know how to approach Millicent with a paper that will not be written for another forty years.'

He shook his head. 'Look at the paper.'

Rebecca opened her satchel and unrolled the parchment. To her astonishment, it was blank. She checked her bag once more and before she had a chance to say anything, the man held his hand up. His long, skinny fingers waving.

'The paper has served its purpose, to engage your dear mother, Meredith and no more. It is now blank and serves no use to you or Millicent. You must step with firmness and engage with Millicent's principles, beliefs, and strengths. You know of her fortitude and capabilities. Empower her through your support. You will not bring forward the dateline. Instead, you are here to make sure she doesn't miss her destiny, her scene in history.'

Within Rebecca's thoughts, she had a distant understanding that during her journeys through time, on most occasions she would be required to make an intervention. Since her time with Millicent in the future, she'd felt destined to alter this woman's route and bring forward females' day of reckoning. She reconsidered her role and as she did, the man again pointed to the page.

'Words have started to appear for today. Only a few of which relate to our meeting. Often, you will be required to turn back the clock and reset some events. This will be because, if allowed, time will take an alternate and often damming route. In your real-time, as today is, you must not alter events. Instead, you are here to encourage them. If the path slips, you go back and try again. This has occurred with you in the past and will again in the morrow. For now, follow your own insight.' He then offered his hand towards the door.

As she approached the door, she turned back to thank him. As she suspected, he was gone. She didn't know why she would be prepared for this, but she was. She was also profoundly aware, faint drifting memories were becoming clearer in her consciousness. As she left the shop and saw Meredith and Rebekha, her thoughts became clearer. She knew exactly what today would bring. 'This is difficult to explain, Meredith, although I suspect, you Aunt, will understand.' She then told them all about her conversation with the elderly man.

'I know this man as the bookkeeper. I met him only once.' Rebekha then turned to Meredith. 'The journey Rebecca must take today must be done alone. I know this. Perhaps you and I can walk around the town and allow Rebecca to follow her destiny.'

Chapter 13 - Millicent

Meredith, although appearing curious, said, 'we can visit the new victualing house for some refreshment. Rebecca, as hard as this is for me to follow, I know you are on a path most others would dare not tread. Go with our love and fortitude. You will find Millicent's yard just around the corner. We will take the horses and return presently. If your time with Millicent is short, you will find us near the river,' she said and pointed.

As Rebecca headed off in the direction of Millicent's yard a strong, yet slightly remote memory told of a time in the future when she visited the victualing house. For some reason though, her subconscious wanted to call it a café. *Hey, café sounds better to me*, she thought and shook her head, increasingly comfortable with these memory episodes. As she turned the corner and saw Millicent having a disagreement of sorts with a robust-looking man, her focus changed.

She quickened her steps and as she grew closer, she could hear Millicent speaking loudly.

'Just because I am female does not mean I will sell my wares to you cheaper. They are not, as you imply, of lower quality. Now pay, or go.'

With a spark ignited, Rebecca stood by Millicent's stall, brushing past the man as she did. Averting her annoyance from the man, she said, 'aha, the best fruit and vegetables in the county. Better than any vender, run by male or female.'

The man turned, grabbed her arm, and growled, 'who asked your opinion, you tiny waif of a girl. Your place is making my bed or cooking my food. Now be off with you.'

Absolutely infuriated, Rebecca just managed to stop herself from kicking his ankle. 'Do not,' she said, stepping close to him and elongating each word, 'do not speak to me in this way.

Release your grip from my arm and step back before I kick you. Just because I am female does not mean you have the right to abuse me physically or verbally. Or indeed treat any other woman disrespectfully.'

Still growling, but showing a tiny shard of surprise, he waved his fist in Rebecca's face. Something though was amiss and Rebecca could see an opportunity to push back. The way he moved one foot back as he spoke suggested he was a bully and no more. Something deep in her memory told her she'd been in this kind of situation before. She pushed hard on his shoulder. 'Wave your fist at me again and I will do more than kick you. I suggest you apologise to Millicent. Then find an alternative source for your food.' The way the man averted his eyes before looking back, Rebecca could again see she perhaps had him on the back foot. She just wasn't sure if this was because he was surprised and unprepared to be challenged, or was just a chauvinist bully who was doing what they always do when challenged, back away.

Stepping back, his eyes flitting between Millicent and Rebecca, it was all too evident he'd never been challenged like this before, certainly by a female. 'I will not apologise to this low life peasant,' he said, his voice raised while pointing at Millicent, 'she is exactly that, and has no rights, legally or otherwise.'

Just then a policeman walked over. 'Is everything in order, Sir?'

In spite of him annoyingly addressing the man only, Rebecca noticed him glance towards Millicent as if he knew her.

'This,' he said, pointing aggressively towards Millicent, 'wench's goods are trash and her outlet should be closed. I was explaining my opinion when this vagrant turned up and started pushing me.' He then pointed aggressively toward Rebecca.

The way this man's tone altered and his bravery suddenly went up a notch when the policeman arrived, told Rebecca all she needed to know about his bully tactics. 'Excuse me, but you grabbed my arm,' Rebecca said and turned to the policeman. 'Actually, he was not explaining anything, he was shouting at Millicent.'

Millicent, glancing between Rebecca and the police officer, said, 'this man has been very aggressive towards me and this lady.'

'Are you going to allow these women to speak? Their opinions matter not.' He then pushed Rebecca so hard, she fell to the ground.

The policeman stepped forward. 'Sir, take your business elsewhere.' He then pointed. 'Now,' he said, nodding resolutely. He then held his arm in front of Rebecca who had got to her feet and was moving towards the man, her infuriation all too evident. Wide-eyed, the police officer looked at Rebecca and shook his head. Turning back to the man, he said, 'Sir, please leave now.'

'Why should I leave? I have priority here, unlike these lowly females.'

'In normal circumstances, you have priority. However, you have an adverse history with our office. Therefore, Sir, this is your final warning.'

Instantly the man's whole demeanour altered. Clearly miffed, begrudgingly, he turned and muttering under his breath, trudged away.

Rebecca turned to the policeman and asked, 'why would he have priority here in normal circumstances?'

The police officer blinked a couple of times. 'Because he is male. Surely you are aware of this.'

Rebecca shook her head, unable to believe what she was hearing. Even though she was consciously aware this was the way things played out in 1827, seeing how male-dominated and prejudiced this society was first-hand went against everything she believed. Infuriated by an almost condoned attitude toward women was compounded by the police officer not stepping in when the man pushed her to the ground. She felt she wanted to argue the point, but had seen a way to broach the subject of women's suffrage with Millicent. 'Yes, I am aware, Sir. My words were brought about because he hurt me when he pushed me to the ground.'

'Miss, the legal standpoint on this would be you provoked him. That is the way it is.' He then turned to Millicent. 'I know you are close friends with Henry Fawcett. This is why I asked that man, James Hoodlum, to leave. He is known to our office and will not return to your stall. I suggest, in future, you have a man working here with you. A woman has no place running a business alone for many reasons, mostly, because it is disrespectful to men who are not in employment. Therefore, consider your position.' He then nodded and left.

Rebecca turned towards Millicent with her arms held up, utterly dumbfounded by what had just happened and how it made her feel. Strangely, a portion of her inner self was half-heartedly accepting of the way things were. This thought just served to intensify her feelings and helped her realise how easily women in this era accepted their position. This realisation was positively invigorating her desire to empower Millicent, which in turn would hopefully open the door for her to take early steps towards a suffrage movement, or at least make sure Millicent followed her destiny. Mysteriously, a thought occurred to her and she found herself wondering if Millicent only ventured down the suffrage path because of today's meeting. To further stimulate her thoughts, a fragmented memory from her life in the 21st century was coming to the surface. The name Margaret Thatcher kept drifting in and out of her awareness. She knew this woman would one day become the head of parliament although right now this very notion was so remote and distant it was almost laughable. Nonetheless, it was starting to dominate her consciousness and make her more determined. 'I cannot believe how ludicrously lopsided society is towards men.' She then raised her eyes. 'Good morning, Millicent.'

'Good morning, Rebecca. Did you hurt yourself when he pushed you over?'

'No, I am fine, thank you. I am just annoyed by how easy it is for us ladies to accept our disadvantaged position in society. The policeman suggesting the legal system would come down on the side of that man even though he pushed me to the ground was ridiculously biased. What was it he said, I provoked him?'

Millicent, wide-eyed, nodded, clearly on the same page as Rebecca. 'It continually maddens me. I need to have a man here on my stall. I do not think so.' She again shook her head.

'It is strange how I feel. I can see how women collectively accept their position. Often this is because they are brow-beaten into submission, or have been taught this is how it is. Then there are the ones who marry into money and are unable to change their destiny.'

Shaking her head, appearing annoyed, Millicent said, 'every woman can change their destiny. They just need to find an inner strength.'

Rebecca thought about Millicent's words for a moment. 'You are right. In fact, it answers my question. I was wondering if it was nurture or nature that made females so submissive. It is nurture. They are taught by their mothers and grandmothers to accept their position in society. It does not matter if you are wealthy or poor, women do as they are told.' Although Rebecca knew about the movement Millicent would play a significant role in forty years, there was a further memory deep in her thoughts. 'I believe, in years to come, women will be treated as equals. If you look through the pages of history, women were revered and respected. I am not sure when or where it changed. I also believe the changes must start somewhere, so why not with the likes of us.' As tempted as she felt to tell her about the likes of Margaret Thatcher, she reckoned the very idea of time travel, would or could, estrange Millicent.

'You are right about nurture. I never had such guidance, if you can call it that. So, I learned to stand on my own two feet. Perhaps that took me down some undesirable roads but ultimately led me to be an independent, free-thinking woman. Like you, I also believe it starts with us. My dear friend, Henry Fawcett, treats me as an equal. He asks for and respects my opinion on many issues. In particular, he is head of the local council and shares his ideas with me. One day, he hopes to be a member of parliament. I must add, he also believes women should have a vote.'

Millicent's words were music to Rebecca's ears. Although she was tempted to say something, she knew she was here to empower this woman and no more. 'There must be so many women who feel the same as we do. You are in an ideal position to speak with other women who come to your stall. Perhaps, we should all get together and form an alliance. In addition, you have an advocate in Henry.' Once again, Rebecca so wanted to tell Millicent she would marry Henry and what would follow in years to come, she also reckoned, especially after her meeting with the bookkeeper, to keep that news to herself.

'I have spoken with a number of women who are frustrated by their circumstances. One lady often comes to the stall baring bruises on her face.' She then looked down briefly and sighed. 'To my mind, it appears as if she has been beaten. I previously spoke to her about it, but she responded in a way that showed an inner fear. As much as I wanted to push her for an answer, she showed too much fear and I felt, well…' Millicent lowered her head briefly. 'The problem we face is the legal system. Men are allowed to beat their wives and the loose term is known as the *rule of thumb*.'

'Rule of thumb, what on earth is that?' Rebecca asked frowning.

Millicent flicked her eyebrows upwards, then showing her disbelief, wide-eyed shook her head. 'Some judge somewhere made a ruling that a married man can legally beat their wife as long as they use a stick no thicker than their thumb.' Again, she shook her head. 'I know, beggars' belief.'

Rebecca grumbled, unable to believe what she'd just heard. As annoyed as she was by this ruling, her mind once more was telling her things will change in the future. The way she felt right now, she was in no mood to wait for things to change, something must happen now. 'I really do not know what to say about this. It strikes me that these men who beat women, either verbally or physically are hiding their own weaknesses. I have always believed all bullies act aggressively to hide their own insecurities.' Inside, she was thinking she would fight back, but at the same time, she also recognised sadly, some women found themselves in a position where they were unable to stand up and fight back. The more she thought about today's events, increasingly, she realised this was about a whole lot more than a vote for women. 'Excuse my ignorance, Millicent. Is there a workhouse or sanctuary for women who are beaten? Somewhere they can seek refuge?'

'I am not sure I follow your question.'

The way Millicent answered, it was clear she had no idea what she'd meant by a workhouse. Thinking about it, Rebecca wasn't all that sure where this reference had come from and now found herself assuming, once more, it was a memory from the future. This wholly unfair, convoluted notion, caused a rather odd perspective. Part of her thought process considered it absurd that there wasn't such a place, whereas a portion of her brain seemed to be bizarrely accepting of this scenario.

'What I mean is somewhere a woman can go to escape being beaten by their husband.'

'A lovely idea, however, it would take a man's influence to build such a place, or even agree to somewhere being constructed. I have no doubt it would be considered illegal by some arrogant fool somewhere. That, sadly, is just the way it is.'

Although Rebecca was aware of how this bigoted world worked, it still angered her no end just hearing those words. Thinking about her emotions, she found herself wondering if her real-time was in the future. If so, was she here to experience first-hand how exhaustingly imbalanced society was. Even then, how could or would her knowledge from the future make a difference now. Either way, rather than show her frustration by swearing, which is how she felt, perhaps she should focus on at least trying to make a difference. The more she thought about this, increasingly she wondered if her job was to empower the likes of Millicent, or actually act herself. This question in itself created an emotional conundrum, increasing her indecision of where she actually belonged. If she acted now this would suggest this was her real-time. Clearly, though, the Book-Keeper was very exact, telling her she was to engage and empower Millicent and should not interfere with the timelines. She frowned inwardly. 'Surely, if this is my real life why should I not act now,' she mumbled.

Millicent, who was now serving another woman some vegetables, glanced at Rebecca with a quizzical look on her face. Rebecca shook her head, raised her eyebrows, and mouthed, 'talking to myself.'

After the woman left, Millicent turned to Rebecca. She narrowed her eyes slightly and lifted her hand in a questioning manner.

Unsure what to say, Rebecca raised her head a little passively. 'I was muttering to myself.'

'We all do that, often.' Turning her head to the side a little, she said, 'however.' She then appeared to think for a moment. 'I have always been aware you are different to the rest of us. The way you speak, the things you say and even the way you dress. When you came to me with Meredith and spoke of my destiny, you seemed to know I was considering taking my life. At the time, I was so down, I did not have time to consider your words. It has occurred to me since you knew what was going to happen before it occurred. Also, my knowledge of this meeting is clear in my head one moment, the next it feels like a distant dream. How can this be?'

Rebecca wasn't at all prepared for this question and thought carefully about how she was going to answer. On one hand, this was an opportunity to tell Millicent the whole story and perhaps engage her to act now. Surely though, if this was the right strategy, the bill of reform wouldn't be blank. Then a thought occurred to her and so she opened her satchel and took out the parchment. Seeing it in its original state should have come as a surprise to her, but it wasn't. Even though she only had fragmented memories of her journeys through time, there was this notion from her life in the future to expect the unexpected. She could see Millicent looking at the bill.

'That looks interesting and reminds me of some papers I have seen Henry with. It most certainly appears to be official and of importance. May I enquire what you have there?

Rebecca glanced between the paper and Millicent, wondering if she should tell her the whole story, or just twist the truth a little. The conundrum that concerned her most was Millicent learning she would marry Henry. She never had an issue with altering aspects of time, but this was different. To her mind, it was like reading the last page of a book before the first. 'May I ask about your relationship with Henry?'

'You seem to be avoiding my question, although it occurs to me, as often in our previous meetings, this is leading somewhere unexpected.' She nodded. 'Henry has requested my hand in marriage. So, to answer your question, we are very close.'

That was all Rebecca needed to hear. 'Your suspicions were correct, and as you suggested, this parchment is official. It is actually a bill of reform.' She then handed Millicent the paper. 'You will see Henry's name at the top.'

Narrow eyed, Millicent took the paper and kept glancing between the bill and Rebecca. The more she read, the more she looked back and forth. 'I see why you asked about my relationship. It has Henry's name at the top alongside his good friend and member of parliament, John Stewart Mill.' Purce lipped she narrowed her eyes. 'Aside from the importance of this bill of reform, two aspects jump out at me. The date, eighteen-flipping-sixty-seven, and Millicent Fawcett. The name is, well... it would suggest I accept his proposal. The date, however, needs an explanation.'

Rebecca looked at Millicent and although she was expecting this reaction, still didn't have an answer other than telling her she was able to jump back and forth between times.

'Having been around your great aunt, I am prepared for any tale you may have. Indeed, I have suspected for some time, as I alluded to just a moment ago, you are different and by that, I mean you are unlike women of this era. You have an assurance which is more than just that of an intrepidly strong-minded woman. You know things you shouldn't. This bill enforces my belief that you are more than different. So, tell me all. I am completely open-minded.'

Rebecca was a little perplexed wondering what had altered since she spoke with the bookkeeper. She decided she had no option but to explain all about her ability to move back and forth through time. Noticing Millicent appeared to be wholly accepting of her tale so far, a thought occurred to her. She paused, glancing around at her surroundings, and again reconsidered if this was her real life. Whatever had happened over the last few minutes had inwardly made her feel different.

115

It wasn't just her indecision if this was her real life, or if her true destiny lay in the future, it was something a whole lot more. She wasn't at all sure what she felt, she just knew something had changed. 'What I am about to tell you may be very difficult for you to accept, or indeed comprehend. This life now is not my real life, my world is two hundred years in the future.' She looked down for a second unsure why she'd said that. Her intention was to, little by little, tell Millicent she could move through time, not say her life was in the future. Thinking deeply about her comment, she was aware Millicent was looking at her in a way that suggested she was accepting of her words.

Millicent shook her head and half grinned. 'I knew all along. The first time I met you it was as if you were not from my world. Your explanation answers every question I had.' She then paused briefly. 'It matters not what the truth is, your story fits. Remarkably, you being here today has kindled a passion within me. From a young age, I have felt the need to change the way women are treated and now I see a way forward. You spoke earlier of a refuge or workhouse for women who face abuse. I now recognise from your words this is something that may be available in the future. I say why not now, why not today? I know I earlier suggested it would require male input, but it just occurred to me that I have advocates in Henry and his good friend and parliamentarian John.' She then narrowed her eyes a little. 'I have one question for you. If your life is two hundred years in the future, how did you get here?'

By Millicent's reaction, Rebecca knew she had to offer this woman an explanation of sorts. Just as she was considering the right words, her thoughts filled with a clear and rich recollection of the future. 'Well, it all started in the year two-thousand and seven. I was a very inquisitive fifteen-year-old and my imagination had no boundaries. One day, while exploring the grounds of my parent's house, I came across an old derelict building. Today we know that building as the servant's quarters. Anyways, I went inside, up a spiral staircase and somehow ended up in this world, this time.' With Millicent apparently so receptive, she decided to explain all about her ability to move through time. For some reason, the more she said, the clearer her previously illusive memories became. When her head filled with thoughts of her two daughters and husband, although this tangled her emotions somewhat, she decided to tell all.

'So, what you are suggesting is in the future you live in a manor house with two daughters, and a husband, and you are forty-one years old. That manor house is the same one you live in now with Meredith?' She then shook her head, but it wasn't in a negative way, instead, it suggested she was actually stimulated by Rebecca's memoirs.

Invigorated, albeit a tad surprised by Millicent clearly accepting her story, she knew she had made the right decision. 'To answer your question, as outlandish as it may sound to many, I have two realities. One here as the daughter of Meredith and one in the future as a mother of two young girls and wife to an adoring husband.' She then thought for a moment. 'It would seem I am here to stay though, which is complex, to say the least.'

'I was just going to enquire how you feel being here, knowing you have two daughters, way off in a future life.'

'I am beginning to think I am here to help you start a female movement towards equality. Then perhaps, once my mission is complete, I may return to that other life.' She then considered her own words. 'If that is my real life because I am not sure. Inwardly, I question why I feel little emotional detachment from my daughters. I do believe that emotion may be protecting me, allowing me a clear site-line for what I need to do now. Interestingly, for most of my time here, my recollections from the future have been distant and remote at best. I'm not sure why but as soon as I started speaking with you today, my memories became clear and lucid. Previously, I had snippets of information that related to a world where women are mostly seen and treated as equals. Sadly, there are still parts of the world where this is not the case. Also, there are individuals who still treat women as second-class citizens. In this country, in the future, there are very strong laws against domestic abuse.' Rebecca briefly thought about the differences between the two eras. 'That world I refer to all started here with you, Henry, and others like you. My understanding though tells me it is another forty years before your Bill of Reform is heard in parliament and a further fifty years before you get to vote on who runs the country.'

'Oh, my goodness, what a tangled story you have. For some reason, my intuition tells me your story is real, even though it would be seen by many as the words of a mad-woman.' She then paused for a moment. 'The way many have labelled your dear aunt Rebekha. So, all things considered, we need to start this women's movement now and the sooner we do, the sooner you can establish where you belong. I believe as we alluded to earlier, a home for mistreated women may be the best starting point.'

'Exactly my thoughts and this could actually open the door for a suffrage movement. Every lady who takes sanctuary would be fully supportive of equality for women. They will be true advocates. I believe the word of our refuge would spread quickly. For sure, there will be those who have negative opinions. However, if as I suspect, most will become supporters and back our ideals. We do face many hurdles though. What is an important consideration is where would we home these women?'

'Start small and spread the word. Henry's family estate has many disused buildings and cottages. Some may need a little repair and the barns will need a lot of work. However, we need to start somewhere. I will speak with Henry this evening.'

'Thank you for accepting my story even though it must sound ludicrous.'

Millicent nodded, 'ludicrous indeed. However, it fits perfectly, so… I think we should keep this between us. I am not sure how others, including Henry, would be accepting of your tale. You only have to look at the way people look upon your aunt, who has often spoken of similar journeys.'

Hearing Millicent's viewpoint was all Rebecca needed. 'I will pop back tomorrow and we can start to build a plan. Hopefully, we can help your lady friend who shows signs of being mistreated. Perhaps speak with Henry this evening.'

'I will indeed. I am rather excited by our plan.'

'Me too. I will speak with you tomorrow.'

Rebecca headed back to the riverside to meet up with Meredith and Rebekha. On the way, she decided to pop in the book shop. She was hoping to find out what had changed, but as she neared the entrance, it appeared as if the shop had been closed for some time, perhaps years. Although this should have come as a shock to her, something inside half expected this outcome. Walking down towards the river, she considered why she would know the shop would be empty, she did though and this fitted with a strange inner feeling. It was as if she had become a different person, and was now thinking like a woman and not a fifteen-year-old girl. To compound this bizarre feeling, she was aware of a thousand memories cascading through her thoughts. Right at the front were strong, tactile memories of her daughters, Gabrielle, and Faith. Considering her thoughts, she wondered if her journey in this time was coming to a close and that was why accounts of her future life were becoming clearer.

Chapter 14 – Refuge and…

As she turned the corner towards the river, she could see Meredith and Rebekha sitting on a bench. In the strangest of ways, this made her feel rather odd. No longer did she feel like she was looking at her mother and aunt. Instead, they appeared in her inner thoughts as if they were characters from a book. It was the most bizarre feeling. For sure, she felt a strong sentiment towards both these women, but something had changed. For the life of her, she couldn't understand what was so different, but different it was. As she walked slowly across the grass, she could clearly remember walking this way with two women named Ruth and Amanda. She stopped for a moment and closed her eyes. She could see the scene clearly and was aware the two women were friends of her mother, Elizabeth, who they were all walking towards. There was something in the scene that was spooking her a little. In her mind's eye she could see the most elaborate building with people sitting at tables drinking, and beyond what appeared to be many carriages in every shade of red, green, and blue, all appearing to be made of some strange material. It was the most bizarre emotion. One side of her brain was saying don't be silly, they are automobiles, whereas the other side was asking, what is an automobile? She shook her head realising once more her thoughts were being jumbled by memories from the future. She headed over and joined Meredith and Rebekha.

'You appear a little at sea,' Meredith said, holding her hand out to Rebecca.

Rebecca shook her head, held Meredith's hand, and said, 'No, I am just fine.' Just holding Meredith's hand felt different and this emotion was a little confusing.

Rebekha looked directly at her with a quizzical appearance on her face. 'Have you been somewhere? By this, I mean, somewhere other than to see Millicent.'

'No, only the book shop.'

With her head slightly on one side, and narrow-eyed, Meredith held her hand up. 'Which Book shop?'

Before Rebecca had a chance to answer, Rebekha said, 'I know where she has been, Meredith. Do you recall me speaking of the Book-Keeper?'

'Vaguely, I do.'

'Yeah, that is where I have been. Odd though, I thought you were with me when I went in.'

The three chatted a little longer about the book shop and about Rebecca's time with Millicent.

'So, potentially, you and Millicent have a big journey ahead of you and it all starts in the morrow. Best we be heading back so you can rest in readiness. Of interest, I find the tales you two tell very interesting, but oh so confusing. So, if occasionally, I appear distant, you know why.'

The three took a meandering route back on horseback, and this allowed Rebecca some time to try and gather her thoughts. By the time they arrived home, she was still none the wiser about where her path lay. She did, however, feel significantly more comfortable believing everything would unravel in the right way. For all her doubt and indecision, there were distant recollections of travelling this road of uncertainty before. Reassuringly, something was telling her she'd always found a way home. 'Wherever home is,' she mumbled.

As they arrived back at the manor, she dismounted her horse and without thinking, led it to a stable named Nadine. Once more, her head filled with the most peculiar emotions. Considering this, she realised she was once more experiencing some kind of unconscious competence leading her and this was being triggered by distant memories.

'How did you know to take your horse to the Nadine stable?' A little louder and touching Rebecca on the arm, Meredith asked, 'Rebecca, did you hear me?'

'Sorry, I was miles away. What did you say? she asked politely, her mind still somewhere else.

'Rebecca,' Meredith said, touching Rebecca's arm gently. 'You really are not with us. How did you know to take your horse to the Nadine box?'

As if she'd just woken from a deep sleep, she turned to Meredith. 'I am so sorry. I really was somewhere else completely. It felt like I was in a dream watching myself scrabbling around in these stables. The thing was, they were dilapidated and neglected. I watched myself find a name plate and it was this nameplate,' she said, pointing to the Nadine plate. 'It was most bizarre. I believe some kind of memory led me to this stable.' She felt sure she'd been watching a different version of herself. That version though felt tangible and real. Considering these emotions, she looked down at the long white lacy dress she was wearing. In the vision she'd had, she was wearing a loose-fitting red top and some kind of tight blue dungarees on her legs. For some odd reason, this distant vision from the future suited her inner thoughts and felt rather comfortable.

'I suspect you were seeing the snippets of a memory from the future,' Rebekha said.

'I guess so,' she mumbled, watching Meredith shaking her head and muttering. This in itself caused a strange emotion in her thoughts. Once more, distant memories were becoming clearer. There was a sense that this Meredith was different from the one she'd always known. This in itself jumbled her emotions because one side of her saw Meredith as a beautifully tactile, much-loved mother. There was now though another vision, which saw this woman as an advocate of her time journeys, a kind of guardian angel who was always there to catch her. She followed Meredith and Rebekha into the house, her thoughts still floating from one notion to the next.

Rebecca then sat all the way through supper, her mind still going in circles. After apologising for being so distant, she decided on an early night. As she lay in bed, she went over everything that had happened today. Although her mind was full of today's events, what with the book shop and Millicent, the incident at the stables was the one that was most prominent in her mind's eye.

The following morning, as she was once more going through the rigmarole of taking a shower, she again considered her life in this world. With her emotions mixed once more, after breakfast, she decided to head into town and meet up with Millicent. She felt a need to push forward with the refuge idea, certain this would ultimately lead to her finding her real existence. 'I am going to head back to town to meet up with Millicent. We have a plan to create a refuge style home for women who need to escape torment at home.' She then explained all about her and Millicent's idea.

'Well, that sounds like a marvellous notion. I suspect as I am sure you are aware this may be greeted by some disgruntled groans. If there is anything George or I can do to help, please ask.'

'Thank you so much. I know we face hurdles, but we must start somewhere.'

'Would you like Rebekha and me to accompany you?'

'Thank you. I feel this is something I need to do alone.'

Rebecca headed outside to the stables and as she mounted Nadine, once more, thoughts from both worlds collided. On her way into town, she tried to dismiss her ambiguity and focus on the here and now. As she was falling asleep last night, she reckoned the only way she was going to find out where she belonged was to complete her mission in this world. Then, perhaps, she would have a clearer line of thought.

As she headed over to Millicent's stall, she could see her standing at the front with a dishevelled, frail-looking woman. As she grew closer, she could see Millicent holding the woman's arm. 'Is everything alright here?' she asked. She then looked down at the woman's arm. 'Oh, my goodness, your arm is very bruised.' She glanced at Millicent. 'It looks as though it is broken.' The woman turned toward Rebecca and offered a weak smile. Seeing this poor creature's face covered in bruises sent a shock wave through Rebecca's emotions. Again, she glanced at Millicent. 'Is this the woman you spoke of yesterday?'

'It is. Her name is Abigail.'

'Hello, Abigail, my name is Rebecca. We need to treat your arm quickly. Millicent, do you have any binding or bandage material? Also, I need two pieces of wood, this size,' she said, indicating with her hands.

'I have the wood you need at the back of my stall. I think I may have some material in the yard.' She then turned and headed off. Moments later, she returned with some kind of hessian like material. 'Will this do?' She then scrabbled around behind the stall and placed two slim pieces of wood on the table top. 'How about these?'

'Perfect. I just need somewhere we can sit comfortably. Also, I need some clean water.'

'Come around the back. I have some seating in the yard and there is a pail of fresh water and some cups.' Just then two older ladies walked over. 'Rebecca, go with Abigail, I will serve these ladies and join you imminently.'

As Rebecca led Abigail around the back, she overheard one of the women speaking.

'Poor lass is Abigail. Her husband is a brute.'

If Rebecca was at all unsure of Abigail's circumstances and if it was right for her to intervene, she now knew she had no choice. She took Abigail inside and started to clean her arm. 'How did this happen?'

Abigail looked at her, her fear all too evident. 'Miss, I fell while attending the goats.'

Rebecca shook her head. 'I need you to be honest with me. If nothing else, I need to know exactly how you did this to your arm so I can address your injuries correctly. You are safe with me and need not fear telling me all.'

Still showing her clear trepidation, she appeared to think for a moment.

'Alright, I can understand your hesitancy. If you do not tell me exactly how this happened to your arm, you may have long-standing issues and could even lose the use of your arm. Who then would tend your goats?'

This seemed to hit the mark. Her eyes changed a little and lowering her head, she said, 'My husband hit me with a fire log. It was my fault though because his supper wasn't warm enough.'

Rebecca shook her head, incensed. 'There is no reason for any person to hit you, and most certainly not your husband.' She averted her eyes, trying not to show how enraged she felt. 'How big was this fire log?'

Abigail looked around and pointed to a piece of wood that was around three feet long and two inches in diameter. 'Like this.'

'How many times did he hit you?'

He punched my face three times, then hit my arm once with the wood.'

Blowing slowly through her lips, Rebecca reckoned it may be a clean fracture that would heal well if treated correctly. She continued to clean the woman's arm. Then as carefully as possible, she placed the two slim strips of wood on either side of her arm and bandaged them as tightly as she dared. 'You do not need to live this way.'

'I have no choice.'

'You always have a choice. Millicent and I can offer you a way out. Somewhere you can live safely.'

With tears in her eyes, she whimpered, 'if he finds me, he will do the same to me as he did to my son.'

'WHAT,' Rebecca exclaimed. 'What did he do to your son?' she asked, her thoughts conjuring up horrid notions.

Abigail looked down, now sobbing, and Rebecca knew she had to push her for an answer. With her mind racing, she said. 'Please help me to help you. You must not live your life like this. I can help you, but you must help me understand your situation. I live at the Manor House just out of town. You can come and stay with us in safety. Alternatively, you can stay with Millicent and her soon to be husband, Henry Fawcett. He is an important man around here and I assure you, your safety will be a priority.'

She looked up, the pain in her soul all too evident. 'I know Henry.' She looked down and seemed to be deep in thought. She then looked up and it was clear to Rebecca this woman's browbeaten appearance had changed. Her tight lips and narrow eyes suggested she was now focused. It was as if a light had gone on in this woman's head. Angrily, but still, with tears streaming down her cheeks, she said, 'he hit my son with a mallet because he dropped a cup.'

Tight-lipped, Rebecca took a deep breath. 'How is your son now?'

Again, the girl looked down clearly unable to answer.

'Take your time, Abigail. I can see you are upset and frightened. You need not be afraid with me; I offer you a solace.'

'My son,' she said wiping away her tears, 'is buried in the woods.'

For all the outcomes Rebecca had considered, she wasn't prepared for this horrid conclusion. 'I am so sorry to hear of the sad passing of your son. How did he die?'

'It was that day when John hit Jimmy with a mallet. He never woke again.' She then looked down and started sobbing again. She took a deep breath, looked up and once more appeared angrily focussed. Her whole demeanour had changed. 'You are right, I cannot live like this anymore. I live in fear every day.' She glanced down briefly. 'I fear one day, I will end up with my son. Some days, I feel I would like to join my Jimmy. Speaking with you, I now know this is not the only way to escape my horrid existence.'

Rebecca continued to speak with Abigail. After a few moments, Millicent joined her with Henry. Rebecca explained the whole scenario, often turning to Abigail, checking to see if she was comfortable with all she was saying.

Henry stood up. 'This is more than unacceptable. I must speak with the local constabulary.'

'Oh, please do not. If John learns I have told you, all hell will be to pay.'

Henry touched Abigail gently on the shoulder. 'Fear not, we can hide you away at our home until the police have investigated further. If your story is true, and I have no doubts it is, your husband will face the full force of the legal system. You never need to cross his path again.' He then turned to Rebecca and Millicent. 'Millicent, poor Abigail is a perfect example of why we need to start the sanctuary we spoke of last evening. I have no doubts there must be many like Abigail and we can offer them an alternative way to live their life. I am going to speak with the police now. I suggest you close your stall for the day and take Abigail to my home. I will meet you there soon.'

After Millicent and Rebecca had cleared the stall away, they headed to Henry's home. Soon after they arrived, Henry turned up with four police officers. A senior looking policeman asked Abigail several questions, often turning to Henry with raised eyebrows.

'Abigail, you will be safe here with Henry and Millicent. We will go to your home and while I speak with John, members of our squad will check the area in the woods you spoke of.' He then turned to the other three officers. 'We have work to do. We have all the evidence we need. A witness, who is showing the obvious results of this man's brutality. We also have records of his previous aggressive behaviour. If Jimmy's body is where Abigail suggests, we will be taking John Scummings into custody.' He then turned once more to Abigail. 'Thank you, Abigail, for your courage. Your fear is all too evident and you have shown great fortitude in sharing your story with us. Henry, I will speak with you soon.'

Chapter 15 – Next Steps

Soon after the police had left, a doctor arrived.

'Hello, my name is Dr Holiday. Chief Inspector Martin Combs requested I attend today.' Glancing towards Abigail, he said, 'I can see why my attendance is prudent.' He then sat next to Abigail and started attending to her arm. 'Whoever put this splint in place did an excellent job.'

While he was treating Abigail's arm, Henry suggested they went to the morning room for some refreshments. On the way along the corridor, he turned to Millicent. 'When we spoke last evening, I totally committed to your idea of a sanctuary for women who have fallen on hard times. Never in my thoughts did I ever consider there were women who were being subjected to Abigail's kind of torturous existence. I have always known women in lower society led hard lives. To my mind, and considering my thoughts further, it would appear it is not just those women on lower incomes who are subjected to abuse. For example, women who marry into money, often because their fathers have guided them in that direction, can and do live loveless lives with no way out. Additionally, abuse can and does take many forms, not just physical but also psychological exploitation. I have also been aware that many aspects of a woman's place in society needs to be addressed. None least, this ridiculous law that rules a woman is the property of her husband and those not married are the property of their fathers. My dear mother often spoke of law changes and an alternative path for women at all levels of society. As the years have passed since her sad death, her vision has become all too evident to me. Thanks to her views, I have always nurtured a desire to somehow offer women an alternative route away from their subservient place within any household.' He then appeared to consider his thoughts. 'Today has compounded my intentions. What a horrid life Abigail has lived. To see her son murdered and then passively live in fear for her own life is beyond condemnation.'

'Henry, you should also know she said she often thought she would be better off with her son. By this, I believe she meant she was considering taking her own life as a way to escape. To live like that is just not right.' Rebecca glanced towards Millicent, aware she had considered suicide and was concerned her words may have had a negative impact. Seeing Millicent nodding, clearly showing she was comfortable with what Rebecca had said eased her concerns. Tight-lipped, considering her emotions, she said, 'we must change society's view of women.' Suddenly, a quote from the future came to her, but she knew she couldn't tell Henry about her time travel. 'I heard someone somewhere once say "behind every good man is a great woman." That will never become the norm unless we alter so many aspects of this ludicrously male-dominated world that we are part of.'

Millicent touched Rebecca on the arm. 'Rebecca, I hope you do not mind. I told Henry of your two existences. For sure, he raised his eyes.' She glanced at Henry and smiled. 'However, I informed him you had proof by way of your Bill of Reform. Would you mind showing him?'

Rebecca took out her parchment and handed it to Henry. 'You do not have to accept that I can travel from one era to another. All you need to understand is that I have information within my hand that pertains to future events. You may consider this story beyond acceptance. The important part is that this paper, irrespective of origin, should act as a catalyst for us to act now'

Henry grinned. 'Firstly, this is a little more than mere information. This is an actual Bill of Reform, dated, I might add, some forty years into the future. Secondly, my dear mother knew your great aunt Rebekha and was close friends with her mother. So, I know of the unique ability that has manifested itself through many generations of your ancestry.'

As he was speaking, a myriad of future memories cascaded through Rebecca's thoughts. 'Henry, you accepting my story makes it easy for me to help you and Millicent advance your vision of equality for women.' Rebecca then spent the next couple of hours explaining all about the suffrage movement, detailing certain timelines of change.

Narrow eyed, Henry said, 'so you are suggesting that it will be another forty years before our bill is even heard in parliament. Then a further fifty years before the vote is in favour. And, unbelievably, an additional seven years before women actually get to vote.'

'Exactly and all the more reason why we need to act now and bring things forward.' She then thought for a moment. 'I believe our initial focus should be on the refuge. The reason I say this is because inconceivably, the first safe-house for women escaping domestic abuse does not exist until nineteen-seventy-one in Chiswick, London.' She shook her head. 'That is another one-hundred and fifty years. Think of all those like Abigail who have no way out, then magnify that by one and a half centuries. I also believe starting our refuge now will open the door for the suffrage movement. It will give it momentum.'

'Both the safe-house, a term I like, and rights for women will face endless objection from men at all levels, from labourers to senior politicians.'

'Yes, but I suggest to you for every man that objects there will be an equal amount, if not more, like you, who are advocates. Significantly, in ten years, Queen Victoria will take the throne in this country and will stay Queen until nineteen-hundred and one. Although she will face condescension from some parts of society, she will become one of the strongest leaders the world has ever seen, male or female.' Rebecca then considered telling them about Margaret Thatcher, but decided that was too much information at this stage.'

Just then the doctor joined them. 'Abigail's fractures will heal well, mostly thanks to your work, Rebecca. She will need a period of convalescence. I am not sure she will find that time if she was to return to her own life.' He then appeared to be thinking. 'I suspect you know about her dreadful existence, or she would not be here with you. Henry, are you in a position to offer her shelter?'

Henry nodded towards the doctor and then glanced in Millicent's direction. 'Millicent and I have initiated work on a couple of the cottages within my family grounds. Abigail can stay there free of charge and we will make sure she is well fed and has everything she needs to convalesce.' Again, he glanced at Millicent and then towards Rebecca. 'I have six such cottages and with some small effort, all will be ready for...' He then narrowed his eyes in such a way it suggested he'd just realised the doctor knew nothing of their plans. 'I best explain our campaign. We three have been considering creating a safe house for women. This sorry situation with Abigail is just the catalyst we needed. We intend to use the six cottages and three of the larger barns to house downtrodden women.'

Nodding, the doctor said, 'What a fabulous idea. I often attend to women who have faced similar ill-treatment as Abigail. I have also been present when woman have taken their own lives, I believe to escape their horrid existences. These poor souls come from all levels of society. If I had the wherewithal, financially, I would have instigated such a...' He nodded, '...safe-house. I like this term. So, with this in mind, I would love to be involved at all levels. I can offer my medical skills, free of charge, and help wherever I am needed.'

Henry, smiling said, 'Thank you, Dr Holiday. We would greatly appreciate your involvement.'

'My mother taught me to respect women as equals. I firmly believe women are misjudged, mistreated, and generally disrespected,' the doctor said with obvious passion.

'We three are advocates for women's equality. Perhaps you could lend your ear to our plans beyond the safe-house.'

The four sat chatting for hours, sharing ideas, and making plans.

Rebecca looked up at the clock. 'Oh my, it is so very late, Meredith will be extremely worried.' As she spoke, the most bizarre sensation came over her. She rubbed her eyes, struggling to focus on the other three. Reckoning she must be tired, she sipped her now cold tea and again rubbed her eyes. That didn't help at all and as the three started to fade further, the strangest thing happened. She found herself standing, even though she hadn't moved. She then stood there with her mouth open, unable to believe she was now watching an image of herself, still sitting, and chatting with the others. To compound this metaphysical scenario, it was clear the others were completely unaware of her presence. With her arms tingling and feeling a tad unhinged, she glanced around the room. In a strange way, although she felt unsettled, there was a calmness coming to the surface telling her she'd been here before. She tried to listen to what the others were talking about but it was muffled at best. She took a deep breath, trying to steady her nerves.

'Your time here has ended for now,' came the words from an oddly comforting and somewhat familiar voice. 'It is I, Ethernal. The wheels are in motion. Those of us who watch over you never believed you were strong enough to alter time with such a positive impact. There were many who suggested this was a bridge too far. However, I always knew you were capable.'

Chapter 16 – What just happened?

Rebecca closed her eyes and stood there for a moment wondering how her emotions could be both calm and jumbled at the same time. No sooner than Ethernal had stopped speaking, she experienced a weird sensation and now felt as though she was a different person. She took a couple of deep breaths and opened her eyes. As if her emotions weren't already scrambled enough, she was now standing in a seriously elaborate hallway. She looked around at a myriad of huge male portraits adorning every wall. Right in the middle was a portrait of a woman she immediately recognised as Queen Victoria. She was considering why her surroundings were familiar and then she realised she was once more standing in the Houses of Parliament. Looking down, she immediately recognised her old blue jeans, and extraordinarily, this matched the strange feelings she was experiencing. Glancing at her slightly furrowed hand, she knew she was once more standing in the shoes of her future life and was again in her forties. What was odd though, she was still somewhere in the 1900s. Looking at the painting of Victoria, she wracked her brain trying to work out what year this was. She knew Victoria became Queen in 1837. Peering at the painting, she reckoned in this image Victoria was perhaps in her early twenties. Knowing Victoria was 18 when she was coronated and reckoning the painting looked fairly new, she assumed it was perhaps around the mid-eighteen-forties.

She glanced around the hallway watching many stately looking men coming and going. To compound her slightly skewed but calm mood, she realised she was once more invisible. Just as she was considering her thoughts, someone touched her on the arm. Turning, she was a little taken aback to see Millicent.

'Hello, Rebecca. It is delightful to see you once more.' She then seemed to think for a moment. 'When we were at Henry's home with Abigail something most strange occurred. One moment I was talking with you and the next I was speaking with a different Rebecca. It caused the most peculiar sensation. Peculiarly, she shared the same passion as you. That was twenty-years past. I often considered what had happened that evening and, in the end, assumed I would find the answers one day. It would seem that day is today.' She then looked Rebecca up and down. 'It would seem you are once more standing here, no longer a young girl, instead a woman, and one from a world I do not know. The one thing that is most confusing, when I spotted you and pointed you out to Henry, he could not see you.'

'Hello, Millicent,' Rebecca said, holding her hand. 'The first time this happened to me, I was spooked, to say the least. It would seem I am invisible to all except you. Because of this, I suspect I am here to observe proceedings only. You being able to speak with me is the only difference, although I did experience this once before with Meredith. Of interest, you suggested the scenario with Abigail was twenty years past. For me, it was just a moment ago. One second, I was with you, the next I was here.' She could see a look of concern on Millicent's face. 'It is okay though; I am used to this happening.'

Millicent smiled. 'Your choice of words also reflects my vision of you as someone from the future. How does it feel being one person one moment and another the next?'

'It is a tad peculiar because, in my mind, my thoughts and emotions feel right, irrespective of which shoes I find myself wearing.' Seeing Millicent appearing a little vague, she considered how best she could explain this. 'You see, I feel I am now back to being the woman I know from the twenty-first century. Now I am that person, I feel this is the real me. Puzzlingly though, when I was just a young girl with you and Meredith, I felt as though that was the real me. This is

135

something I have been confused by all through my time with you and Meredith. I felt I was getting mixed messages and at one point felt I had to decide who I wanted to be, the young girl or this woman.' Rebecca then considered her own words and realised every aspect of this journey was like no other she'd experienced, what with the loss of memory, not knowing who she really was and not knowing where she originated. It was testing every aspect of her heart, mind, and virtues, creating a slightly chaotic mindset. 'What year is it?'

'It is eighteen-forty-six. So, we are twenty years ahead of schedule, thanks to you.' Thinking for a moment, she said, 'going back to what you said, the scenario you find yourself in must be so confusing for you. So, because you jumped, if that is the correct word, from being with Abigail and me to here, I assume you have not been back to your future life yet.'

'No, indeed, and that is most odd. And yes, it is the most conflicting and confusing journey I have been on.' She then grinned. 'Jumped is a good word. So, what happened with Abigail?'

Smiling, and squeezing Rebecca's hand, she said, 'Abigail recovered well. Her husband was found guilty of killing their son and imprisoned for life. As for Abigail, she still lives with us to this day. Indeed, she is a nanny to our two beautiful children, Ryan, and Samantha. As for the safe-house, within months we were homing thirty-eight women.'

'How wonderful on all fronts. And, congratulations on your two children.'

'Sadly, Henry and I were unable to have our own children. Then one day, a woman named Judith arrived at our door. Both she and the young children showed horrific signs of being beaten. Wretchedly, Judith lost her fight to survive. So, we adopted her two children. We love them as if they were our own.'

136

'What a wonderful outcome. I am so delighted for you and Henry. How old are Samantha and Ryan?' Before Millicent could answer, two huge doors opened at the end of the corridor and the hall filled with a din of noise. Rebecca stood there trying to work out if people were cheering or booing, then realised it was a mixture of both.

Millicent held Rebecca's arm tightly, glancing between the commotion and Rebecca. 'This will be the result,' she exclaimed excitedly.

'What result?' Rebecca asked.

'Of course, you do not know. I am so sorry, instead of waffling earlier, I should have realised you were oblivious to recent events.'

Rebecca was thinking, out with it, woman.

'So, today is our fifth amendment to our suffrage Bill of Reform. The fourth, just five months previous, lost by one vote.'

'Oh, my word, that is music to my ears. How wonderful.'

'Well, it is largely down to you. Your notion to start the safe-house and then showing us the Bill of Reform, started us on a mission. As Henry said, "I am not waiting forty years for equality." The intriguing aspect, as you alluded to, I might add, was no sooner the safe house was up and running, than a number of women came forward. Within a couple of weeks, we had a suffrage movement with seventy members. In what felt like the blink of an eye, there were movements springing up all over the country.'

Of all her exploits in the past and indeed future, for Rebecca, this was the most enjoyable journey. 'How wonderful. It is also very reassuring to realise that in some small way I was able to influence you and Henry and bring events forward.' She then thought for a moment wondering if Millicent actually knew this vote was ahead of schedule. She shook her head,

137

realising she didn't actually know what year she was in and if they were ahead of schedule. Once more, she found herself questioning not only her path but her thought process. In the past, she'd always had a clear site line and her thoughts were never jumbled in this way.

'It was more than a small part you played. Henry said to me often, if it was not for the likes of you, altering people's mindset, we would still be in the dark ages.'

As Rebecca was considering Henry and Millicent's rather profound take on events, Henry walked toward them waving a piece of paper in his hand.

'We won. Unlike the previous votes, today's victory was by an overwhelming majority. Two hundred and thirty-eight in favour, a mere thirty-one against.'

Cuddling Henry, Millicent said, 'how fabulous and we owe much to Rebecca.'

Henry then turned towards Rebecca and appeared somewhat taken aback. Shaking his head, a little, he pointed at Rebecca. 'Last time I saw you, you were a young girl. Where have you been for the last twenty years?' He then shook his head again. 'I am confused because, after our last meeting with Abigail, and Dr Holiday, you seemed to change. One moment you were this fearlessly intrepid young woman, the next you were a young girl who seemed to know nothing of our venture. Although you or I should say the person who took your place, quickly engaged with the aspect of our venture, and became a true advocate. Yet here you are, although a little older, you appear to be that valiant, free-spirited female again.'

'I know exactly what you mean, Henry. When I spotted Rebecca earlier, I knew I was again in the presence of the Rebecca I once knew. What is odd, when I pointed her out to you previously, you were unable to see her, yet now you can.'

'This is strange for me also.' Deep in her thoughts, Rebecca had a peculiar notion simmering. She now found herself wondering if somehow, she lived the last twenty years in some kind of oblivion, missing out on all events in between. And maybe this was her world. That didn't make any sense though, because she was wearing clothes from the future. She then looked down and took a sharp intake of breath, seeing she was no longer wearing her jeans, instead, she was in an elaborate beige lace dress. Just as she was considering this bizarre scenario, Henry spoke.

'I will be back shortly.' He then turned and headed off.

Rebecca turned to Millicent and couldn't work out why she hadn't reacted to her sudden change of clothing. She was certain when Millicent first came over, she was still in her jeans and t-shirt. Clearly, though, that wasn't the case. Considering this, she guessed her clothing had altered before Millicent had come over. Thinking about this, it made sense because she wouldn't have appeared out of place that way, or at least once she was visible to Henry and perhaps others. *Hmm*, she thought, racking her brains, fairly sure Millicent had mentioned her clothing. 'Umm, Millicent, when you first came over, do you recall mentioning my clothes?'

Millicent raised her eyebrows. 'I did, and…' She then seemed to think for a moment. 'After that evening with Abigail, I spoke often with your great aunt. She suggested our paths might cross again. She also warned me your appearance may alter in some way. I never really understood what she meant, but seeing you as a woman of the future, in unrecognisable clothing made it a little clearer. But then you manifested into a woman of this era before my very eyes, well, it all became clear I should expect the unexpected.'

'I wish it was that clear for me. Over the years, I have gotten used to changes of direction, the era I found myself in and such like. I've never experienced physical changes like this before.' She then thought for a moment. 'Thinking about it though, I have gone through changes but never like this.' Seeing Millicent appearing a little confused, she knew she had to be clearer. 'There was this one time where I stayed in the nineteen-forties for thirty-odd years. Then in the blink of an eye, I was back in my world, well at least I thought it was my world, anyways, as a twenty-something woman. Here, the changes have been ludicrously abrupt. By this, I mean, one minute I am wearing clothes from the future and without noticing or feeling any change, I am back wearing clothes of this era.'

'It is not just your clothes that changed. When I first spotted you a few moments ago, you were wearing some kind of blue dungarees, an odd vest type top that looked like an undergarment and your hair was blonde. Now, your hair is brown.' She shook her head. 'That is the thing that unbalanced me most.'

The notion that her hair had changed colour came as a total curve ball. She pulled her hair in front of her face, and seeing it was a mousey brown colour should have unhinged her emotions completely. She could recall her hair colour being mentioned when she first arrived in this era and seeing how she'd changed from blonde to brown actually made sense of the earlier comments. It didn't however tell her where she actually belonged and this was something that was starting to affect her thought process. On one hand, there was this notion, as so often in the past, once her job was complete, she would find her way home. Here though, no sooner than one mission is complete, she was on to the next. She couldn't help but wonder if she would stay in this bizarre limbo, going from one era to the next, never settling, perpetually in this no man's land. The more she thought about this, the more intense and unstable her emotions became. What was confusing her most were her feelings of detachment compounded by this disconnected, almost loveless existence she was ostensibly lost in. Part of her was actually missing Meredith and being a young imaginative girl. Of late though, she also felt detachment issues from her husband and two daughters. Then to compound this, thoughts of her young brother, Tommy and his flipping ball antics had upset her to the point of her involuntarily crying.

'Are you alright, Rebecca? You look sad and I do not recall you ever appearing this way before.'

Rebecca really wasn't sure what to say. Part of her didn't want to burden Millicent with her fragile emotions, but just seeing the empathy and care in her eyes was actually compounding her feelings further. 'I am alright, just confused by my sudden changes.' Just as she was reconsidering telling Millicent how she felt her vision became blurry. Unlike before when she was with Millicent and Abigail, this was different. Then everything went dark as if she was standing in an unlit room. She rubbed her eyes a little and tried to focus. The silence and darkness were causing the most peculiar feeling and a little unsteady, she instinctively put her hand out to steady herself. As she did, she felt her hand touch against a cold, metal-like rail. In the strangest way, this metal rail felt inexplicably familiar. She blinked a couple of times and slowly as her eyes adjusted to the darkness, she realised she was standing on the old spiral staircase in the summerhouse. She took several deep breaths, trying to compose herself.

Chapter 17 – The Spiral Staircase

Over the years, she'd experienced many sudden changes of direction. This though was testing what little balanced thinking she had left. Not that she was a fan of applying rationality to any aspect of her journeys, but the events of today had left her emotionally bewildered and feeling misplaced was heightening her anxiety levels. In the past, events always followed a similar route, she'd complete her missions and then be back home. The problem was, she just didn't know where home was. As she stood there in the darkness, she tried to steady her nerves and reconsider her thought process. Throughout all of her journeys, no matter how complex, she'd never felt this anxious before. For sure, there were many times when her nerves were frazzled, and her sight-line blurred but she'd always managed to steady her thoughts and focus. The summerhouse and spiral staircase were part of her make-up and being in such a passionately tactile and familiar place should help calm her anxiety. The problem was, although this was a place she loved, something was wrong. She couldn't put her finger on it, it was just wrong.

As familiar as this place was, there was no smell of almonds, no odd whoosh of air, and even the hand rail, normally covered in dust, felt clean to the point of being polished. To compound this, she was still standing here not having a clue where she should go, up or down. Over the years, she'd learnt to trust her intuition. Today, there was nothing, no gut feeling telling her which way to go. More recently, whenever she'd been confused or lost, very quickly, Ethernal had whispered in her ear. In the early days, Meredith had appeared as a shining light. Either way, there had always been something or someone to catch her or nudge her. She considered the up or down limitations of her surroundings for a moment and was aware she'd perhaps been standing here for ten or so minutes now.

She rubbed her forehead considering her options. The events of the last couple of days, oddly now felt like distant memories, and she knew this normally meant she'd completed all she could and was now moving on. Evaluating this notion, and glancing up into the darkness, she knew she had just two choices, go up or go down. Although standing on the old spiral staircase was familiar, it had been many years since she'd actually used these stairs to go anywhere.

Then as if a light had come on in her head, she realised whenever she'd climbed the stairs in the past, at some point, Meredith or the spirit of Meredith would be there. Down had always led her back to Elizabeth. Although her choice was a little clearer, she was once more facing the conundrum of where she belonged and who was her real mother, Meredith, or Elizabeth. Although it felt like a lifetime ago, she could recall her emotions when she'd thought about Tommy while in Millicent's company. Rebecca was never one for emotional reactions, it just wasn't part of her make-up. However, when she had recalled his silly antics with that damn football, it had stirred her emotions like no other, causing tears to fall involuntarily. 'Maybe that is where I belong,' she mumbled as once more vivid tactile memories of the Twit had filled her thoughts.

She closed her eyes and thought of all the people who had been a part of her life. Briefly, Étienne came to mind, but any emotions evaporated quickly. She then considered Millicent and Henry, but these two also felt like part of her journey and no more. She then considered her time with Matilda and Princess Rebekah. Again, these women emotionally felt like scene players in her life's journey and no more. This left her with Meredith or Elizabeth, and as she considered her feelings towards both these women, a thought occurred to her. No matter where she'd ended up and no matter who she'd been in the company of, be it four-thousand years ago, or a thousand years into the future, she'd always ended up back with Elizabeth.

She glanced back up into the darkness and whispered, 'I love you Meredith but my home is with Elizabeth.' Slowly, she eased her way down the stairs, opened the door at the bottom and as she did, she experienced an overwhelming inner feeling of warmth. Heading towards the front door, she stopped briefly and looked in the room on her right. She didn't know what she was expecting to see, but never could she have prepared herself to see the room appearing like a bedsit. With her thoughts going in circles, she looked in the room on her left, and it was the same. She glanced back up the hallway and spotted a wooden plaque on the door that led to the spiral staircase, labelled room 3 and room 4. With her curiosity overriding the need to see Elizabeth, she headed back along the corridor, wondering where this door would now lead. Gripping the handle, she considered what she was expecting to see behind the door. Her conscious thoughts were telling her it would be the spiral staircase, obviously. Something though, in her subconscious thoughts, was preparing her for the unexpected. She considered this emotion for a moment and although her curiosity was on edge, she felt relaxed knowing the unexpected and her journeys went hand in hand. She opened the door and although seeing a normal staircase instead of the spiral stairs should have come as a surprise, her response was to chuckle, shake her head and mumble, 'well, no surprise there.' She looked up the stairs and could see two rooms labelled 3 and 4. Reckoning that both of these rooms were similar to the others, left her inquisitive curiosity a tad edgy. *I'll find out soon enough,* she thought.

She closed the door and headed back along the corridor. Now standing at the front door, she started thinking about all that had occurred in this building over the years. In her memories, she had three distinct recollections of the summerhouse. The first was as a ramshackle old building that first led her to Meredith, then next as a servant's quarters, which briefly served as Meredith's temporary home, and eventually, as the home that she lived in with Duncan and her two daughters being the third. So, to find it like this should have unbalanced her completely, but as strange as this was, she felt at ease and relaxed. There was a thought now rumbling at the back of her subconscious, wondering if, during her time with Meredith and Millicent, she'd involuntarily altered something that led to changes in this world. The pressing question now was what else had changed other than the summerhouse. 'Only one way to find out,' she mumbled and opened the front door.

As she stood on the veranda looking across the lake, the warmth of the midday sun kissed her cheek. She took a deep breath, as an overwhelming feeling of being home settled any doubts she might have had. Then, to unbalance her again, something caught her eye off to her right. She stepped off the veranda and was shocked to see two further summerhouse like buildings, plus a third partially built. It was now evidently clear whatever she'd done in the past had changed this world dramatically. Then she spotted a plaque on the wall of the summerhouse that said "In Memory of Millicent Fawcett," and this just confirmed her opinion. The question now at the front of her thoughts asked if her intervention in the past had had a positive or negative outcome. To her mind, it appeared positive, but there was something making her feel a little uneasy. As she considered why she felt like this, she suddenly wondered if she was back to being 15-years-old again, or in her forties. She looked at the skin on her arm, but in the bright sunlight was left none the wiser. Not knowing was daft to her mind, because if she was still in her forties, surely, she'd know, or at least be able to see. This thought then brought forward another question asking if she was still married and had two daughters. She breathed out deeply, having to think for a moment what her husband's name was. This gap in her memory made her reckon she probably wasn't married at all because if she was, she wouldn't have to search for her husband's name. She thought of looking at her reflection in the water in an attempt to gauge her age, but it was too choppy to see. Her clothes weren't offering an answer either because she had spent most of her life wearing skinny jeans and a t-shirt. *This is ridiculous* she thought and decided to head up to the main house in search of answers.

On the way, she considered her surroundings. Everything seemed just so, with the exception of the summerhouse and adjacent new builds. Then as she approached the main house, she flinched as she spotted a ball flying towards her. 'Blinking twit,' she grumbled involuntarily. 'Oh, my goodness,' she mumbled, realising she was fifteen again and Tommy was a twit like 12-year-old once more. Briefly, she thought about his life as a professional footballer and wondered if she would once more experience his journey.

Then as his ball flew towards her once more and nearly hit her on her leg, she turned and hollered, 'Twit.'

'Rebecca, your brother is a lot of things, but please do not call him names.'

Hearing her mother's voice, Rebecca's eyes filled with tears. She turned and seeing her mum overwhelmed her emotions. 'Mum, I love you with all my heart,' she said and cuddled her tightly.

'I love you too, Sweetie. To what do I owe this pleasure?' She then stood back and with a hand on each of Rebecca's shoulders, asked, 'whatever is the matter, Hunny?'

'Oh, Mum, I don't know, I am just so pleased to see you.'

Elizabeth flicked her head up a little. 'Where have you been this time? On another of your imaginative jaunts through time, I suspect.'

Her mother asking this question came as a relief to Rebecca in an odd way. As soon as she had realised, she was back in her teens, a notion had occurred to her that no one would know about her journeys through time. As much as she'd been happy talking about her time jaunts, she'd forever been frustrated trying to convince her mother she could actually travel back and forth. 'Oh, Mother, what an experience I've had.'

'Well, best you come inside and tell me all about it.' As she turned to head indoors, Tommy's ball once more headed towards them. This time though, it hit Elizabeth on the arm. 'Tommy,' she shouted, 'stop behaving like a twit.' She then turned towards Rebecca and grinned in the most delightfully familiar way.

As they entered the kitchen, Rebecca took in her surroundings. For the first time in what had felt like an eternity, she knew she was home where she belonged.

After her mum had poured some tea, she said, 'so, tell me all.'

Over the next couple of hours, Rebecca told her mum everything in as much detail as possible. There were a couple of times when her mum appeared a little puzzled, but mostly, she seemed to be delighting in Rebecca's story. This in itself reassured Rebecca she was where she was meant to be and in the company of her real mother. Often, while with Meredith, she'd found herself feeling a tad frustrated, having to explain every detail many times in different ways. With Elizabeth, this was never the case. For sure, in the early days, there had been times she had become frustrated convincing her mum, but she never had to find several different words to get her point across.

'I spotted you walking up from the summerhouse and the new buildings.' She then seemed to think for a moment. 'I suspect these may be new to you. I am not altogether sure why I know this. Perhaps it was something you said.'

'Seeing them came as a complete surprise. The last time I was here was...' She then thought for a moment, realising her mum wouldn't know anything about her living in the summerhouse with her husband and the girls. That was many years into the future. Just thinking about this made her realise being married with children wasn't a reality and may never occur. Although this came as a bit of a surprise, it didn't impact upon her emotions. More so, her emotions not being affected hit her hard, realising everything she'd ever experienced away from this house was not real. For sure, she'd altered events, changed people's lives, and affected their destiny, but none of it was her life or reality. These thoughts made her re-evaluate what she should say to her mother and importantly how she should tell her story. 'Well, let's just say, the last time I saw the summerhouse it was a derelict old crumble down building.' Just speaking out loud about her perspective reiterated the need to pick her words prudently. She had to think strategically about relaying recollections of past events that may have changed or future situations that haven't occurred yet and may actually never occur.

'Well, from what you have told me about the suffrage movement and your time with Millicent it would appear those events have left a legacy. That legacy is prevalent today and known as the Millicent Fawcett Foundation.'

Although Rebecca's eyes were open, all she could see was a vision of Millicent standing in the hallway of Parliament. Many times, over the years, she'd thoughtfully considered her journeys and questioned the impact her intervention would have on future events. Although she'd never doubted the path she was on, hearing her mother's words today was a clear message to her consciousness. Shaking herself back to the here and now, she held her hand out to her mum. 'There's been many times when I have not only doubted the reality of my journeys, as in have I imagined everything, especially in the early days.' She then thought about her comment and realised this was the early days as far as her mother was concerned. 'What I mean by that is when I travelled the first couple of times. Anyways, there have been many times when I have asked myself if I should intervene in past events, wondering if my actions could alter the future in some way. There is a term they use in some time-travel films, "space-time continuum" and all that. So, the point I'm making is you mentioning the Millicent Fawcett Foundation is a very powerful message, which suggests I may have made the right choices.' She then thought for a moment about her involvement with global warming. 'Thinking about it, I had a big impact when I got involved with global warming.' As soon as she said it, she suddenly realised she was in her twenties when that happened and her mum wouldn't have a clue what she was talking about.

'Funny you should mention that because when you said you'd questioned if your intervention was right, I immediately thought about you getting the award from the Queen on your twenty-first birthday.'

Although she heard very clearly what her mum had just said, it came as such a shock she actually needed to hear it again. The moment she'd seen Tommy as a twelve-year-old twit, she'd just assumed she was still 15 or 16 at most. Thinking about what she'd just said about the space-time continuum and also it being 1827 rather than 1853 when she was with Meredith hit her thoughts like a clap of thunder. For sure, it appeared on the surface that her involvement in the past supposedly only led to positive outcomes, she had nonetheless altered events throughout history. This led her to wonder what else she'd changed and how she might have altered the timelines of other people. She then realised she didn't actually know how old she was. Rather than ask her mum something that might come across as a stupid question, she got up and looked in the mirror. Although she could see she might be in her mid-twenties, she was still left wondering. 'Err, Mum. This is going to sound like a stupid question, but…' she then hesitated for a moment.

'I have sat here watching your brain going in circles. Considering all you have been through what with you jumping back and forth between this year and another, no question would come as a surprise. So, ask away.'

Still unsure if she wanted to ask, and knowing her birth certificate was in a picture frame in her bedroom, she decided to change tact completely. 'Mum, do you recall events with the boiler?'

Her mum narrowed her eyes. 'How could I forget, your dear father tried to fix it and it exploded taking his life.' Elizabeth then lowered her eyes appearing very tearful.

Rebecca's heart started beating so fast that she felt like she was going to pass out. She took several deep breaths, trying to regain some composure, aware her mum was looking at her. She looked at the tears on her dear mother's cheeks and knew she had to go back to the summerhouse and try to find a way to a world where her father was still alive. She held her hand out to her mum unsure what to say. 'I love you, Mum.' She then spent the next few minutes trying to console her mother. After she'd made her mum a cup of tea and spotted an empty bottle of scotch on the side, she knew she had to act now. 'Mum, I left something important in the summerhouse that I need to show you.'

Although her mum appeared a little quizzical, she held her hand out and said, 'hurry back, Sweetie.'

Chapter 18 – Finding James

Rebecca hurried out of the front door and rushed down towards the summerhouse. Passing Tommy doing some tricks with his football reiterated this was her world. Not that she needed any assurances, seeing him and knowing the impact losing his father would have had, she knew she had to somehow rebalance this world, her world. As she made her way down towards the summerhouse, although hearing about her father came as a horrid shock, she was feeling unquestionably focussed and determined. All she could think about was finding a route back to a place where her family was as she knew it.

Arriving at the summerhouse, she glanced back at the other summerhouses and for a second wondered if her path lay here via the original summerhouse or through one of the new ones. She shook her head, realising that they were part of this world and her reality must be via the original old building. Standing at the door, she reached out and touched a sign she had missed earlier labelled "Millicent Fawcett Foundation."

As she opened the door, there was a delightfully familiar whoosh of warm air brushing her cheeks. This was quickly followed by her nose filling with the smell of almonds. At no point had she hesitated to look for reassurance but these two significant signs sent a clear message of comfort to her consciousness. With her fearless head-on and positively focused, she headed down the corridor. Halfway along, something stopped her in her tracks. She stood there for a moment gathering her thoughts. She then turned back and as soon as she did, she could see she was back in the summerhouse in its original, delightfully rickety state. She paused looking at the dust-laden hallway and for a moment wondered if just entering the door was all she needed to do.

This notion got her to wonder what lay ahead and question her next move. On one hand, she had been certain all she had to do was climb the stairs and find a way back to the world where her father was still alive. The issue was if she climbed the stairs, where would she end up, and then what would she find when she came back. Over the years, she'd faced many conundrums, none of them though had involved the very existence of her family. There was the time when she saw into the future and was given a very clear message about the boiler and her mother. Her path though was never in question and what she needed to do was clear. Today, she was facing a whole different scenario and it was clouding her focus like never before.

She stood there for a moment considering her next move. Catching her completely unawares, the second she'd closed the front door, her surroundings changed. Over the years, she had become acclimatised to this almost seamless shift. Even so, she just wasn't prepared for the summerhouse to be back in its original state of disrepair. To her mind, it felt the same as it was when she first entered the old building, which suggested her home life could also be back as it should. She was feeling mixed emotions though. Part of her brain was telling her to just go back to the main house and everything would be fine. At the same time though, she was experiencing feelings of trepidation, reckoning it couldn't be that easy. She was also feeling somewhat alarmed, and a little frightened of what she may find, which was further clouding her decision making. She'd come to the summerhouse with the intention of climbing the stairs. This though would be a step into the unknown, albeit she'd be doing it with a profound hope it would lead her back to the world where both her parents were still living. Although there had been many times when she'd felt the need to consider her next move wisely, there'd never been a time when she was this unsure. As she stood there considering these emotions, another move came to mind. Thinking about the time she'd travelled into the future and witnessed the horrid episode with her mother and the boiler, she'd eventually found her way home by entering the summerhouse via the old kitchen at the back, kind of retracing her steps.

With her thoughts and emotions going in circles, she stood there trying to refocus her thoughts. Gradually, she started to realise her uncertainty was being completely driven by the world she'd found herself in. The loss of her father had hit her harder than anything else she'd ever experienced, even though her conscious competence should have told her she can fix this dreadful scenario. Nodding, she took a deep breath and mumbled, 'one step at a time.' She glanced around, still with shards of hesitancy flickering around in her head, took a deep breath and headed to the front door. She grasped the handle, mentally slapped her cheek, and opened the door.

It was mid-summer when she'd entered this old building, but a bitter chill hitting her cheeks left her with no doubt she was stepping into a different world. This in itself should have triggered more uncertainty, but instead, it actually stimulated her focus. *After all*, she thought, *I came here in search of change.*

As she headed up towards the main house, it felt somehow different. In a strange way, it felt like she was seeing this old house for the first time. *Hang on a minute,* she thought, *dad had the brickwork cleaned years back.* 'Did he, though,' she mumbled, realising that was when she was thirty or so and that recollection may be from a world that she'd only experienced and wasn't her reality. 'Damn, this is confusing,' she grumbled, not knowing what to think. *This must be what writers feel like when they are creating a story, this way or that way,* she thought. As she arrived at the front door, it was evident the house was empty. She now found herself wondering what time period, or scenario she'd stepped into. Partly, she was thinking she'd just stepped back to a time before her father bought the house, almost to the point where she expected to see her mother's Volvo pull up for the first time with her and Tommy inside. Something though was nagging at her, asking what if her parent's never actually bought this

153

house, which in turn may lead her back to the Whispering Pond.

This is stupid, she thought and decided to head back to the summerhouse. Wherever she was, it wasn't a world she knew. Ever since she'd arrived back and seen Tommy and her mother, she knew instantly that was her world. The major issue though was that life was without her father. Because every aspect of her mother and Tommy and living here felt right, all she needed to do was find this same existence, just the version where both parents were alive.

As she approached the lake, she felt a horrid nudge of reality, asking if her true existence was one without her father. 'No, no,' she grumbled, thinking I don't care if that is my real world, I want to find the one with Tommy, Mum, Dad, Amanda, Ruth, and my best friend Roxy. 'I want that world,' she said out loud.

'You will find that world.'

'Ethernal. Where were you when I needed you?'

'I am here now. Earlier, you found your own way. I had to leave you time for your thoughts to focus on what you truly want and to know your exact and rightful existence. You will find your way home. There is, however, one journey you must follow before. Go, climb the stairs, and distillate on that alone.'

From the moment she'd focussed on finding a way back to the world where both her parents were living that was all she'd thought about. Hearing she now faced another journey first scrambled her brain a little. 'When I do find my way home, will my father be alive?' she asked, thinking to herself, *what does distillate even mean.*

'Distillate means focus. Go now and all your questions will be answered.'

'But what about my dad?' There was no answer and she was kind of ready for that, knowing he never answered such questions. She glanced back at the main house, then turned and continued towards the summerhouse.

For a moment she thought about how she'd felt being around Meredith, and at the time had been sure that was her world. On the flip side to that, she was now certain her life was with Tommy, Elizabeth, and her father. This got her to thinking about all of these superficially similar worlds, that were actually all so different. *Does Meredith live in 1827 or 53*, she thought. Then there were the different scenarios she'd found her mother living in, and was now wondering how many worlds there were and if she'd ever find her way back home.

Chapter 19 - Osgyth

She stepped up on the veranda and immediately her attention was drawn to something unusual off to her right in the distance. As she tried to focus through the gentle mist around the lake edge, she spotted some kind of animal moving. Before she had time to consider this any further, her question was answered as a white deer started moving towards her. Although she'd read about this almost mythical creature, often referred to as a White Hart, she'd never really believed they were real, let alone seen one. This in itself was unusual because she always believed in such creatures, reckoning all you ever needed to do was open your eyes with a little belief and see what was in front of you. She loved telling her mother about the fairies, pixies, and elves, often suggesting adults lose their ability to see with an open mind. Watching this beautiful creature made her wonder why she'd never really believed in them. The more she considered her unusual perspective, it got her to wondering if this was a message of sorts and perhaps a prelude to her next journey. The creature, now so very close, looked up, almost as if it was looking into her soul. It was the most peculiar feeling. Then, in the blink of an eye, it was gone. She was now left wondering if it was some kind of mystical apparition, or, as her common sense was suggesting, it had simply vanished into the mist. She stood there for a brief moment asking herself why there was a mist in the middle of what was a warm sunny day. This in turn got her to think about the day she saw the lady on the boat all those years before. *Or was it years before*, she thought?

She took a deep breath, trying to focus on the job at hand. She shook herself down, entered the summerhouse and headed straight for the door at the end of the corridor. Without any of the usual hesitation, she opened the door and entered the tiny, dust-laden room. Just as she did all those years earlier, she felt the slightly spooky, but oddly calming whisper of air around her ears, followed by the delightfully familiar smell of almonds. With concerns for her father's wellbeing now parked up, she climbed the stairs into the darkness, sure this was the only way she could alter events for the better.

As she stood at the first door, she briefly considered climbing to the next landing. That thought quickly disappeared as she gripped the handle, felt a positive vibe, and knew she was right to follow her intuition, something that had always served her well. Although she was embarking on a new journey into the unknown, as always, her fearless mindset was optimistically focused. She opened the door and stepped into the pitch-black room, and as she did, the door slammed shut behind her. As she stood there waiting for her eyes to focus, she considered how she must have felt the first time she followed this route. Somehow, she'd gotten used to the door slamming behind her in that way, but considering it now, she couldn't help but wonder how she would have felt all those years ago. *There it is again, all those years ago,* she thought, now unsure how long ago it actually was, what with her being so young again. Gradually her eyes focussed, but unlike her previous ventures, the room remained in darkness. Once more following her gut, she made her way across the room, hoping and kind of expecting to find another door that led down to the kitchen.

Fumbling around in the darkness, all she could feel was a lightly damp, musky smelling wallcovering. *That's odd*, she thought, turning back towards the door she came in by. Every time she'd entered this room, there had always been two doors. Again, she scrabbled around feeling for a door. There was nothing. She then headed towards the window, but that too was missing. Now a little uneasy, she tried to evaluate her situation. *Got to go back and retrace my steps*, she thought and cautiously made her way toward the door she'd entered by. She took a deep breath, and although a tad apprehensive, she opened the door. The door opening easily, in spite of it

157

slamming a moment earlier, surprised her a little but was kind of reassuring.

Without hesitation, something that had clouded her view earlier today, she fumbled her way downstairs, out into the corridor and straight to the front door. Now on a mission, she stepped straight outside, and fell to the ground, landing on long straw-like grass. *Where's the veranda*, she thought, rubbing her elbow. Gathering her thoughts, she looked at the knee-high grass wondering what had just occurred. As she turned around to try and work out what had just happened, nothing could have prepared her to see no sign of the summerhouse. Standing up and looking around, there was no summerhouse, no lake, no spry wood. There was nothing remotely recognisable. Over the years, she'd stepped into some unusual scenarios but it had been via the stairs or followed a seamless transition as she'd approached the summerhouse. She considered this for a moment and thought about her journeys within a journey, and rarely did that involve either the stairs or summerhouse. Still rubbing her elbow, she thought, hey-ho, shrugged her shoulders and glanced around trying to find a focal point.

Surveying her surroundings, she glanced up at the watery sun to get her bearings. A couple of miles to the east she could see what looked like an ocean or sea. It would seem she was standing near the top of a small hill, with the land beyond being fairly flat. To her right, in the south was an estuary where she could see what looked like a handful of boat masts near some kind of shed type building. She then turned slowly to the west plotting every inch hoping to see some kind of recognisable landmark. In the distance, there were a couple of small buildings scattered amid miles of rough grass-like grounds, but certainly nothing of significance. She wasn't at all sure what she was looking for, but reckoned she'd know it if she saw anything other than these outwardly inconsequential farm type dwellings. She tightened her lips and asked herself what she was hoping to see, and as she did, something to her right caught her attention. As she turned, less than a couple of hundred yards away stood a magnificent priory type building with a central elaborate clock tower. There were also many surrounding buildings all with the appearance of grandeur. The important aspect for Rebecca was how new these buildings appeared. Remembering her time with Matilda at Perth Priory, she reckoned she might be somewhere around the 11th or 12th century.

Stepping into another era like this wasn't unusual for Rebecca, but the way she got here was unlike any of her previous journeys. To then find herself alone, in the middle of a field added to this unusual scenario. As she made her way towards the nearest building, she reconsidered what Ethernal had said about following her intuition, when she'd been unsure what she felt. There was a shard of apprehension because of the way she got to this timeline. Mostly though, she felt animated by her surroundings and Ethernal's words were helping. It wasn't just the grandeur of the buildings that was creating a mood you could almost smell. Far from it, this place had a distinctly tactile almost spiritual atmosphere.

As she grew closer, she could see a number of women going about their business, all dressed as nuns, which to her mind answered why this place felt the way it did. What was immediately obvious to her though, was once more feeling as though she was invisible. She'd been in this situation before in the past, and it always followed a similar pattern. She'd step back, and be invisible to most, with the exception being Meredith, who'd always been able to see her. Whenever Meredith hadn't been there, invariably there had always been one person who could see her. Today there was no one to greet her. As her thoughts circled, she again thought about her time with Matilda. Not too dissimilar to this situation, she'd stepped back and found herself alone. What was different was her hearing Matilda's whimpers very soon after she'd arrived. Today there was nothing.

Reckoning there must be a message here abouts, she made her way across the yard between two elaborate looking buildings. For some bizarre reason, as she walked past several women all outwardly oblivious to her, something was telling her this was a kind of stepping stone. However, whenever she'd been in transition mode before, she'd always been greeted by someone who served as a protagonist. Never had she found herself in an era purely to observe, or find a message and certainly not just as a step between missions. Considering this notion, she wasn't at all sure why she would think she was here purely to find a message because that had never been the scenario previously. There was an odd thought fragment in the recesses of her brain telling her she had to look for a plaque. Some distant emotion though was also preparing her for an unfamiliar situation. This notion was putting her nerves slightly on edge, which was weird because her whole life had been fuelled by the unexpected.

Really unsure what she was looking for, she continued to walk around. To her, she was wandering aimlessly and this was annoying her, the problem was she just didn't have a clue what she was looking for. Certainly, in the past, she'd never had to search for an answer, not like this anyways. She stood still for a moment looking around. Although her conscious thoughts were telling her to head towards the grand building with the clock tower, something at the back of her mind was saying ignore that place and instead head around the back. Her whole life had been fuelled by gut feelings and intuitive emotions, so she shrugged her shoulders and made her way down a narrow walkway between the clock tower building and a slightly smaller, but still elaborate adjoining building. Although the walkway was narrow, it was still bright and certainly didn't have any unusual vibes. Halfway along was an arch adjoining the two buildings. Although small by comparison, in an odd way, it reminded her of the Bridge of Sighs in Oxford. It was somewhere she'd visited as a 12-year-old, on a school trip when she still lived in Cheshire. She stood looking up at the arch remembering how in her mind she'd renamed the arch, the Whispering Bridge after the whispering pond in her garden. She looked down at the ground considering where her thoughts were going. She could now recall exactly how she'd felt that day and remembers hearing a voice whisper something. At twelve and surrounded by other 12-year-olds, screaming and shouting, she'd been unable to focus. She now found herself wondering if that was what she should be looking for, or indeed, listening for today.

A little more focused, but still a tad apprehensive, she approached the arch. As she did, a large oval plaque on one side immediately caught her attention. The inscription appeared to be written in Latin, and to her mind was illegible. The image though, of a female essentially carrying her head, chilled her to the bone. It caused the most peculiar emotion sending her mind scurrying for an answer. Although she hadn't a clue why she was here, she felt this message held a kind of answer. Just as she was coming to terms with how she felt, she heard a chilling, whispery, voice behind her once more sending her emotions spiralling.

'My name is Osgyth. Help me find an alternative road,' the female voice said.

She took a deep breath and turned slowly. She couldn't help but blink a couple of times; her vision blurred by this woman's presence. In front of her stood a stunningly beautiful, elegant woman, whose appearance immediately reminded her of the woman she'd seen in the boat just prior to her first journey. Again, she blinked trying to focus. The woman, who was now holding her hand out, seemed to drift in and out of focus almost as if she was surrounded by some kind of mist. Again, thinking about the woman in the boat, the mythical White Hart, and now believing she was perhaps in the presence of an apparition, Rebecca felt weirdly peaceful and calm. Reckoning this woman's overwhelmingly kind aura was creating this peaceful ambience, she held her hand out towards her.

As the woman's hand touched Rebecca's, it felt as if she'd just been kissed by some otherworldly breath of air. It was the most peculiar sensation, the likes of which she'd never experienced before. Mysteriously, although the sensation of this woman's hand touching hers should have raised her anxiety levels, it was enchantingly calming and reassuring.

'Rebecca, my soul has stumbled and floated aimlessly for three centuries,' the woman said, her voice engagingly soft. She then pointed at the plaque. 'This was my forced destiny and only you can alter my undeserved path.' Again, the woman's hand caressed Rebecca's very being.

The woman calling her by name should have come as a shock, but for some reason, it further helped settle Rebecca's mood. At the front of her thoughts was this woman's sad plight and lost spirit. Although she had so many questions, she somehow knew she only needed the answer to one. Pointing at the plaque, she asked, 'why were you beheaded?'

'I refused marriage to the King of Essex. After he had hunted the spirit of a White Hart, he returned and ordered my sorrowful demise. I had asked the nunnery for help, but they turned me back to him.'

White Hart, Rebecca thought, shaking her head, surprised but not. She closed her eyes trying to recall the image outside a public drinking house she'd visited with Duncan. 'White Deer,' she mumbled and as she did, she felt the strangest sensation. It was the same feeling she got whenever she stepped from one era to the next. She narrowly opened her eyes just enough to see, curious where she'd find herself. Sure enough, the sensation she'd just felt was right. She opened her eyes completely and looked around trying to work out where she was. Only three of the mews of a dozen or so buildings were still there. Gone were the clock tower and the two adjacent grand buildings. Looking around, and seeing the sea and an estuary in the distance, she knew she hadn't changed locations, perhaps just changed eras.

She stood there for a moment considering what may lay ahead of her. *Okay, what do I know for sure*, she thought? She then realised the trigger point for her movement was when

Osgyth spoke of the White Hart. That was the message, loud and clear.

Chapter 20 – White Hart

Rebecca glanced around considering her next steps. Although she had a clear notion of what may lay ahead of her, she nonetheless felt a little uncertain. She then heard what sounded like several people speaking around the back of the building nearest to her. Without any hesitation, she headed in the direction of the voices. Passing a couple of people, once more, it seemed she was invisible. As she entered a large courtyard area and saw around 30 or 40 people, mostly men, her attention was drawn by their clothing. Throughout her many journeys, she'd come across many differing outfits, but nothing like this. Drawing on memories from something she'd done at school, to her mind these people had an early medieval appearance. In spite of it being a very warm day, the handful of women were all dressed in heavy-looking, dark red, green, or amber coloured dresses that draped on the ground. Over the top, they had substantial cape affairs, equally as long. The fact that all women wore an abundance of jewellery suggested these folk were from the upper courts of society. By contrast, the men wore brightly coloured tunics and elaborate waist jackets. All brandished swords in waist slings. The combination of male and female clothing, plus the lack of male jewellery, and overstated female jewellery, to her mind, put her sometime around the 10th-century.

She stood there for a moment considering her brief meeting with Osgyth's spirit. Recalling she'd said her soul had been lost for three centuries, she closed her eyes and tried to recall anything else that would tell her if she was in the right era. Then the plaque on the wall came to mind, and she was sure she'd seen the number 903. At the time, she hadn't considered this to be of any significance, just a reference number. She now felt sure it was actually the year 903. She opened her eyes, feeling she was possibly at the time when Osgyth had met her tragic end. Then, as was more often the case during her journeys, she spotted a woman who looked identical to the apparition she'd met, assuring her she was in the right place at the right time.

Watching the movement of people, it occurred to her she was perhaps at a pre-wedding ceremony or something similar. As she observed the toing and froing, it appeared to her that Osgyth was outwardly being guarded, to the point where it was clear she was there under duress. The way one man, who was sporting a crown, was gripping her arm, annoyed her to the point she wanted to go over and intervene. However, the one thing she'd learnt over the years was there would always be a non-emotive signal indicating her time to move. Just as she was weighing up the situation, she heard a man at the back of the group shout what sounded like "whitered ro-buck." Although her knowledge of medieval English was non-existent, she was fairly sure he was referring to a white deer. Immediately, seeing a white deer near the summerhouse came to the front of her thoughts and linking that manifestation to her current situation assured her she was where she needed to be. The thing was, she couldn't see any sign of a deer. Before she had time to think any more, the man shouted again, and all the other men gathered at the back of the courtyard. Seconds later, several coarsely dressed, dishevelled looking men appeared, each leading a horse.

Within seconds, all the men mounted the horses and as they did, Rebecca just caught site of a white deer in the distance. Although this creature was at least a couple of hundred yards away, inexplicably, it felt as though this gracious being was looking directly at her. This in itself was bizarre because she couldn't even see the animal's eyes. It was just an intense feeling she got in her stomach. It was peculiar in so many ways, but mostly because she'd gotten the same feeling when she'd seen the white deer by the summerhouse. She puffed out her cheeks as a strange notion came to mind. At the time, having never seen a white deer before, she wondered if this grand creature was a messenger. She was now questioning if

165

the two animals were one of the same, a time messenger if you will. As she was thinking about this, a conversation she'd had with Roxy, her school friend, came to mind. *Oh, my goodness,* she thought, remembering Roxy going on for days about seeing a herd of white deer. At the time, Rebecca had never even heard of such animals, let alone seen them, so smiled politely. She was now trying to defuse a hand grenade that had just gone off in her memory. Roxy had also talked about a fabulous abbey that was being restored, having been derelict for many years and that abbey was called St Osyth Priory and was in North Essex. She took another deep breath and exhaled slowly through her tightened lips. With the combination of the white deer at the summerhouse, the white deer today, Osgyth, and Roxy visiting what she now believed was this exact place made her wonder if her whole life was set out in front of her, with subliminal messages of what to expect scattered throughout her existence. This combined with the sudden appearance of Ethernal, the Book-Keeper, Meredith's spirit, so many aspects, all ostensibly leading her to certain points throughout her destiny. Her emotions, although a little wobbly, were actually settled by this belief. To her mind, it was strangely reassuring.

While still considering her frame of mind, she noticed that Osgyth was standing alone by a wooden post. Heading over, she could see this woman was actually tethered. As she approached Osgyth, the way this woman turned and looked directly at her, she knew she was not only visible to her but also in the right place and importantly at the right time.

Osgyth then said something to her in a language she hadn't heard before. Knowing she was in North Essex in 903 AD, and recalling her memory of history, she reckoned this woman was speaking in a variant of Anglo-Saxon English. Then, just as it was with her time with Matilda, who spoke with an odd mixture of Germanic English and Celtic, she was able to understand exactly what Osgyth had just said.

'Help me. I must away from here, afore their return,' she said, her eyes tearful and full of dread.

166

Knowing this woman's appalling fate, Rebecca looked around considering her next move. She started to untie Osgyth's hands, which was proving difficult at best. 'Please do not be concerned, I will help you get away,' she said, increasingly frustrated by the tightness of the knots on the cord. She glanced around looking for something that would help her, then noticed a broach type object on the woman's dress. Pointing, she asked, 'may I use this?' The woman nodded and so unclipping the broach, she used the edge in an attempt to cut through the cord. Gradually, she started to make headway, all the time considering where she would lead this woman. From what she'd seen on the plaque and her brief conversation with Osgyth, she knew this woman had turned to the nearby nunnery seeking help. It was all too evident this hadn't been the right choice and Rebecca knew she needed an alternative. Then, just as she freed one of Osgyth's hands, she thought about the boats moored in the estuary. More than once, this method of transport had served her well and she was now certain this was her best option. After a few more seconds, she freed both hands. She glanced around and other than a couple of women standing at the far side of the courtyard, they were alone. She put both hands on Osgyth's shoulders, and looking directly at her, she said, 'follow me.'

She then glanced around once more and headed across the yard towards the open countryside. As they arrived by a picket fence, she looked around once more. The two women at the far side of the yard were now looking directly in their direction. Reckoning she was probably invisible to them she knew they were watching Osgyth alone. Unsure if they were friend or foe, she quickly helped Osgyth over the fence, not that this frail, but clearly feisty woman needed any help. On the other side, Rebecca pointed in the direction of the boats in the estuary. 'This is our best option of escape.'

'The nuns will help me though,' Osgyth said, pointing back towards the buildings.

Knowing she couldn't explain she'd seen her spirit 300 years from now and knew of her fateful demise, Rebecca shook her head steadfastly. 'I cannot explain. However, you need to trust me. The nuns are controlled by the King of Essex and they will turn you over to him. Trust that I am here to help you find an alternative path to follow.'

Osgyth appeared to consider Rebecca's words for a moment, then nodded. 'I cannot sail, but we can row perhaps.'

'I can sail, and very well. Now, let us go, with haste.' As quickly as possible, trudging over the heavy ground, the two made their way towards the boat masts in the distance. Often on the route, Rebecca turned to make sure they were not being followed. Seeing the two women standing by the fence watching their every move, she knew she needed to disguise their route. Noticing a small wooded area next to a sprawling lake, she reckoned although a diversion may slow them a little, it would disguise their chosen escape route. 'We are being watched and need to hide our direction.' Osgyth nodded and they made their way towards the lake. As they entered the woods, Rebecca glanced back once more. She could see the two women had turned and were now pointing in their direction while talking to a man on horseback.

Knowing time was of the essence, Rebecca looked around. To stay within the woods would considerably delay them reaching the boats, whereas the boats were actually only a couple of hundred yards away. She looked back and could now see several men on horseback. Reckoning, even if they ran directly towards the yard, they wouldn't be able to outrun the horsemen. She had no choice but to stay hidden in the woods. The problem was, the two women had seen them enter the woods and they would be found easily.

Osgyth grabbed Rebecca's arm and indicated for her to follow. 'I know of a sanctuary and we can hide.' She then led her through the woods around the edge of the lake. Moments later, they arrived by two enormous willows clinging to some

huge moss-covered rocks, right by the edge of the lake. The
ground under foot was very boggy and Rebecca wondered
where they could be heading. With the sound of men shouting,
she followed Osgyth down towards the lake edge. Osgyth,
indicating for Rebecca to follow, paddled through the water and
under the hanging branches of the willows.

As soon as they were beneath the willows, Rebecca
experienced a peculiar sensation of quietness and calm, to the
point where she could no longer hear the men. Again, Osgyth
beckoned her to follow. Right by the lake edge, there was a
constant stream of water coming from a small gap in the rocks.
To Rebecca's mind, this was exactly the kind of place you'd
see water fairies or such, and in an odd way, it reminded her of
Fairy Glen in North Wales. Although this place was tranquil
and quiet, she reckoned they'd still be found easily and this was
troubling her. She looked around for somewhere that might
hide them better and then noticed Osgyth had clambered down
towards the small opening in the rocks. She stood there and
watched as Osgyth sat down in the stream with her feet facing
the opening. She then eased herself feet first through the gap
and before she disappeared from view, turned, and beckoned
Rebecca to follow.

As Osgyth vanished from sight, Rebecca was a tad uncertain
about what to do. She then saw Osgyth's hand appear through
the gap waving her in that direction. Without hesitation,
Rebecca sat down in the stream and followed her. Although
the hole had appeared too small, she was surprised how easily,
aside from a wet bottom, she got through.

Now standing on the other side, Rebecca took a sharp intake
of breath, marvelling at her surroundings. They were standing
in a grotto-like cavern that was about ten feet wide with room
enough for her to stand up straight. Every rock was covered by
an inspiring myriad of multi-coloured moss, lichen, and
toadstools. To compound her senses, as she peered towards the
back of the labyrinth-like cave that seemed to go on forever,
she could see a maze of amber and red coloured stalactites and

stalagmites. Although her feet were still in the water, she could see Osgyth standing on a dry rock. As she stepped from the water, animated by her surroundings, she was aware of how silent this place was. She then kicked a small stone and the sound of it hitting the water echoed around the chamber creating an almost choral like sound.

With her eyes wide open, Osgyth held her finger to her mouth and indicated for her to sit next to her.

Although this place would serve them well as a hideout, Rebecca's inquisitive side wondered where this cave might lead. As much as Rebecca wanted to ask, she knew she had to say nothing. She briefly thought about trying hand signals, but reckoned all would be clear in time. She actually felt comfortable sitting in silence next to this tiny framed, but enormously valiant woman. She was also aware that at some point they would have to leave the cave and although she was happy sitting there, for now, she knew she would become fidgety at some point.

They'd been sitting there for what felt like an age, with no sound other than the meandering trickle of water caressing the moss-covered rocks on its route to freedom. *Freedom*, she thought, wondering how long they should stay put. Osgyth then tapped her on the shoulder and narrow-eyed, pointed to the cave entrance. There were whispered voices on the other side of the entrance, but due to the conducting powers of this labyrinth, they could hear what was being said clearly.

'I am not sure I want to find Osgyth,' one of the male voices said. 'If she does not want to marry that abhorrent narcissistic man, I do not see why she should.'

'I agree totally,' the other male voice said.

Wide-eyed, Osgyth glared at Rebecca and shook her head. She then picked up a stick and scribed "NO" into the soil. She put her finger to her lips and indicated for Rebecca to follow her as she headed further into the cavern.

170

Rebecca got to her feet as quietly as possible, avoiding kicking any more stones. She then trailed Osgyth as they eased a route through the ever-increasing stalactites and stalagmites. They'd walked for around ten minutes and although to Rebecca's mind they should have been in complete darkness, the ancient natural columns somehow reflected what little light there was, shining a path before them. Although their route was narrow and delicately awkward, this place had a divine, almost otherworldly feel to it, inexplicably feeling like the aisle of some ancient basilica.

After another few minutes, the pair entered a huge antediluvian gallery. From the upper limits, there was a shard of sunlight cascading on an expanse of water ahead of them, reflecting like a thousand celestial crystals. The emotional noise created by this wonder of mother nature broke the eerie silence manifesting itself in a divine, almost spiritual way.

Being in this subterranean world made Rebecca reflect on her many experiences. She'd been witness to some amazingly wonderful journeys over the years but never had her senses been stimulated like this before. Even during her time in Mesopotamia at the cradle of civilization, her emotions were never affected like this. She'd long forgotten any notion of sailing to safety and was now wholly focussed on the path ahead of them. Both her conscious and subconscious thoughts were banging on the door asking what next and where to.

Osgyth indicated for Rebecca to follow her to the left around the water's edge along what appeared to be a well-trodden path. This unexpected scenario stimulated Rebecca's senses to no end leaving her with many questions. As desperate as she was to ask Osgyth about this path, and in spite of reckoning they were beyond any earshot, she knew this woman would speak when she felt it was safe. Then, just to kindle Rebecca's mindset further, she noticed what appeared to be tiny, almost baby-sized footprints in the sandy like soil by her feet. She tapped Osgyth on the shoulder, pointed to the ground and knelt down to get a closer look.

Osgyth knelt down beside her, smiled and nodded very slightly. She then pointed ahead, and mouthed, 'soon.'

The mixture of anticipation and bewilderment cascading through her thoughts like the pages of a book took Rebecca's breath away. Feeling weirdly unsteady, she stopped and held onto one of the columns. As if her senses needed any further stimulation, the column was warm to the point of feeling like a radiator. As she tried to regain a smidge of composure, she suddenly realised the air was icy cold when they'd first entered the cave, now though, it was warm. Reflecting on this experience, she realised unlike any of her previous journeys, she was being led, rather than leading. She then noticed Osgyth some way ahead of her, so took a deep breath, rebalanced her composure, and hurried along the path.

Chapter 21 – Beyond Reason

She caught up with Osgyth, tapped her on the shoulder and held her hands up in a questioning manner.

Osgyth turned, and holding Rebecca's hand, said, 'we will see my friends soon.' She then indicated for Rebecca to follow her.

With her senses a miss-mash of questions and wonderment, she followed her as the path meandered around this subterranean lake, their way lit by the shards of sunlight reflecting from the crystal-like stalagmites. After another few yards, Rebecca could see ahead of them a gothic-like doorway. It was forged into the wall of this eerie, yet peaceful, almost otherworldly labyrinth. To her mind, it was truly a world where anything was possible. For years, her senses had always been aware of a world beyond the one everyone knew. Often, when she'd spoken of a place where fairies, pixies, elves, and other such mythical folk lived, her words were greeted by a passive, somewhat unreceptive smile at best. Her mother had always delighted in her stories, but even so, Rebecca had known she'd only ever considered her words imaginative tales. Here she was though, in a mystical world where nothing was beyond reason. Now being greeted by this ethereal arched door just stimulated her wonderment further. Although breathless with an eager expectation, she felt a calmness, the likes of which she'd never felt at any time during her journeys.

As they approached the door, Rebecca was more than a tad surprised by the size of this entrance. From a distance, its stature offered the presence of a grand mythical gate-keepers ingress. Well, that was how Rebecca's inner thoughts perceived this entrance. Up close, it was actually no more than five feet tall. For some odd reason though, it still maintained its imposing, yet calm gesture. She stood back and watched Osgyth bend down, and pick up an odd-shaped shell, not dissimilar to an oyster shell, just larger. She then tapped the shell gently against an almost translucent stalactite hanging from a rock over the entrance. A tender harmonic sound seemed to evaporate gently around the labyrinth of corridors, only to echo back like a choral chant.

Although Rebecca's senses were overstimulated, her excitement was tempered by calm anticipation. To her mind, she was on a journey, the likes of which she'd never experienced previously. For some bizarre reason, it was as if her subconscious had waited her whole life to be here and was now revealing itself through her every thought. Ever since she could think, she'd seen the world unlike those around her. She'd never allowed her vision to be stifled by the condescending frowns of onlookers. In an odd way, part of her spirited inner self was now shouting at those doubters. That said, her practical side knew those very people would never be able to open their minds enough, no matter how loud she hollered.

Just as she was calibrating her thoughts back to the here and now, the door started to move, turning any fragment of balanced thinking she'd mustered on its head again. With her emotions once more invigorated by what may lie ahead, she made a conscious decision to ignore attempts to apply rational thinking and just go with whatever this wonderous place had in store for her.

Although the door had a heavy granite-like appearance, it opened silently. A curious, stimulating mixture of light and a constantly changing odour cascaded from the entrance, taking a stranglehold on Rebecca's senses. The light was a shimmering surreal mix of translucent yellow, rainbow-like amethyst and a weird lustrous turquoise. The way the meandering, misty light moved seemed to be in some kind of sequence with and somehow stimulate an ever-changing odour. Rebecca had always had an excitable, open mind but this was beyond her wildest dreams even with her child-like imaginative head-on. The twisting, shimmery light was an exciting, almost eerie spectacle, but the way its movement seemed to alter the smell was the one thing that was bewildering her thoughts the most. One moment the air seemed to fill with the smell of honeysuckle, but no sooner she'd recognised this odour, it changed, not always for the best. In just a few seconds her nostrils filled with the smell of flowers, freshly baked bread, almonds, as you'd expect, newly cut grass and then rotting mushrooms, well, at least that is what she thought it was.

Just as she was trying to get some kind of balanced foothold, Osgyth tapped her on the shoulder and again held her finger to her lips. Although this woman's tactile, obviously gentle mindset should have settled her disposition, the almost whispery, surreal appearance Osgyth had taken on made Rebecca feel like she was dreaming.

Before she could gather her thoughts and any kind of composure, Osgyth bent over slightly and kind of stepped through the doorway, although it was more like she'd floated. She then turned and beckoned Rebecca to follow her. No sooner she was inside, the door closed silently behind her. Weirdly, both the smell and light seemed to settle, followed by a constant smell similar to honeysuckle and a continuously moving, greenish-blue shimmering light. Ahead of her was a long corridor affair that seemed to be carved into the rock, rather than natural. Narrowing her eyes, she could see the path had a slight downward gradient, but with the constantly moving light, she was unable to follow its route too far. For a second, she tried to consider her feelings. Although her mindset was animated with intrigue and ideas of what might lie ahead of her, part of her consciousness was struggling to come to terms with the bizarre, surreal world she'd entered.

'The men outside were the King's brothers. I suspect they knew we were hiding inside and their words were designed to hood-wink us out. The entrance we came in by opened for us, although once we were through, the recess would have narrowed again. I found this sanctum when I was a child, while out walking with the white hart. We can speak freely now.'

175

She then touched Rebecca on the hand. 'I knew from the moment our paths crossed your spirit was strong and with good intent. They would not have allowed you to enter if my judgement was incorrect.'

Rebecca's mind was now going in circles, wondering how she had failed to notice the entrance narrowing behind them. Mostly though, Osgyth had said they, *so who are they*, she thought. She then followed her down a gentle gradient. Although under foot, the ground felt sandy, she could hear a crunching sound every couple of steps. When she stood on something a little bigger and it made the same crunching sound, she bent down to investigate. Although she'd considered various options, she was a little surprised to see a large oyster shell. Reckoning they were a couple of miles from the sea and around a mile from the estuary, she now found herself wondering if this subterranean world was once closer to the sea. To her mind, this didn't fit though because although she was no geographical expert, she was sure this cave was filled with fresh water and stood at least one-hundred-foot above sea level. Considering how these shells found their way here, she then noticed Osgyth turning to the left some way ahead of her. She hurried her steps, once more treading on shells and at one point, nearly losing her balance.

With her thoughts jumping from one question to the next, she turned the corner. Osgyth referring to "they" had stimulated Rebecca's thoughts with what and perhaps who may lay ahead. Never, in her wildest dreams could she have prepared herself for this vision of wonderment that was now in front of her. They had entered a huge, almost cathedral-like gallery. In front of her was a sprawling warren of tiny odd-shaped buildings. The surreal miss-mash of shapes and colour was a delightful feast for her senses. As she tried to focus, she could see many sprights, nymphs and elf-like characters scurrying around, all outwardly oblivious to her and Osgyth. Over the years, Rebecca had always believed these mythical creatures existed, but to her mind, they were tiny critters, no

176

more than a few inches tall, and importantly, they rarely mixed together. Yet here they were, outwardly living in harmony, and from her viewpoint, it would appear they were at least three-feet tall, perhaps more.

Before she had time to consider this mystical ecosystem any further, she was aware Osgyth was standing some fifty or so feet below her. Looking around, she could see a meandering flight of steps carved into the granite-like rock face leading down to Osgyth. Watching her every step with care on this narrow, uneven stairway, she made her way down to join her. As she drew closer, she could see Osgyth speaking with three characters. Her attention was immediately drawn to one character who was around four feet tall, very slim, with the most amazing translucent amber coloured eyes. His features were harshly sharp and wispy, yet still, his overall appearance was tranquil, offering an approachable demeanour in spite of his animated arm-waving. Standing with him, appearing to be listening, was a slender male around three feet in height. His weathered features and long white beard reminded her of the bookkeeper. The third individual, standing at the back had much harsher characteristics, and to her, his overall demeanour and disposition were exactly how she'd imagined an Elf leader. To compound his appearance, she was also aware he appeared to be peering unreceptive towards Rebecca.

She stood back a little and tried to listen as Osgyth and the taller character spoke. Due to the constantly swirling strange mixture of light and mist, it was difficult to see or hear clearly. One moment she was able to focus on their body language and hear clearly, the next their voices sounded echoey and their appearance unclear. From what she could hear, their conversation seemed to be heated, even though they were speaking in a language unrecognisable to Rebecca. It seemed to be a weird mix of clicks and sounds. It reminded her of a previously undiscovered tribe of Amazonians she'd seen on a television documentary, even though this was a distantly vague memory and she wasn't at all sure what a television was, the memory was there though. As difficult as it was to hear, or indeed understand, the temperature of the conversation seemed to cool a little. Catching her completely off guard, the one at the back who reminded Rebecca of the bookkeeper, stepped to the front, and beckoned her towards him.

To her mind, she'd sensed her presence wasn't welcome, so she tried to hide her uneasy appearance and as receptively as possible joined the group. At this point, she was trusting her intuition and drawing closer, lowered her head passively.

The taller of the three men, tapped her chin, indicating for her to look up. As she did, all three looked at her almost as if they were reading her thoughts and somehow judging her disposition. This triggered the most mysteriously weird feeling inside her. The way the taller individual's amber eyes scrutinized her, it felt as if he was reading her like words on a page. In a bizarre way, it felt like he was summoning distant memories from her subconscious. To compound this inexplicable feeling, the group were joined by several others, young, old, male, and female. One female, in particular, caught Rebecca's attention. She was slightly taller than the others, her skin, a seamless mixture of pale greens and blues generating a shimmering aqua appearance. To Rebecca's mind, she had an amphibious appearance and the demeanour of someone of importance.

The way she moved through the group with a firm, but calm manner, easing the men at the front to one side, clearly demonstrated a position of authority. Now standing eye to eye with Rebecca, she looked her up and down. Slowly, she moved around Rebecca as if she was scrutinising her soul. Now back at the front, she gently, but firmly, gripped Rebecca's jaw and moved her face to one side.

The way this female then flicked her hand in Rebecca's direction left her feeling a little apprehensive, but curiously still relaxed.

She said something unrecognisable to the group, then turned to Rebecca and spoke with broken English. 'World you from is self-images, confliction, and disdain. Our creation is amity.' She then gripped Rebecca's jaw again, and asked, 'will you amend our system with types of negativities? I doubt not.' She then turned and again spoke to the others with a series of clicks and sounds.

Rebecca watched this woman gesticulate with the group, trying to not only work out what she was feeling herself but at the same time analyse this woman's stand-point towards her. Although she should have been way out of her comfort zone, weirdly, she felt calm, mesmerised by not only this world within a world, but also fascinated by these folk. Although at the outset, she kind of felt like she was within the pages of a fantasy book, no sooner than she'd clambered down the stairs everything became tactile and oh so very real. For sure, it was the weirdest scenario she'd ever experienced. Something though, inside of her, was telling her she belonged, even though she was still a tad unsure if her presence was welcome here. Oddly though, in spite of her calmness, there was something deep within her thoughts that was a little uneasy. This had come close to the surface a couple of times but was quickly watered down by this amazing place and these mythical, yet oh so real folk.

'They are deciding if they should allow you to stay,' Osgyth said.

Stay, Rebecca thought, wondering how long she would be, or, was meant to be here. When she'd entered the cave, she only ever considered it a hiding place and no more. To her mind, she was still planning to escape with Osgyth in a boat, and her only consideration was where they would end up. At no point, even when they entered this subterranean citadel, did she believe it would be anything more than a passing visit. As much as she was invigorated and stimulated by both her surroundings and these folk, it wasn't somewhere she planned on spending much time. Considering this, she reflected on the thirty years she'd spent with Etienne. Indeed, her life had been littered with journeys that outwardly and inwardly lasted weeks, months, and often years. Each time though, she had returned to the exact point where she'd left. That was with the exception of this entire journey, which started in the secret garden when Meredith suggested she was home now. Since that episode, which felt like eons ago, she'd never actually found her way back to where her journey had started. So, the idea of spending a week here, let alone months or years was leaving her a little uneasy and unusually uncertain. 'Osgyth, you said stay.'

Narrowing her eyes, a little, she smiled. 'Of course, you are unaware of the parameters of this place. When we entered, our path behind us closed. It has often offered me a sanctuary from the world we know. My existence has been fraught with misguided lights. Often, I unwittingly chose or was ushered along fated paths. For two hundred years, I was lost to an unfulfilled and miserable destiny. One day, I stumbled upon this sanctuary and was welcomed by these folk.'

Hearing her speak of living for two hundred years, although startling, for some strange reason it did not come as a surprise to Rebecca. Recalling her time in Mesopotamia, she was aware Rebekah's life seemed to cover several generations. At the time, she had unwittingly accepted it as part of the path she found herself treading. Now, that concept was manifesting itself in her consciousness. 'You mentioned this place had often offered you a sanctuary. 'So, when you first entered this world, how long were you here for? Also, how many times have you been here?'

'I have taken refuge here many times. I stay each time until it is safe for me to return to my world. I have trodden my path for seventeen epochs, twelve of which I have spent here.' She then seemed to think for a moment. 'In your world, my life has spanned seven centuries.'

Osgyth's words were a little confusing for Rebecca because this woman appeared to be thirty at most. The unsettling factor was her spending more than half of her life here and to her mind that equated to over four hundred years. That notion and the idea of her being stuck here was uncomfortable, especially with these folk appearing more than a little unreceptive to her presence. For sure, this place was a delight for her senses, but the concept of being here any longer than a day or two was not ideal. As uncomfortable as she felt, something in the back of her thoughts was telling her it was what it was and she needed to focus on the here and now. Dragging this thought to the front, she found solace knowing she would, at some point find her way home. After all, not only was she way out of her timeline, but she was also in a place that only ever existed in her imagination. She nodded and decided to try and go with it and wait for something to happen.

Chapter 22 - Labyrinth

Aware Osgyth was looking at her, she smiled but knew her uneasiness was all too evident.

'You appear a little disordered. I suspect this is because you are considering a way back to your future world.'

'You know of my world?' Rebecca asked.

'I have made company with others of your making. Some appeared from worlds long past, and some like you, from a future existence.'

Although her words caught Rebecca a little off guard, for some reason, she wasn't as surprised as she should have been. The question foremost in her thoughts wondered why others like her had visited Osgyth. 'You said you have met others like me from the past and future.'

'Over the years many who share your making have entered my life. Often, when my world becomes unstable and takes a damning route, they visit and alter events. Although I know of your kind, I am unsure of their exact purpose. To my thoughts, it would seem they visit to reset time. I have thought often about the changes they create and wonder how events would have unfolded without their intervention. I was informed of my destiny at a young age and without fail, your kind has smoothed my route.'

'You said you were informed of your destiny. May I ask who informed you, and what is your destiny?'

'A character I have yet to see visits and speaks with me. His name is Ethernal. I was recently informed by him someone would visit me and aid my next step. He also said that same person would need my help to find their rightful path. I, therefore, believe part of my destiny is to guide that individual. The equilibrium of time is dependent upon that person following their own destiny. It was said this individual would be the strongest of their kind, but their route wavering in indecision. Immediately our paths crossed, I considered you as that individual.'

Over the years, Rebecca had been presented with many two-way scenarios like this. So, learning she was here to help this woman as much as this woman was here to help her wasn't really a surprise. As she considered this, in an odd way, it reminded her of the first encounter with Meredith. Also, realising Ethernal transcends all time wasn't really surprising either. However, learning he had visited Osgyth, who didn't appear to be of her making, left her with questions. She now found herself wondering if this woman was some kind of link between Ethernal, her world, and this mysterious place she now found herself part of. All that this woman had said, got Rebecca thinking about her own situation, rather than Osgyth's. Ever since that day in the secret garden with Meredith, Rebecca had felt as if she was in some kind of limbo, not knowing where she belonged. In fact, that notion had plagued her every step. Even after seeing Elizabeth recently, although she'd instantly felt an absolute love, her father not being there once again raised emotions and feelings of not truly belonging. So, hearing this woman would ultimately serve as a guiding light for her eased this constant underlying feeling of uncertainty. Before she had time to consider her position any further, the tall woman who had firmly gripped Rebecca's cheek, gently took her hand, her disposition now clearly open and engaging.

'Come, sit. We speak. Jolinga is my title.'

Now back in the here and now with a jolt, Rebecca followed this woman, weaving a path between dwellings of every shape, height, and colour. Some were unevenly round, others square with slanting roofs, but one, in particular, caught Rebecca's eye. It was an uneven hexagon-shaped, blueish building, with a tall spire that appeared to be made from some kind of yellowish-brown material. It really felt like she was in a magically enchanted land, the kind beyond most people's imagination. To her though, it was how she'd imagined it would be, just grander, and more elaborate. Even so, the one thing she'd never envisaged was this mix of cultures, the almost human-like interactions, and certainly wasn't prepared for the size of these characters.

At the front of every building were a number of folks, their clothes befitting of this subterranean creation of wonderment. The one thing that struck her was their oh so intriguing variation in appearance and dress code. A few, in front of the bigger buildings, were slim individuals, around five feet tall, dressed in tight-fitting, and to her mind, Mayan like warrior outfits, all in a mixture of reds, oranges and yellows. Other folks were short and rotund, but in no way appeared over-weight. All sported what could only be considered farm-like hessian clothing in browns and fawns, which oddly matched their appearance. There were also several individuals whose appearance seemed to fit somewhere in between. They were however clearly unique, their clothing a rainbow of colours and styles but nonetheless very individual. In Rebecca's mind, here was a blended society befitting of this inspiring underground system. As she approached the hexagon building, there were a couple of folks who had a mysteriously celestial appearance with a fitting demeanour. To her, they not only appeared to be some kind of spiritual leaders, but the aura coming from them exaggerated this notion. Their imprint and demeanour actually manifested as an odd sensation the likes of which Rebecca had never experienced. The nearest she'd come to feeling like this was when she visited St Albans Cathedral with Roxy.

As her eyes danced between the buildings and their residents, she couldn't fail to notice her every step was being watched to the point of scrutiny, which made her feel a little uncomfortable. This feeling made her realise they were perhaps seeing her kind for the first time in the same way she was witnessing them. Although it was clear Osgyth had visited this world before, she seemed to manifest into some kind of divine being as soon as they entered this environment. This realisation and perception altered Rebecca's outlook completely, and it was now clear they were inspecting her in the same way she was examining them. Considering this, she tried to be mindful of her body language and outward response to their scrutiny. At university, one of her lecturers, Sam Pochard, who'd become a good friend, said to her it wasn't about how an individual reacts to you or your comments, it is how you respond to their reaction. She went on to say that in that situation you have two routes you can take. Irrespective of it being a negative or positive scenario, your response should be considered, tactile and friendly, but never defensive. A defensive response will take a positive situation and create a negative situation. She also went on to say that most people's negative responses are a matter of nurture, not nature. Their unconscious incompetence recalls a similar scenario with a bad outcome and brings that distant memory to the front of their mind, causing an involuntary reaction, which is invariably negative. You are not born negative, she suggested, in most cases, life's hurdles make you negative if you allow them to dictate your mindset. Considering this, Rebecca inwardly shook herself and tried to appear receptive, approachable, and considerate. Mostly though, there she was with another vivid memory from a life as an older 21st-century individual. While considering this, she forced herself to stop looking each individual up and down and instead smiled and nodded with as much sincerity as she could muster. Within seconds, she noticed their demeanour had changed and was noticeably tactile. It was really rather weird because she could not only see the change, she could physically feel their altered perception of her. Earlier, she was unwittingly giving off a defensive appearance, and they were feeling this and then responding accordingly. There and then she realised just how fervently spiritual these characters were. They didn't judge you by your appearance, they judged you by your emotional intelligence. This then triggered another memory of Sam talking about the mood when you walk into a restaurant. You feel it, you don't see it, but most people don't think about it, or understand it, just accept it, when in reality, it can sometimes be you who is creating the mood. It was clear to her now these people had an inimitable understanding and grasp of this mindset.

To compound this emotional journey she was experiencing, one of the taller females stepped forward and touched Rebecca's cheek gently with one hand while brushing her arm with the other. The feeling it created inside Rebecca was as if her soul had just been kissed by some kind of serenely tranquil being. Over the years, Rebecca had witnessed some incredible situations and been in the company of many truly inspiring individuals. Never though, had she felt or experienced anything remotely similar to this.

Just as she was thinking about her frame of mind and all she'd learnt since entering this world, she was aware Osgyth was standing with Jolinga. Both were grinning to the point of almost laughing. To her mind, although they were appearing to be laughing at her, it was clear it wasn't at her expense. In the most peculiar way, Rebecca recognised their smiles were a positive response to the way she was reacting to her situation. The only time she'd felt this confident about someone's standpoint was with her mother Elizabeth. Even when her mum had outwardly responded to one of her stories with laughter, Rebecca just knew it wasn't at her expense. It was only now looking back she recognised an emotional correlation. The thing was, her trust was born over a number of years with her mother. These two individuals had only been in her life for a short time, yet here she was inwardly trusting these two in a similar way. This notion in itself made her realise she was here to learn about herself as much as anything else. Alongside this, she was aware of how often her thoughts had brought forward recollections from a life with Elizabeth. At no point had she considered her time with Meredith. For her, this notion offered her a little more clarity. Perhaps, this was how her meeting with Osgyth was helping her.

Without thinking, she smiled back and rolled her eyes, then instantly realised how this involuntary reaction may have been perceived in a negative way. All she was actually trying to do was respond to them in a positive way. This inward acknowledgement of her own behaviour made her realise how far she'd emotionally travelled today. The Book-Keeper had said to her, as had Ethernal, she had more to learn. Their comments were all too prevalent today. To her mind, she'd always considered herself a receptively tactile individual. Because of this, she'd never really considered her behaviour and how others would see her. With this in mind, she joined Osgyth and Jolinga. This time, she was much more aware of her body language and facial expressions.

'You journey far today,' Jolinga said, touching Rebecca's hand. 'You joined us with mind fastened. You open now. You see me and I see you.'

Rebecca had never considered her mind as fastened. Now though, she was all too aware of the way she'd initially reacted to this unfamiliar situation. She'd felt everyone was watching her with uncertainty. Her fastened response mechanism would have countered this perception in an unreceptive manner. This wasn't because she felt unreceptive. Her conscious mind was overwhelmed by her surroundings and the onlooking eyes. Subsequently, her subconscious was giving off an air that could be considered negative. Reality was, she was delighting in her surroundings and her true feelings were anything but negative. 'I feel I have travelled a long emotional road today with just a few steps.'

Nodding, Osgyth said, 'I have seen this. I knew the moment our paths crossed your spirit was full of goodness. This is why I brought you here. Aside from hiding from the King, I had to be sure I was right in allowing you to enter this sanctuary. At first, I was ready to escape with you in a boat. Once we were boxed, I had little choice but to escape into this solace. I could have done so, and left you behind. I knew however, you would learn from these people, which clearly you have. They do not interact with our world for good reason and it will always be that way. On the surface, our lives are driven by greed and an inability to consider those around us. Here, it is the opposite.'

Rebecca considered Osgyth's words carefully before answering. She nodded, trying to show her agreement, and said, 'I was bewildered when I first entered this place, by my surroundings mostly. With each step, I have felt my way wisely. It has become clear to me these folk walk a spiritual path of goodness. They judge individuals by their demeanour only. If you have a kind integrity and manner, it will be felt and reciprocated. I have always been aware of how others perceive me, my inner feelings and emotions. Today, this understanding has been magnified.'

'I have watched you learn,' Jolinga said. 'I looked into your inner being. I saw good. You welcome. You first to be welcome.'

This confused Rebecca a little. 'The first, surely Osgyth was before me.'

Jolinga smiled. 'Osgyth has become one of us. She has chosen to live some of her creation in your world to better her understanding. She was conceived and born into your world. She then transcended to this place. Physically, she is of your world, mentally she is one of us. Her spirit is strong and brings a light to our unique world, unseen by those conceived here. You are clearly not of this world, although you have been received well.'

These few words alleviated some of Rebecca's concerns about being here for a long time. Although she was excited by this place and its people, the notion of spending years here had concerned her. This idea had been triggered by Osgyth's suggestion she'd been here for four centuries. She now realised that was unlikely to be the case. Aside from this, it also explained her perception of Osgyth. She'd known right from the moment she'd met this woman there was something about her that was unlike anyone she'd ever met. That feeling had left her with many questions. Those questions were now

188

answered. 'May I ask how many years you have lived for Jolinga?'

Jolinga frowned and turned to Osgyth. She then spoke with her in that series of clicks and sounds. After a little back and forth, she turned to Rebecca. 'I am young compared to our priestess,' she said and pointed to one of the two characters who'd caught Rebecca's attention earlier. 'I have trod this path for eleven centuries. Mala,' she said and again pointed, 'has seen over three-thousands of your years. She has watched your people's greed weaken your destiny.'

Although Jolinga's words should have come as a shock, for some reason Rebecca wasn't at all surprised. She was actually more astounded by her lack of surprise. As she considered her reaction, she thought about everything that she'd been through in her life. The last couple of surreal hours had been beyond amazing. Even so, despite the odd emotional reaction, she'd taken it all in her stride. It mysteriously felt as though her life's journey had somehow prepared her for this moment. The question now dominating her thoughts was why did she feel this way and what was next. Inwardly, it felt as though she was about to face a significant challenge and this was actually heightening her anticipation. A remote, rather odd thought was telling her it wouldn't be a physical challenge, more a mental test. Thinking about this and reflecting upon all the conundrums she'd faced throughout her life left her with many questions.

'I see you thinking,' Osgyth said, holding Rebecca's hand. 'The first time I entered this kingdom, I too was overwhelmed with questions. With every step, I questioned my very being, often considering my next move and its subsequent influence and impact. That very consideration endeared me to these people and their way of life. They tread a spiritual path, which considers their every word and its subsequent effect. We see in you that same consideration. In your world, your people have lost their connectivity to those around them. Their only thought is for themselves. It was never meant to be that way.

A ravenousness and thoughtless greed had altered their views. Through time, many of your kind have entered our world. They have returned back with a greater understanding. Their mission, to bring about change. Although some affected an alteration within your society's direction, it was never of significance. Some were met with disdain and eventually lost their direction. Some, in years to come, will be considered evil sorcerers and murdered by this belief. Mostly, none of them showed your vision, only appeared in this world as an apparition. You are the first here in the physical form.'

Although this answered some of Rebecca's questions, in turn it actually created more. 'So, if I follow you correctly, I am not the first to be here? There have been others before me.' She then thought for a moment. 'Also, you alluded to others in the future?'

'So, there are two futures. The world you know, and the world we know. Also, to answer your question, as I alluded to, you are the first in the physical form.'

'I am not sure I follow,' Rebecca said, narrowing her eyes and shaking her head. She then realised how she'd just responded. 'Sorry, I shook my head and squinted. It was not in response to you. It was caused by my own confusion.'

Jolinga touched her on the arm, again triggering the most delightful sensation. 'Firstly, no need to be sorry. Unlike others of your kind, you are aware. So, the future we see is from now, this world, this place. Your future is from your world, your place. Your future will ultimately be our future.' She then looked at Rebecca almost as if she was interpreting her thoughts. 'The morro for us is the next day. The true and rightful morro for you is in eleven hundred and thirty of your years.'

A little taken aback by this exact timeframe, Rebecca did a quick sum in her head and realised this woman was specifically referring to the year two-thousand and thirty-three. Ever since the day she sat with Meredith in the secret garden, Rebecca had questioned her true reality. If this woman's maths were accurate, and she had no reason to doubt it was, especially as she'd been so specific, that meant Rebecca belonged with Elizabeth as a forty-one-year-old married woman. This notion brought instant comfort to her emotions. Of late, she'd felt sure Elizabeth was her true mother, and in particular, her reaction to Tommy had compounded her thoughts and feelings towards that existence. The one question now burning in her thoughts was if she returned back would she have any knowledge of her time movement. Also, would she be married, would she have two daughters? This then stimulated another thought whereby she may actually end up in two-thousand and thirty-three as a single forty-something woman or perhaps even as a fifteen-year-old girl. She glanced at Osgyth and Jolinga and realised they were watching her thinking. 'I understand. I have a burning question though. Why am I here? Am I here to simply learn from you? Am I here to help Osgyth avoid her ill-fated tomorrow?' She then thought for a moment. 'Am I here only to find my own true path?' Again, she paused as another notion occurred to her. 'Or, am I here to learn from you and alter my people's destiny?'

Both Jolinga and Osgyth looked at each other and chuckled. Jolinga then turned to Rebecca. 'All four, and more besides. The White Hart is our guiding spirit and he led you to us this day. He to us is the same as Ethernal is to you. A guiding light who sees all and only knows of truth.'

'So, are the White Hart and Ethernal godly creations?'

Shaking her head, Jolinga said, 'No, not at all. Your God is your God and yours alone. Both the White Hart and Ethernal are driven by our inner thoughts and are displays of our fears, trepidations, and beliefs. They are ours alone and created by our own conscience. Their aura manifests to guide those like us and you.'

This came as a shock to Rebecca's thoughts. She'd always believed Ethernal was real and appeared when she was lost. If

Jolinga was right, he didn't actually exist and was essentially a subliminal creation. Although this answered why she'd never actually seen Ethernal, the reality was still just beyond her reach. 'What about the Book-Keeper? Is he real?'

'You have much to learn from us. Although you are the most receptive of your kind, your journey with us is one of continued learning.' Osgyth then spoke with Jolinga briefly. 'In time, you will understand all and return to your world stronger.'

Rebecca pursed her lips and although she was once more wondering how long she'd be here, asked, 'is the Bookkeeper also a manifestation of my own inner thoughts?'

'The Book-Keeper happens in an alternate existence to us all. There is the world you know. There is this world. There is another dimension where Queen Matilda, Princess Rebekah, the Book-Keeper and those like them belong. There are others who exist in that in-between world, such as Meredith and her aunt. It is a place between the past, future and all possible timelines that exist.'

Once more, Osgyth's words, although complex, shone a semblance of light on Rebecca's own true reality. It actually created a strange and many-sided realisation. Through every step of this protracted journey, even when she'd questioned if Meredith was her real mother, inwardly, she had always known it was Elizabeth. It was only now, hearing Osgyth's and Jolinga's words that she realised she'd essentially known all along. Although learning that Meredith and her aunt were not of her world was a bit of a shock, she'd kind of known all along, and to discover they belonged alongside the Book-Keeper fitted perfectly. Thinking about how Meredith and her aunt drifted in and out of her reality, it made sense now. 'When I return to my world, will I be back to the beginning with no knowledge of my journeys?' This question raised another query in Rebecca's thoughts. 'Will I still be able to travel back and forth through time. Or will I go back to being a young woman who just sees the world differently and whose notions are just that, imaginative notions?'

'You are a time-keeper and always will be. As for your memories, that will be your choice.'

How can that be, Rebecca thought? To her mind, her memory was exactly that. She couldn't see or understand how she could choose to remember something or not? It didn't make sense to her mind. Then she thought about her time in 1827 with Meredith and the way her memories fleetingly came and went. At the time, she'd never really come to terms with the situation, instead just chose to accept it for what it was. Thinking about it now, she kind of realised that very notion was her own, choosing to just accept it, without any debate. It just occurred to her that towards the end of her time with Meredith, she needed to remember so she did. 'I get that and I suspect this is exactly the kind of thing I am here to learn.'

'It is part of your journey. You have always accepted your ability to travel through time as your destiny. Never have you questioned its reality. You have just moved from one experience to the next without ever asking why.' Jolinga again spoke with Osgyth. She then again turned to Rebecca. 'Time is on your side. I see you are deeply concerned.'

'How do you know this?' Rebecca asked, once more taken aback by Jolinga's ability to read her every thought. Just this notion alone reminded her how Meredith appeared to be able to read her thoughts also. She'd never really questioned it at the time, just accepted it for what it was. She now found herself wondering if Jolinga belonged to the same group of people.

'It shows in your eyes and facial reaction. In our life, we read those around us by their manner. This way, accidentally negative comments are not taken incorrectly.'

'I am not sure I follow this, Jolinga. Surely if I say something negative it is what it is.' In the back of her thoughts, Jolinga's comment offered an alternative perspective of this woman. Perhaps she didn't belong to the same group as Meredith, instead was purely a social expert and could easily read people's behaviour patterns. To her mind, some of the things Jolinga had said were ambiguous and almost weighted in some way. She wasn't at all sure how this was, however, there was a tangible difference between what she said and what Osgyth said. It wasn't anything she could put her finger on, it was just there, nudging at her inner thoughts.

Shaking her head. 'Not at all. Consider how many times you have chosen the wrong words and it has been misinterpreted,' Jolinga said, frowning and smiling at the same time, which again nudged at Rebecca.

Rebecca thought for a moment about the way her father behaved when she was young. She had a belief her father was dysfunctional and arrogantly dismissive. Considering how quickly he changed after the boiler incident, she now found herself wondering if he was initially responding to Elizabeth, who was, in turn, responding to him, causing a downward spiral. *Hmm*, she thought, *but he used to refer to her mother as, "woman," which is inexcusable.* Closing her eyes and taking herself back to a particular incident in the kitchen, she had a huge reality check. Her dad had called Elizabeth woman, but only after he had heard her mother refer to him as that man when speaking with her about dinner choices. In her minds-eye, she could now see him grimacing as Elizabeth had said, in a rather hostile way, "that man," and pointed. All those years of believing her mother was annoyingly passive when actually her passiveness was an unwitting guise to subterfuge her father. To her mind now, neither were to blame, they just started down the wrong road and couldn't turn off, both being unintentionally responsible. It was essentially all about delivery and perception. As she was about to speak, she thought about her calling Tommy a twit. Her mum didn't like it, even though Tommy didn't care. In reality, Tommy knew it was a term of endearment, whereas her mum was just hearing the word. More so, he kicked his ball at her, so she would call him a twit and get in trouble. 'Crumbs. I know exactly what you mean. I was just thinking about my world and your words have given me a completely different perspective. It is not what you say, it is how you say it. You can call someone a derogatory name that to onlookers might come across as negative. Reality is, it's a term of endearment. Also, your body language will alter the meaning of your words to those who do not know you, or know you mean well.' Rebecca then thought for a moment. 'Importantly, if you misread a situation and respond in a negative way, that then causes a harsh response and you end up heading down a path you can't get off.' Through every word, she kept thinking about Jolinga and the way she spoke, held herself and importantly the way she scrutinised Rebecca's every movement. In an odd and indistinguishable way, it was almost like she was looking for weak points or some kind of frailty. The one aspect that was becoming increasingly clear to her was that Jolinga's demeanour, unlike Osgyth, was contrived to the point of being subliminally controlling.

Jolinga turned to Osgyth and again spoke in a series of sounds. For some reason, this time she understood every word, "She has learnt quickly. Her time with us will move quickly, but still, be long. We need to slow her movement."

Chapter 23 – How Long?

Hearing that word, long, refocussed Rebecca's thoughts. Considering what had just been said, and unsure if she was supposed to understand their private conversation, Rebecca felt she had no choice but to say something. Not knowing how long she would be in this place was the one thing that made her feel a little uncomfortable. 'I completely understand what you just said. Throughout my journeys, I'd always just accepted each turn was just that, another turn. The one thing I am struggling to understand is why I will be here for a long time?'

Narrow eyed, Jolinga turned to Osgyth. She then turned back to Rebecca. 'It is clear you now understand our words. You are the first of your kind to do so, aside from Osgyth. Your unique receptiveness will shorten your time with us. Ahead, there are many turns for you. If your mind remains open, your days will shorten and the next page will be written. Fear not. You have learnt much today. None least, where and with whom you truly belong. For hours, days and eons, you have followed a path with no consequence or fear. Each conundrum was flawlessly held and dispatched by you. Your mission here may take a little longer than you feel comfortable with.' She then turned her back once more on Rebecca and whispered something to Osgyth.

Hearing Jolinga's words of encouragement kind of helped alleviate Rebecca's concerns a little. Nonetheless, she was left feeling a little uneasy and now found herself wondering what lay in front of her. It wasn't so much the words, more the way they were delivered. From the moment she had encountered Osgyth, she felt certain she was here to help her escape a dreadful destiny. Considering this, and thinking about how easily Osgyth escaped to this labyrinth, she wondered why she would have needed her help, other than to untie her hands. Surely there was more to her journey other than apparently helping someone who possibly didn't need help. Surely, her journey wasn't just for her to learn from these folk. To her mind, and thinking about every step she'd taken, it had always been about helping others, who in return helped her in some way. Never had she been in a situation where she was somewhere just to learn. In fact, the more she thought about her journeys, she'd never questioned why she had been somewhere. Even her time with Etienne and Duncan was part of a journey whereby she altered the direction of history in a positive way. The one overriding aspect was she always knew once her mission was complete, and would know she was returning home. This current scenario apparently had no mission to complete, other than helping Osgyth, which she'd done. 'How will I know when my mission here is complete? To my mind, I do not have a mission.'

She then watched as Jolinga whispered to Osgyth. Initially, she thought she was simply hiding what she was saying because it was private. However, seeing Osgyth frown uncomfortably raised concerns. To her mind, it was more than just a reaction. To compound this, Osgyth glanced at Rebecca from the corner of her eye without moving her head. The look suggested all wasn't as it should be. This instantly put Rebecca's mind on alert.

Jolinga then turned to Rebecca and indicated for her to follow. She led her past a couple of hexagon-shaped buildings before arriving by a flight of steps carved into the rock face.

Still a tad apprehensive, Rebecca glanced up to see where these steps led. Looking up, she followed the step's path until it entered a hanging canopy of unrecognisable trees. To her mind, the trees had an almost rain forest type appearance, surrounded by a peculiar swirling mist. In most scenarios, this scene would have invigorated Rebecca's imagination. Right here and now though, her gut was telling her to keep her guard up. She wasn't sure if this was purely because of the look Osgyth gave her, or if there was something else. She turned to Osgyth, glanced at the flight of stairs, and back, raising her eyebrows a little. In the back of her thoughts, something was stirring. When Osgyth had spoken earlier about her time here and her time above, there was something in her voice and tone that was a little scratchy. At the time, Jolinga had spoken of Osgyth's unique light and that it had not been previously experienced by those conceived here. It hadn't raised any concerns at the time, but now that same sentence was starting to take on a different meaning. She couldn't really put her finger on what had changed or why she was feeling the way she did but was feeling increasingly uneasy. There wasn't anything in particular, but from the first second Jolinga had gripped her face and then scrutinised her body language had caused a little ripple. There was something in her gut telling her not to climb the stairs. Seeing Jolinga now standing with one foot on those very stairs, looking in her direction caused that ripple to become a wave.

'Come, join,' Jolinga said, beckoning Rebecca towards her.

There was an expression on this woman's face and it was raising alarm bells. Rebecca looked at Jolinga, before glancing at Osgyth, all the time not having a clue how she was going to get out of this. In normal circumstances, she'd just say, "nope," not going up there." For some bizarre, inexplicable reason, she was intimidated by Jolinga, which in itself was not only annoying but also baffling. She glanced again towards Osgyth, who in turn glared wide-eyed at Rebecca. The look on her face didn't need words, and she knew there and then she was possibly in danger. She glanced around and could see several of the people watching, almost with baited breath. She didn't know why but felt they were watching her with trepidation. This alone would have been enough to put her on guard. The way she felt now, there was no way she was going to climb these stairs. Something though was telling her she couldn't belligerently refuse, which in itself was completely against the grain. If her initial concerns were right, and the more she thought about it, the louder that apprehensive alarm bell was ringing, she knew she had to think on her feet and try to find a way out of this situation. Glancing down, she looked for some kind of subconscious inspiration. Then, just in front of her, she noticed a large shell type object. That was what she was looking for. She smiled at Jolinga, stepped forward, deliberately put her foot on the shell, and fell to the floor. The way she went down nearly made her laugh, reminding her of a time Tommy was booked for faking a dive during a football match. This whole notion actually reset her mind and she now felt as if she was back in control, which was the one thing that was annoying her. She then grabbed her ankle and realised she'd actually hurt herself a little.

Osgyth knelt down and the look in her eyes clearly acknowledged Rebecca's dramatics. She touched her gently on the arm and mouthed, 'we will talk.'

Jolinga came across and to Rebecca's mind, she looked cross to the point of being angry. This actually got Rebecca's back up to the point of her feeling unusually aggressive towards this woman. In an odd way, but perhaps actually not that odd, it reminded her of some larger-than-life girl at school who had decided Rebecca was her next target. In one incident in the school corridor, this girl, with her hanger-on mates, had approached Rebecca, clearly with a hostile mindset. Rebecca had prepared herself for this moment and was ready. As the girl angled toward Rebecca, she stepped to one side and tripped the girl, causing her to fall. She then turned to one of the friends and gripped the girl's hand with all she could muster. She then lent over the bully girl and snarled a warning at her. There were two more incidents, but each time Rebecca had gotten the upper hand. She looked at Jolinga trying to work out if she should take this woman on now. Oddly, although she was clearly in a minority here, a notion was stirring. Something occurred with the bully girl over the next couple of weeks whereby the hanger on friends had found alternative avenues. She now found herself wondering if Jolinga was somehow running this place with a kind of tyranny and autocracy. Glancing around at the people now standing over her, she was aware they had a look on their faces that had altered the second Jolinga had stepped forward. As she sat there, while Osgyth tended her ankle, she could see Jolinga's eyes deepen as she watched on. In an odd way, the look in this woman's eyes had a malevolence befitting of the sorcerous she vanquished at Perth Priory.

This thought instantly rang a bell in Rebecca's mind. *Priory, Priory*, she thought. She now found herself wondering if the absolute goodness of a priory somehow attracted an evil counterbalance. Something had definitely changed in the last few moments with Jolinga's body language, which had become hostile. To compound this, her skin tone and its colour had altered in some bizarre way. Instead of the engaging aqua marine radiance, it was now more of an insipid, characterless bluey-green shade. To compound this, she suddenly became aware this woman had no shadow. One of the things that had surprised Rebecca earlier was in spite of no sun, everyone had a distinct shadow, mysteriously always in front of them. She glanced around and it was clear everyone else still had a shadow. She inwardly narrowed her eyes, stretching her memory. Then in a flash, she recalled Queen Matilda's exact words, "that malevolent, shadowless creature," she said when speaking of that evil woman.

Rebecca glanced at Osgyth wide-eyed, wondering how she was going to get out of this ugly predicament.

Osgyth turned to Jolinga and said something again using a series of clicks and sounds. This time, Rebecca only managed to understand part of what she'd said, but it seemed as if Osgyth was suggesting she needed to tend to Rebecca's ankle.

Jolinga knelt down and gripped Rebecca's cheek between her fingers. The look on her face of utter contempt left Rebecca with no doubt she had to find a way out of this place and quick. The question was how. Whenever she'd been in a difficult situation, there'd always been a fairly obvious route out. Being in this predicament, with so many onlookers, all clearly advocates for Jolinga, she just couldn't see her next steps. To compound her situation, she remembered the cave entrance seemingly opened and closed on its own and was now thinking Jolinga had some kind of control. She shook her head inwardly, wondering if that was even possible, although she was in a world where everything came as a surprise.

Osgyth gripped her hand and indicated for her to stand. 'Come, I will dress your ankle.'

Faking her injury, Rebecca got to her feet grimacing and yelping quietly, making sure the onlooking Jolinga could see and hear. She then followed Osgyth, leaning on her shoulder for support. The way Jolinga followed them was to Rebecca's mind menacing to the point of being threatening. She then noticed Jolinga push a couple of onlookers to one side and the way they responded triggered a notion in Rebecca's head. It was obvious right from the first moment she encountered this woman, she was in charge, but she was now thinking her seeming authority was born from fear. Osgyth led her right back to a small cabin affair near the steps where they first climbed down into this world. Observing individual reactions to Jolinga left her in no doubt this woman ruled this place with terror. Considering this, Rebecca could see a possible way out, reckoning she could perhaps win the trust of these people. To her mind, though that would take time and the way she felt now, she wanted out sooner rather than later. Whenever she'd been in a difficult situation before, she'd always relied on her intuition, today though required action of some sort. Thinking about the small cave entrance they'd entered via, and Osgyth's suggestion this closed behind them, she couldn't see a way out. She then recalled the shard of light coming from above when they entered the middle section of the cavern. Even though the light coming from it was relatively small, it was perhaps big enough to fit through. The only issue was how high up it was, but there were a number of tree type shrubs clinging to the rocks nearby, and she reckoned she might be able to use these to help her climb out.

As she entered the small cabin with Osgyth and spotted Jolinga stalking their every move, she couldn't see a way of escaping via that route without facing off with Jolinga. She sat on a small wooden chair and as Osgyth nursed her ankle, she looked at Jolinga standing at the door, sneering. She then saw her push one of the onlooking, smaller folk to the ground who was also looking on. Watching this enraged Rebecca. 'Maybe she rules with fear and no more,' she mumbled quietly.

'She does. The mist by the other steps takes away an individual's ability to act for themselves and makes it easy for her to rule with fear. That mist enslaves all, including me,' she whispered.

Jolinga's actions angered Rebecca and instead of being afraid of this woman, her attitude changed to one of determination and empowerment. This emotion was intensified by Osgyth's words. Aware of her altered mindset, she recalled a time at school when she was around thirteen and was being verbally bullied every day. It was something that never really bothered her but when that same bully reduced a younger girl to tears, Rebecca's whole mindset changed. Challenging the bully and seeing her back down so easily left Rebecca with a life-changing feeling of empowerment. She was now aware that very empowerment could be her way out. Reckoning the last thing Jolinga was expecting was Rebecca to jump up and fight back verbally, she thought, *now or never*.

She took a deep breath and nodded to Osgyth as she put her foot on the ground. She could see Jolinga watching their every move and was aware her expression altered a little as she placed both feet on the ground. *Now*, she thought and moved resolutely towards Jolinga waiting at the door. To her surprise, although Jolinga's face showed utter disdain, she was aware of an element of apprehensive fear. As she reached the door, Jolinga held her arm across the exit, but it oddly lacked conviction. Without thinking, Rebecca grabbed her hand, twisted it back and pushed her to one side. The look on

Jolinga's face was a mixture of aggression and surprise, with a hint of inert weakness.

As she ran towards the stairs they'd entered by, she was aware everyone moved to one side, almost as if they were clearing her path. If she had any doubts about the response of these folk, she now knew they wouldn't step in her way. As she started climbing the stairs, aware Jolinga was following her at pace, she couldn't help but feel an element of concern about leaving these people and Osgyth under Jolinga's charge. Even so, she reckoned she had to get out now, and started scrambling up the staircase. In her hurry, she slipped on one step near to the top and this allowed Jolinga to reach out and grab hold of her ankle. Without thinking, she turned and, in an attempt to free her ankle, pushed Jolinga.

Jolinga balanced for a second, and with an anguished, but also aggressive look on her face, fell backwards. Rebecca watched as she dropped to the ground. Although she was concerned that her kicking out resulted in this woman falling, possibly to her death, her concerns were overridden by an element of astonishment. Jolinga had fallen without making a sound, her eyes wide and fixed on Rebecca. Even when she couldn't focus on this woman's eyes, Rebecca could feel them burning into her like a knife. As she stood on the step looking down, she was half expecting Jolinga to stand up as if nothing had happened. What she wasn't prepared for was to witness a mass of individuals surrounding this woman, ostensibly led by Osgyth. Even though Jolinga hadn't moved, she watched on as they hurriedly tied her hands and ankles together. The moment Jolinga had hit the ground, the whole mood of this place altered. To Rebecca's mind, the way Jolinga had hit her head and then not moved, she believed this woman had fallen to her death, so to see the way these folk responded came as a surprise.

Rebecca was desperate to escape this place but her intrigue was now in control and was telling her to climb back down. She stood there for a moment considering her options but her

203

clear line of sight was now being overridden by a need-to-know. Cautiously, she made her way back down. As she approached the bottom, she was aware everyone was watching her every move. What was immediately obvious was a peaceful, almost still posture resonating from these people. To her mind, when she first entered this place, her thoughts were enveloped by the wonderment of her surroundings and it was only now, she realised that although the place felt calm, there was a whitewashed, almost vague mindset coming from these folk. Now, she could feel personality and an atmosphere that only now on reflection, was missing earlier.

As she approached Jolinga's body, every eye watched her every move, but unlike when she first joined these folk, they were clearly seeing her with different eyes.

Osgyth walked over and gripped her hand. 'Thank you. We have all been locked here controlled by her spell,' she said, pointing towards Jolinga, frowning to the point of almost growling. 'Had you entered the mist, you too would have become caged. Those with inner strength like you, once under her spell, adds to her power and control. She is Ethernal's malevolent counterpart. Her destiny is to unhinge time and this is why you and those like you exist, to stop her kind. I belong above. I lost my verve and soul to Jolinga's spell. Every time I returned to my world I was pulled back. I could not alter my path. Now I am free and feel free, as does everyone here.'

Although these words should have come as a surprise to Rebecca, in an odd way, she'd kind of worked out this scenario in her head. If, as it would now seem, she was here to save Osgyth from Jolinga, rather than the King, she couldn't help but wonder why she was still here. She'd faced this mental situation before and always, there was more for her to do. The question was what because she couldn't see what else there could be. Just then, a notion manifested in her thoughts. 'May I ask if you will return to your world, or stay here now?'

'I am unsure,' she said, narrow-eyed and clearly thoughtful.

Inwardly, Rebecca nodded, reckoning this might be the answer she was looking for, waiting on Osgyth's decision. That didn't quite fit though, because she'd never found herself in a situation whereby, she had to convince someone to follow a life route or path. For sure, she'd led Malinda to safety and there'd been other such situations, but none that ever involved setting out someone's destiny. Thinking about this, it occurred to her that to some degree, she'd guided Millicent, but that was towards a path already set out in time. This was a whole new concept for her and one she was struggling with. *Hey, maybe that's it,* she thought, *I need to help her find her destiny, rather than lead her.* 'May I also ask why you tied Jolinga's hands and ankles. She appears dead to me.'

'She fell once before and appeared lifeless only to return.'

Hmm, she thought and headed over to what looked like the lifeless body of Jolinga. She then bent down and felt for a pulse or some indication of life. There was nothing in her neck, chest, wrist or anywhere else she could think of trying. What did occur to her was although apparently lifeless, her body wasn't cold. She then checked her chest for a heartbeat, and her nose and mouth for breathing, all to no avail. It was weird because this body seemed lifeless, aside from the skin being warm to the touch. To her mind, it was as if she was at some kind of midpoint between life and death. She turned back to Osgyth, unsure of her next move. 'I was aware there was a mood change when Jolinga fell. When we first entered this place, although vibrant with colour and wonder, there was a feeling of lifelessness. Now, I can almost feel an energy that was missing earlier.'

'She,' Osgyth said, and pointed, 'took our soul, vigour, and life. The mist she manifested from within, whitewashed our ability to think for ourselves. Many were unaware they were under her control. I was different and knew I was under her rheostat because I was born to the world above. Even so, I was unable to leave her mental grip.' She then seemed to think for a moment. 'Now, everyone feels as if they have been in a dream, and only now awake.'

A female with elf-like characteristics walked toward them both. She nodded to Osgyth. 'On behalf of my people, thank you, Osgyth. You brought this woman to us. Her actions have awoken us from our psychological and cerebral slumber.'

Rebecca stood up and smiled at this female. 'May I ask your name?'

'I am Kiffany.'

Rebecca smiled again. 'Hello, Kiffany. You said my actions awoke you from a psychological slumber. How did it feel before compared to now?'

'Before, our spirit was absent. Sadly, we were inwardly unaware. Only now do we feel this. I am, like others here, unable to reflect on our world under this creature's control,' she said and pointed, her disdain all too evident. 'She owned our mind. We have no memory of days past. We do all know we were broken before and now are fixed. You fixed us.'

This female's comments had a profound and intriguing impact on Rebecca's spirit. Her actions though were self-motivated. 'You need only thank Osgyth. My actions were born from a need to escape.'

Kiffany turned sharply towards Jolinga's body and pointed.

Rebecca stood with the others and watched as an inexplicable swirling mist appeared to leave Jolinga and in a second, vanished, along with her body.

Kiffany then turned to Osgyth and nodded. 'You will stay and be our Queen or you will turn back?'

Osgyth turned towards Rebecca and held her hand out.

As Rebecca stretched out her hand, she was unable to reach Osgyth and instantly knew what was happening.

Chapter 24 – The Dream

Rebecca sat up, aware the back of her blouse and jeans were damp. She felt really quite peculiar and a little unsure where she was or what had just happened. Glancing around, it seemed she'd perhaps fallen asleep on the grass in front of the summerhouse. Seeing the sign "Millicent Fawcett foundation," confirmed she'd just nodded off, but there was something rather odd stirring in her thoughts. She actually felt as if she'd been part of a dream, rather than just dreaming. This notion was causing the most curious mindset and was leaving her a little uneasy. She knew for sure she'd come down to the summerhouse in an attempt to find a way back to a world where her father was still alive. To now find herself lying on the grass in front of the summerhouse didn't add up. She had come down here with intent, so she couldn't get her head around how, or why she would end up on the ground asleep. It was just plain daft and to compound these feelings, there was a bizarre notion rumbling in her thoughts that she'd actually been part of a dream. None of it was making any sense and the more she thought about it, the more scrambled it all became. Trying to work out what she was actually feeling, she was suddenly aware of something digging into her side. She rubbed her hip, could feel something in her pocket and putting her hand inside, pulled out what looked like an oyster shell.

She sat there gazing at the shell as a thousand thoughts scurried around in her head. Whenever she'd been anywhere in the past, at no point did any of her journeys feel like this. To her mind, it was very confusing because here she was looking at this shell, which clearly was evidence she'd actually been somewhere, but every emotion in her body was telling her it was all a dream. She glanced along at the other two partially built summerhouse buildings. This along with the sign was clear evidence she hadn't been anywhere, or if she had, she'd returned to the exact same place and time.

This in itself was confusing because when she'd discovered her father had died, she'd known she was in the wrong place and timeframe. So, she'd come to the summerhouse with clear intent, just as she had many times before. Each time in the past, she'd found a way back to the place where she belonged. To go anywhere and return back to the wrong life just wasn't how it worked in her mind. She got to her feet and reckoned she needed to go back to the main house where things may become a little clearer.

She walked slowly up to the manor, trying to put her thoughts into some kind of order. Never, throughout her journeys had she ever felt like this. The closer she got to the main house, the more confused she felt. The thing dominating her thoughts was why she'd somehow managed to find her way back to a world where she didn't belong. What was contradicting that thought was an odd feeling that she hadn't actually been anywhere, other than via this dream? *If it was indeed a dream,* she thought, which actually offered her a different angle on things. She looked at the shell again thinking slightly differently, wondering why she was finding it so difficult to work out what was going on. Especially as the shell was evidence she had obviously been somewhere. She stood at the front door and again looked at the shell. Just then a car pulled in behind her and for some reason, she recognised the sound it made on the gravel. She turned knowing it was Ruth's car. As if her emotions weren't already frazzled, here she was recognising the sound of someone's car, someone she hadn't seen for many, many years. Well, that was what her consciousness was telling her, yet, it felt as if she'd seen her yesterday. Before she had time to juggle her state of mind, Ruth got out of the car and walked over.

'Hi ya, Bex. Have you seen your father? I tried to call him this morning. He and your mother were supposed to meet Amanda and me in town to sort out the final aspects of the planning application.'

Ruth's comments were a complete curve ball, but before she had time to think, she heard her father's voice behind her.

'Hi, Ruth. I tried to call you but we didn't know your number. Ridiculous, I know, but Elizabeth and I mislaid both our phones and both sets of car keys. Doesn't make any sense. Moreover, neither of us knew either your or Amanda's number off the top of our head.' He then held up his hands in a questioning, oh so familiar manner.

Listening to this caused the strangest sensation in Rebecca's head, which really unbalanced her emotional state of mind. No sooner than her father had said car keys, she recalled a conversation with Tommy. He'd hidden both their phones and keys and she'd told him several times it wasn't funny and he had to put them back. The thing was, she recalled this conversation as being yesterday. That didn't make any sense though, because when she was last here, her father was dead. This, like every other aspect of today's events, wasn't adding up. To confuse her state of mind further, part of her wanted to rush over and cuddle her father, whereas another part of her brain didn't feel the same urgent need. It was as if one half of her brain was in the here and now and everything was just dandy and the other half was on a rollercoaster. 'Dad, I know how important that meeting was regarding the planning for the other Fawcett buildings. You go with Ruth, I will go kick Tommy until he tells me where he hid the keys, which he did, twit.' She then shook her head, not having a clue what made her say that. To her conscious mind, she didn't know anything about the planning application, yet here she was talking about it, with a clear understanding. It was as if her thoughts were full of memories of a world, a world she hadn't been part of until now. It was as if she had two consciousnesses, one from a world where her father was dead and this one where he was alive. To scramble this inexplicable notion, here she was with knowledge from both worlds. It was as if she'd been in two parallel worlds at the same time, in the same body.

'Right, I will go with Ruth, and you can tell Tommy he is in for it when I see him.'

'I will join you all with mum once I've found the car keys.'

Just then Elizabeth came out with Tommy. Holding his ear, she led him across the car park. 'Right,' she hollered, 'where are the keys and phones?'

Rebecca had never seen her mum this cross, which in the strangest way actually made her smile. 'Dad, we can all go together now. By the way, I love you and I am glad to see you back.' The second she's said that she knew she'd have to come up with an explanation. That was until her father responded.

'Been somewhere, have you?' he said and chuckled. 'Looks like our girl has been jumping around again, Liz.' He then turned towards Tommy. 'No football training for a week. Get in the car, now.'

As Rebecca sat in the back of the car, she experienced a rather mysterious change in her thought process. All of a sudden, although she still had a clear recollection of her time with Osgyth, something quite peculiar had altered. Mysteriously, it now felt as if she'd been there and experienced every moment, but somehow wasn't there. She'd had this before with her memories of events, whereby she had felt like she'd watched a film, but at the same time, it had felt like she'd dreamt every second. To compound this, any thoughts of her father's death now also seemed like a dream. All the way into town, she considered her altered perspective and recollection of events. It was as if her whole outlook was finding a new understanding of her journeys through time. Instead of a world where her father was no longer alive and dominating her thoughts, that memory was a progressively distant notion. It was there but felt as though it didn't belong to her. For sure, she knew she'd been in an ugly place where her father was dead, but just like the incident with her mother and the boiler, it was something she'd seen but wasn't physically part of. Although she was struggling to fully comprehend this new outlook, the feeling that she'd perhaps only witnessed this type of event actually settled her emotions.

To keep her on her toes, there was something else really quite surreal in her thoughts. To her mind, she was a young woman, yet here she was with memories and recollections from journeys covering thirty-odd years. In some strange way though, this notion didn't unbalance her feelings in any way. Instead, she knew she'd witnessed and been part of many events over many years, some as a young girl and some as a mature mother. For a few moments, she sat there silently as her mind went over many varied events.

Unwittingly, she found herself focussing on the life she'd on the face of it experienced as the daughter of Meredith. She could clearly recall every detail and specifically found herself concentrating on the events with Millicent. The present-day Millicent Fawcett Foundation was clear evidence her recollections were real, and to her mind, had clearly affected this world almost two hundred years later. Although she could recall being confused about where she truly belonged, she now knew she wasn't Meredith's daughter and that world wasn't hers at all. With her altered outlook, it now felt as though she'd only witnessed it as an onlooker. For sure, at the time, as with many other episodes, she'd felt she was there and living every emotion. With her altered mindset and reflecting back now, although every journey was uniquely different, there was a constant theme, whereby it felt as though she'd seen that world through the eyes of another. As she sat there thinking about this, she recalled her father suggesting something very similar. Indeed, he'd actually suggested she was perhaps seeing these various events through the eyes of another. What was oh so strange about this memory was part of her brain was telling her that the conversation with her father was years before today. Weirdly though, her recollection was telling her she'd been in her twenties when it occurred. Just to compound these conflicting accounts, it now felt like this was actually a recent event. Although her recollections were jumbled and mixed, that conversation with her father was now offering some clarity and oddly, it actually didn't matter when it occurred.

With her thoughts a little clearer, she was suddenly aware her father was standing by the car door beckoning her out.

'You look like you've been on another of your journeys into the past,' he said and chuckled. 'You have that same look on your face every time, almost as if you are with us, but your brain is somewhere else.'

'Funny you should say that, Dad. I was just thinking about a conversation we had where you suggested perhaps, I was only seeing the worlds I travelled through the eyes of another. That chat is very clear in my memory and now makes complete sense to me.'

'Well,' he said and patted her on the shoulder, 'I should think so too, especially as it was only yesterday when we talked about it.' He then shook his head. 'How long have you been gone this time.'

Her father's words caused a weird feeling for Rebecca, but one that peculiarly made sense, especially when he asked how long this time. 'Dad, this might sound ludicrous, but...' She then thought for a moment. 'I feel like I've been gone for years. I don't just mean a couple of years, I mean, err, I dunno, forty, maybe fifty years.'

Her father narrowed his eyes a little. 'That must feel very unsettling. We need to sit down and talk all about it after the meeting, which,' he said and glanced at his watch, 'is in eleven minutes. Come on, Madam, let's go.'

On the way to join the others, he mentioned all the years she'd spent with Etienne. This offered her a little perspective, and she now found herself wondering if she'd always been 15-years-old throughout all of her journeys. This standpoint meant everything she'd witnessed, Tommy playing football for England, her years at university, being married to Duncan and indeed, Etienne didn't actually occur. Before she had time to consider her emotions, she heard her father calling her.

She followed her father, mother, Ruth, Amanda, and Tommy, who had been told to behave, into a room with three stuffy looking, local council officials in what Rebecca considered a rather stale feeling room.

Rebecca sat at the back of the room drifting in and out of the meeting, as the councillors and her father went through page after page of detailed, somewhat boring paperwork. Then she heard someone mention Rebecca Hewison, which instantly captured her attention. One of the councillors produced what appeared to be a sealed, unopened envelope, which was encased in glass.

'This letter,' he said, 'has been held by the council offices in a vault since eighteen-sixty-seven. It came with explicit instructions, signed by Queen Victoria. It states that this envelope should not be opened until the seventeenth day of June, two-thousand and seven in the year of our Lord, in the presence of Rebecca Hewison,' he said and glanced up and shook his head. 'It also states it will form part of the Millicent Fawcett Foundation. I do not understand how this can be.' Again, he shook his head.

Rebecca held her hand up. 'Umm, you said Millicent Fawcett and kind of hesitated before saying foundation. May I ask, did you hesitate because it says Millicent Fawcett-Black?'

He glanced at the other councillors, then at Rebecca. 'How can you know that. I did hesitate but only because we know this as the Millicent Fawcett Foundation. There has never been a mention of Black before and well, I thought it might… I don't know actually.' He shook his head once more. 'How can you know this?'

James, Rebecca's father said, 'it is a long story. In essence, Rebecca has been doing a lot of research on this matter.' He then glanced wide-eyed at Rebecca, and mouthed, 'we need to chat.' He then turned back. 'So, shall we see what's inside?'

The councillor handed the glass case, along with a small key to Rebecca. 'It specially states that it should be you who opens and reads this letter. It also says you should read the letter once in private, and then decide if you wish to share this with the group.'

Although this was curiously stimulating, and clearly mind-numbing to onlookers, Rebecca felt very calm and in complete control of her emotions. The only thing she was unsure about was where she should read the letter. 'Umm, should I leave the room to read the letter first? I am actually happy to read it here. It is not as if any of you are going to look over my shoulder, other than my brother, Tommy,' she said and glared in his direction.

'I reckon read it there Rebecca,' her dad said, glancing around the room.

Rebecca slotted the key into the lock at the front of the glass case. As she removed the letter, which puzzlingly felt as if it was new, a thousand thoughts went through her mind. Aware everyone was watching her she carefully broke the seal and took out a rather formal looking letter. Although it started with "Dear Rebecca," her eyes were immediately drawn to the names at the bottom. It was signed off, by Millicent Fawcett-Black and Queen Victoria. She stared at the names for a few seconds feeling the strangest emotions, recalling every moment with Millicent and their time in Parliament. She then started reading.

"Dear Rebecca.

You entered my world when my life was lost and my spirit broken. Your words gave me focus. I have never understood, or been able to grasp how you were able to be with me. Nonetheless, you were and every word you said came to fruition. You set out in front of me a vision of how my life would unfold and where it would take me. I accepted your insight, even though I was unable to comprehend how you could, or would know. As you suggested, I married Henry, and we started a safe house for beleaguered women. Also, you foretold of events in Parliament whereby women would be given a vote. This vote gave females a voice and positively altered their position in society, immeasurably.

On the day of writing this letter, in the presence of Queen Victoria, the first female member of parliament was voted in. As a result of my work, which occasioned directly from our time together, some forty years prior to the writing of this letter, the Millicent Fawcett Foundation was set up nationwide.

This letter was then put in trust, to be safeguarded until you were in a position to follow on the work, which you and I started in eighteen-twenty-seven. The timeline for you to read this letter was set out by our mutual ally Meredith Hewison. How Meredith would know to set the date was beyond mine and our Queen's comprehension. We did, however, accept her farsightedness. Indeed, Queen Victoria stated that although it was beyond our knowledge it should not be disregarded.

There was a trust fund put in place by Queen Victoria within the Bank of England. It matures on the seventeenth day of June, two-thousand and seven. It will offer enough finance for you to continue the work we started. Within this envelope are all the details you need to access these monies.

How you deal with this letter or share these words lies with you and you alone. I suspect, like me, your ability to wear the shoes of someone two hundred years before your time, is beyond most people's belief. Therefore, I suggest you will consider your actions carefully, as you always have.

You gave my life a clear mission and for that, I am and will be forever grateful. It now falls back to you to continue what you started.

I pass my best to you in the knowledge our paths may cross once more. Your forever advocate, Millicent Black."

Rebecca read through the letter once more, aware her every breath was being scrutinised. She looked up at her father, unsure what to say. Inwardly, she felt a need to show the letter to her father but was also aware she had to say something to the group. 'Would you mind if I spoke with my father alone briefly,' she said, looking around the room.

The Councillor who handed her the letter glanced around for a second, and then said, 'You can use my office,' and pointed to a door at the back of the room.

Rebecca looked at her father, indicated towards the door with her eyes and nodded. Her father, James, followed her into the room.

'Dad, I felt I needed to share this with you first. I am not sure how comfortable I am sharing this letter with this group of people.' She then handed her father the letter.

James read through the letter a couple of times. He then looked up at Rebecca and shook his head slightly. 'It seems you have been on another long journey. To some degree, I have learnt to expect the unexpected with your adventures. Nonetheless, to learn you changed female history to such an extent is, well, let's say, incomprehensible to most. To some degree, to me also. So, I would suggest you only share the basics with this group.'

'I was thinking something similar. However, I keep thinking how a trust fund, from Queen Victoria no less, in my name would need some kind of explanation.' She then thought for a moment and reckoned her ability to think rationally was being complicated by all the other things she'd learnt today. To some degree, this cleared her head a little. 'Thinking about it, I really do not need to offer them an explanation.'

'What you could say is one of our distant relatives was an ally of Queen Victoria, hence the trust fund.'

Rebecca agreed totally and with her father joined the others.

She then explained as briefly as possible that Queen Victoria had set up a trust fund in the name of the Millicent Fawcett Foundation. She also threw into the mix a made up distant relative who was an advocate of the Queen.

Her words were accepted mostly, although she was aware the councillor who handed her the letter was raising his eyebrows a little. As tempted as she was to explain a little more, her common-sense side was shouting it was none of their business.

'Rebecca, thank you for your explanation,' the councillor said. 'I am sure there is a rational reason why, or how, Queen Victoria would be in a position to address the letter specifically in your name.'

'I can answer that to some degree,' her father said. 'There is a long-standing tradition, still followed to this day, that every generation of the Hewison family has a Rebecca, Rebekha, or Rebekah.'

'Thanks, Dad. That is exactly what I was going to say.'

The councillor nodded, but Rebecca could see he was still unconvinced and was now frowning in a way that didn't sit comfortably with her. In the past, because of the incomprehensible nature of her time adventures, she'd always felt the need to explain every detail of her journeys. Perhaps, for the first time, she didn't feel that need. Thinking about this, she was aware that her thought process was twofold. On one hand, having spoken to her father, she realised she didn't need to explain anything, whereas, in this situation, she had no intention of offering this slightly aloof, frowning individual a full-blown explanation. 'Well, it is what it is. So, with the seal of approval from Queen Victoria, our planning application should be straightforward.'

The councillor turned towards Rebecca, and frowning to the point of giving his appearance a positively disagreeable demeanour, he said, 'I do not need planning advice from a child.'

James, appearing angry, got to his feet. 'This meeting has just concluded. I will take our application to my friend, MP, Malcolm Latten.' He then headed towards the door. Holding the door open, he said to Rebecca and the others, 'shall we?'

The moment her father had mentioned his friend, Malcolm, the councillor's expression changed. 'Um, we can continue the meeting,' he said, appearing very uncomfortable.

'Insult my daughter, you insult me.'

'I am sorry, I never meant to offend anyone,' the councillor said, appearing rather flustered.

'You can say whatever you want, there is and never will be an excuse for your bigoted behaviour.'

As they left the office and headed downstairs, Rebecca held her father's hand. 'Thank you, Dad.'

Ruth touched Rebecca's shoulder. 'I've met him before. It struck me he was, and still is, to use your father's words, bigoted. I believe he has an issue with females in general. Ludicrous in the twenty-first century.'

'You should have witnessed what it was like in the early eighteen-hundreds. The apathy towards women, who were deemed second class citizens was mind-numbing,' Rebecca said, without thinking.

Everyone stopped and looked directly at her, their surprised curiosity all too evident. Just as her father was about to say something, Tommy piped up.

'What's she on about?'

'Nothing, Tommy. Just something I was reading up on.'

He narrowed his eyes in a very unlike Tommy way, which caught Rebecca off-guard a little.

218

'I was watching some old footage of the suffrage movement.'

'But that was the nineteen-hundreds and you said eighteen… I know because my mate at football, well, his mum is related to Emily Pankhurst.' Again, he narrowed his eyes and shook his head. 'I heard mum and dad talking the other day and I know what's going on. All I want to know is what does it feel like.'

Rebecca, slightly on the back foot, glanced at her father, then her mum. 'What are you on about, Twit?'

He laughed. 'Not as much as a twit as you think.' He then pointed to his ears, 'see these?'

'We can talk about it when we get home,' her father said. 'I just need to make a phone call.' He then spent a few minutes talking to his MP friend on the phone.

As Rebecca stood there, she suddenly realised what Tommy had said about Emily Pankhurst and it being the nineteen-hundreds. The way she'd left things, women had gotten their vote in 1867, so what was Emily doing in the nineteen-hundreds. 'Tommy, your mate's mum. Does he ever talk about Emily and do you know much about her?'

'He never stops talking about her. Boring, but kinda interesting, I guess. She had something to do with women losing their vote in, err, I dunno, eighteen summit.'

This completely scrambled Rebecca's thoughts. 'Thanks, Tommy,' she said and reckoned she needed to look it up on the internet when she got home. To her mind, it had all been sorted in 1867, so whatever happened would mean she hadn't completely succeeded.

Chapter 25 – What Happened?

Sitting quietly in the back of the car Rebecca's thoughts were going in circles. On one hand, she had a profound legacy left to her from Queen Victoria, in the name of Millicent Fawcett, yet somehow the women who'd gained their vote ahead of time subsequently lost that same vote. Coming to terms with the notion she'd probably be heading back to the 1860s, she suddenly noticed Tommy looking at her with an odd expression on his face. 'What's that look all about, Twit?'

Tommy leaned across and whispered, 'I know all about your time jumping so no need to keep it a secret anymore. Strikes me that you are gone more than you are here. I hear Mum and Dad talking about where you are. I may be a twit but I'm not stupid. My mate said his mum has an old letter from her great, I dunno, three times great aunt with your blinking name on it. He keeps asking if you are related to his whatever she is.'

A little taken aback, Rebecca asked, 'so, what do you say when he asks.'

'I just say I dunno. I do know but like I ain't gonna tell him my sister is related to Marty McFly.' As if he had just read the look on Rebecca's face, he said, 'err, hello, Marty McFly, Delorian, Back to the Future.'

'Right, Twit, but funny. Seriously though, you know everything?'

'Pretty much. Known since you found the key and went off to, what was 'er name. Meredot or summit.'

'Right, but you never said anything, how comes. And it was Meredith.'

'Look, Sis, I've always known you were different. Sometimes, even when I was like six, I used to think you were so different you might as well have been a fish or a cow. Well, sometimes you literally are a cow,' he said and pinched her arm gently. 'Your secret is safe with me. If I blab, they'll lock me up, not you, coz they won't be able to find you.'

Rather surprised but oddly pleased Rebecca sat quietly in the back of the car, chuckling every now and then thinking about Tommy's analogies. Mostly, her thoughts jumped between Tommy, what happened with the vote in the 1800s and in the background this rumbling notion that all of her memories were just distant accounts from events she'd only ever witnessed as an onlooker. When they got stuck in some traffic by road works that were distantly familiar, as if she'd sat here before, her mind focussed on this notion that she'd only ever seen, through the eyes of another, those worlds she'd felt so much a part of. For the first time, this new way of thinking about her time in the past and indeed the future was rather unsettling. It got her thinking about how she'd helped stop global warming, and how meeting Rebekah in the Cradle of Civilisation had ultimately led her to alter humankind's road of self-destruction. This opened the door for her mind to reflect on her time with Queen Matilda, and also how apparently years later, she'd help stop child trafficking. The more she delved into her memories, the longer the list became, scrambling her thoughts, even though every step was clear. In spite of her clear recollections, the way in which they were all muddling together, she now found herself wondering if any of these events had actually taken place. When they finally arrived home, she started to list her thoughts in a different way. There were proceedings, such as today, where clearly, she'd been there, in whatever form, and altered events. There were others, such as her time at university, and sadly, Tommy playing for England, where she now believed she'd only seen those chronicles from afar. Importantly, her time and actions during these events had ultimately no bearing on their outcome. Just this notion alone, helped her re-evaluate everything into two categories. There were events that actually had a place in history and could apparently be altered for the good. There were other events that hadn't yet occurred where she'd seen a world yet to occur. Perhaps through the eyes of her older self. The one thing that was an emotional sticking point for her was the global warming problems society are yet to face. To her mind, she was in her twenties when she received the award from Queen Elizabeth and that was at least 7 or 8 years off yet.

She was deep in thought when she looked up and realised that she was sitting in the car on her own. Tommy was, as usual, kicking his ball around in the yard. She sat there watching him, wondering if he'd ever follow the footballing path she'd seen. Thinking about one incident where she'd embarrassed herself by shouting his name, she felt a little saddened by the idea it may never happen. Then watching him doing some amazing tricks with the football, she reckoned his destiny was all too evident. She shook her head, wondering how long she'd been sitting there.

As she got out of the car, her father, who was standing by the front door called over, 'back with us now, are you?'

'How long have I been sitting there?'

Chuckling, her dad said, 'maybe an hour or so. When I opened your door and you didn't look up, I realised you were deep in thought, so…'

'You know what is weird, the last thing I remember was us sitting in that traffic jam. I felt as though I'd been there before.'

'What do you mean?' her father asked, his curiosity obvious.

Rebecca shook her head. 'It was uncanny because I felt as though I'd been in that exact jam, at that exact time. It's difficult to explain, and I'm not sure I really got to grips with how I felt, but it got me thinking. Being there provoked so many memories from my journeys, but what made it weird was some of those memories were, well, from the future, if that makes sense, which I doubt it does.'

Her father narrowed his eyes a little. 'let's go have a cup of tea and talk about it.'

She followed her father into the kitchen where her mum was making tea.

'Would you like a cuppa, Rebecca?' her mum asked, standing by the kitchen table.

'Love one, thanks, Mum.'

'So, Rebecca, tell me more,' her father asked, his curiosity evident.

'Well, I have lots of memories from different episodes, all in the past, as in meeting Meredith in eighteen-fifty-three, and so on. While thinking about those events, I remembered an occasion from the future when I was in my twenties. I am struggling with this concept.'

'Well, you have shared a lot of journeys with your mum and I. Mostly from the past but there have been a couple from the future. One, in particular, your mother and I were only talking about the other day. We wondered how it felt for you, where one day, you're are fifteen, the next you're twenty-four and receiving an award from the Queen for your work with global warming.'

A little taken aback, Rebecca wasn't sure what to say. 'Umm, that was the one episode I was thinking about. What I can't get my head around is if I was twenty-four as you say, that's like nine years from now.' She then thought for a moment. 'Thinking about it now, what bothers me most is the idea that I may have to go through every step all over again to stop us from burning the planet. Surely that can't be the scenario.' She considered her own words briefly. 'Unless I have to actually wait until I am twenty-four to fix it for good.'

'That, Rebecca, is exactly what we were talking about. You came back from your journey into the future, including meeting the Queen when you were aged twenty-four and gave us a detailed timeline of your journey. Now, here is where it got weird for your mother and me. The very next day, you got an invite to meet Queen Elizabeth. Subsequently, you received an award for something that wasn't going to happen for another nine years, according to your recollection. The thing was, it would seem, in spite of your accounts relating to you being twenty-four, you were actually fifteen when it happened.' He then narrowed his eyes a little, clearly thinking. 'The thing is, that event was just last week.' He then shook his head. 'I have seen you confused and a little at sea when you've returned from your trips, but never like this before.'

'I was thinking exactly that,' her mum said and put the tea down. She sat down opposite Rebecca and asked, 'How long do you think this has been going on for?'

Wide-eyed, and feeling really quite odd, Rebecca glanced back and forth between her mum and dad. 'I'm not sure, because I have years, and I mean many years, of memories. For example, in one memory, I can recall living in the summer house with my husband and two lovely daughters. I was in my forties. So, I really do not know or have an answer.'

'Well, Rebecca, you found an old key,' her mum said and glanced at her father, 'around four weeks ago. Since then, you have been away on your adventures and returned with amazing stories so many times, we've lost count. There was one day when according to you, you went on five very different excursions if that's the right word,' she said and chuckled in a heart-warmingly familiar way.

'What is bizarre,' her father said, 'you never go missing. It is something we've struggled to understand. One minute you are sitting right here chatting about school, the next, you are talking about spending six weeks with Queen Matilda. It's like you go and come back seamlessly. For sure, the first story followed you going to the summerhouse and finding yourself back with Meredith. Since then, well… The only one who ever seems to notice you've been missing is Tommy. When I quizzed him about it, he just shrugged his shoulders, suggesting he feels you go, rather than sees you go.'

Her father's words came as a surprise to Rebecca, but at the same time made sense. To her mind, it gave a little credence to what is a bizarre notion at best. Her way of thinking was that time travel was a thing for the movies, as Tommy said, Back to the Future. Her father suggesting, she went and returned without outwardly going anywhere made sense of this notion that she was only ever seeing her journeys through the eyes of another. 'That must be weird for you and Mum,' Rebecca said, a little unsure how she felt. The one aspect that raised questions was how Tommy knew, or felt it, to use her father's words. *Not so much of a twit, after all,* she thought.

'Mum and I were chatting about this yesterday. You get a blank look on your face for a few seconds at most, then bam, you're back with another story. Like just now, when you were in the car. I looked at you, turned to Liz and said, she's off again.'

'Dad, Mum, what I cannot get my head around is feeling like I am actually there. No debate, I truly feel every breath and witness every incident. I can't dream of giving birth and knowing what it feels like. But what makes it weird is coming back to the real world and feeling no emotional detachment. There have been two journeys that have lasted years, as in twenty plus years. In the one I mentioned earlier, I had two daughters and lived in the summerhouse. There was another time when I had two sons. The strange bit is I can recall talking to you and Mum about me having two sons with a Canadian Red Devil army officer named Etienne. To my mind though, I was in my twenties when I had that conversation with you.'

'We have also had this chat before, Rebecca. Just last week, you told me all about Etienne, importantly, you told me you could remember having the same chat when you were in your twenties.' Her mum shook her head. 'Neither your father nor I understand what happens to you.' She then glanced in the direction of James.

'I think you move around, almost as if you open a door, find yourself in one world, open the next door and find yourself in another time or place and eventually, you find your way back here. All this seems, to us anyway, to happen in your head somehow. As if you go into a dream-like state. The thing is, in most incidents, there is evidence you have been somewhere in the past.' He seemed to think for a moment. 'Or the future, as with the global issues. You then come back to us and it is clear, whatever you did, wherever you've been, however, you got there, it happened. Just this morning, by example. We had to make up a story, to cover up you affecting events in the eighteen-hundreds. The point is, as is often the case, there is a clear evidence trail. To most, it wouldn't be so obvious, but because your mother and I know the back story, we are able to correlate the two.'

To Rebecca's mind, everything her father was saying made complete sense. If sense could be made of her time-jumping. The aspect she was struggling with was the notion she'd only ever seen the places she had visited through someone else's eyes. She sat there for a moment, then remembered her time with Matilda. One night when they were hiding out, she'd scratched the back of her arm on a bramble, which was rather deep. The thing was, this was the first time she'd physically hurt herself. 'Dad,' she said, feeling under her tee-shirt sleeve, 'To your mind, how long ago was I with Queen Matilda?'

'Last week, why?'

She stood up, turned sideways, and said, 'if I wasn't there physically, but only there seeing it through somebody else's eyes, how did this happen?' She then lifted her sleeve,

226

revealing what felt like a deep scratch on the back of her arm. She then stood in front of the kitchen mirror, surprised at how deep it actually was.

James glanced at Elizabeth.

'I wondered where the blood on your white tee-shirt came from. That actually looks rather deep, as in needs stitches.' She then glanced at James. 'Well, it is mostly your father who has the answers but I have a solution.'

Rebecca looked at her mum waiting for her to finish her sentence. She then glanced at her father and lifted her palm.

'You can put your eyes away, Sweetie. I am thinking about how best to explain my idea. So, on some of your journeys, you, as your father suggested, see that world through the eyes of another. Some, as with Queenie, you have to physically be there, so, yeah,' she said, and shook her head, clearly a little uncomfortable. 'Perhaps you go into some kind of time loop if there is such a thing. By that, I mean you can be gone for years and come back and pick up exactly where you left off. This is your real, stable world. The other places are a hole into the past or the future. Somewhere you go, sometimes mentally and sometimes physically.'

'Mum, that answers everything and I really do not know why I hadn't considered that myself. A time loop is a good notion. Perhaps, while I am gone, this time, this world, somehow stands still awaiting my return. No dafter notion than me actually time travelling in the first place.'

Her mum smiled in a delightful way that knocked at Rebecca's conscience forever thinking this woman wasn't her real mother. 'There have been many situations whereby I have found myself questioning where I truly belong. I spent a long time with Meredith and wondered if that was my world. I am sorry for that, Mum. Sitting here now with you and dad has made me feel... well, this is where I belong. When I was with Meredith, I continually questioned why I felt the way I did.

Never once did I feel as though I belonged. Today, I feel like I belong here with you, dad, and even the twit, bless him.'

'Well listening to you and your father made me realise you'd both lost your way because you were trying to find a "one answer fits all," solution. How can there be a definitive answer to something that, well, to most people, is make-believe.'

'That also makes complete sense, Liz. With you, you only offer a complete solution. You never speculate, you never dither, you think, and find a concrete answer. Even for this most bizarre situation, we find ourselves blessed with. Nobody else but you would be able to apply some rational explanation.'

'Well, thank you, James,' her mum said, looking very pleased with herself. 'The thing is, I need a rational mindset. It is the only way I can deal with Rebecca's ability. I know only too well that there is no tangible explanation and to avoid me being spooked, I look at the questions and find tactile answers. I never think about it as a sci-fi movie. I take each incident and accept it as real, then try to apply some foundations. It is how I cope.'

'He is right, Mum. Ruth said something very similar,' she then realised Ruth might not have said it yet, 'umm, in three years' time, or so,' she said and chuckled. 'Anyways, Ruth said you are the most rational, clear-thinking person she knows. It doesn't matter that she hasn't said it yet,' she chuckled again, 'she will.'

Chapter 26 – Real or Not

After Rebecca had finished chatting with her mum and dad, she decided she needed to find out what happened with the women's vote and so headed upstairs to her laptop.

As she sat there searching the internet, her focus was constantly interrupted by her mother's words. The notion that sometimes she saw the worlds she visited for real, and sometimes she was just seeing that world through the eyes of another was a little unbalancing. She'd always been aware that mostly, she was physically there, and occasionally, she was invisible but had felt she was always herself. At no point had she ever felt she was in someone else's shoes. After a few fruitless minutes, she decided to go for a walk to clear her head.

'Hi, Mum. I'm just going for a walk.'

'Let me have a closer look at your arm before you go off galivanting.' She then bathed her arm gently and asked, 'when did you say you did this?'

'In eleven-twenty-three,' Rebecca said and laughed, which in turn made her mum laugh out loud. 'Err, I'm not sure to be truthful.' To her mind, her time with Matilda was years ago, clearly though it was recent. The way she felt right now, she wasn't sure how she would ever get her head around the notion that she'd only found the key four weeks ago.

Her mum raised her eyes, 'well it looks about a week old, but it seems to have healed well. Looks better now I've bathed away some of the blood. Be careful this time, wherever you end up.'

Thanks, Mum,' she said and stepped out into the kitchen courtyard, unsure where she was heading. Part of her subconscious was telling her to have a look in the secret garden, whereas something was telling her to head straight down to the summerhouse and maybe then to the Spry Wood. She stood there for a few seconds and reckoned on visiting the secret garden as she was so close. She made her way around the wall and pulled at the small door behind a shrub that she didn't really recognise.

This kind of threw her a little and when the door felt stuck, she stood there, her eyes back and forth between the odd-looking shrub and the door. The thing that was confusing her most was this shrub. It was a rhododendron, which was one of her favourite plants and she had no recollection of any such plant, other than in Meredith's time. This thought made her stand up straight and look back at where she'd come from. Something was telling her at some point between the kitchen and here, something had happened. To her mind though, she still felt she was in her own time. Then she heard several voices and knew she wasn't at home. The thing was, the voices seemed to be coming from behind the wall. She eased her way past the shrub and tried the door again. This time it opened easily and to compound her already slightly unbalanced feelings, the door looked new, as in, it had just been hung.

She narrowed her eyes and stepped into the garden. There was no one there, which was plain daft because she definitely heard voices coming from the other side of the door. She stood there for a moment trying to focus. The thing was, the voices now seemed to be coming from the other side of the door. 'This is ridiculous,' she mumbled.

'All is to test your resolve,' an all too familiar voice said.

'Ethernal, about time, where have you been. My brain has been like scrambled eggs.'

'I am not sure what scrambled eggs are, but I understand your concept. Your thoughts are at sea. Know your mother's notion is correct. You, like today, are here in the now, and on other occasions, you observe only.'

'Where am I then?' she asked, but felt he was gone once more. *Oh well*, she thought, *let's go find out.* She opened the door again and as she did, she could once more hear the voices coming from inside the garden. *This is stupid*, she thought, turned, and could see several people standing by some fancy white, iron, garden furniture. *Where am I*, she thought, glancing around for a face she recognised. Just then she spotted Millicent, and it appeared to be at the same time Millicent spotted her.

Waving, Millicent headed over. 'Something inside said you'd be here today. I mentioned this to Meredith and she'd had the same thought.'

Why today, Rebecca thought.

'Our bill of reform was overturned in Parliament. It was the day after the first female member of parliament was inducted. Some arrogant backbencher on the opposition side had found an anomaly in our original reform.'

'Anomaly must have been a big anomaly to get the bill overturned.'

'Well, here's the thing, it was just the date. Actually, two dates, one at the beginning and one at the end. They didn't match. Everyone recognised it as a mistake, however, the legal system is such that this was enough.'

'That is blinking ludicrous. Surely, if everyone knows it's a genuine mistake, then...'

'Doesn't work like that and sadly, had Margery Smith not become an MP, no one would have noticed and if they had, they wouldn't have been too concerned. It's that male ego getting in the way again.'

Rebecca was a little taken aback but not surprised to hear how the male ego can, in some cases, try to keep women in their place. 'What concerns me most is it isn't a lot different in my time. What I have noticed is most men actually embrace equality for their female counterparts. It is the noisy minority who shout the loudest and this is where the problem manifests itself. Those who believe in equality lose their voice, fearful of condemnation for speaking out. It is not a lot different from that minority who go around picking on people and the quieter ones feel unable to stand up to the bully-boys.' While speaking, Rebecca's brain was trying to work out how she could actually fix the date issue. To her mind, everything that had been achieved was lost just because there was a discrepancy with the dates, and that was just too frustrating to let go.

'I have always been aware of this and in particular, when Henry spoke out about women losing their vote because of a mistake with one date he was ridiculed and told he was prejudiced in favour of women.'

'I got your letter, by the way, the one you left in trust, signed by Queen Victoria.'

'I must say, I struggled with the whole concept of writing a letter for someone who wouldn't be born for another two hundred years. As was the Queen. We did so, with an assurance from Meredith. In the end, we decided there was no harm in writing the letter.'

Listening to Millicent speak, Rebecca couldn't help wondering why she was here and what she could do to alter things. To her mind, she should be back at the beginning or at least when the bill was about to be submitted so she could change the date. To think that women lost their power to vote for fifty-odd years just because of a mistake with one date was actually very annoying to the point of clouding her thought direction. She shook her head inwardly, trying to focus on the here and now. There was obviously a reason why she was here. 'When was the bill overturned?' she asked, wondering what, if anything, she could do now to affect some kind of change.

'It was yesterday and that was why Meredith and I kind of expected you to make an appearance. I am not altogether sure how it works, however, Meredith explained that consistently you turn up when things were likely to go a little awry.'

'That is always how it works, but normally, I arrive before it goes wrong. Kind of keeping history on its rightful track, if that makes sense.'

'It does make sense and I am beginning to comprehend your role in all of this.'

'What I do not understand is why I am here today. What can I change?'

The two continued to chat, searching for an answer of sorts to no avail. Then the subject moved on to the Millicent Fawcett Foundation. When Rebecca brought the subject up, Millicent had a rather unexpected reaction.

'I am so pleased you mentioned this. Henry and I were considering bringing our attempts to create a nationwide foundation for women to a halt because of the autocratic obstacles we constantly faced. It has been one step forward, two steps back. Hearing you speak of our foundation still running in two hundred years has totally refocussed me. Knowing this, no matter what, we will strive through all the obstacles.'

Hearing Millicent talk in this way, Rebecca realised she was perhaps here just to offer some kind of reassurance. She then watched as Millicent began to fade, and knew she was about to move on to the next step. Before she had time to consider this any further, she was standing in the walled garden, in the pouring rain, alone.

What now, she thought, her clothes soaking wet. Normally, whenever she moved like this, she found herself among other people. There was no one, no sound, nothing, which made her feel a tad edgy. Now becoming cold, she stared aimlessly across the garden trying to work out what she should do next. Her common-sense side was telling her to head indoors and get some dry clothes. The problem with this was she didn't know what she would find when she went indoors. Unlike every other journey, she'd been on when she'd always known she was in another era, this was different. There was nothing to tell her when or where she was. Although rationally thinking, she knew her only option was to go inside in search of an answer, but something was overriding this idea and telling her to stay where she was.

She stood there for a few minutes and was now starting to shiver. When she'd left home, it was mid-summer, and when she was speaking with Millicent, it was clearly a similar time of year. This was winter and this notion alone was enough to put her on edge, aside from being totally alone. She wracked her brain trying to remember if she'd ever jumped from summer to winter before, or vice-versa. For sure, there was the time when she'd jumped into the future where it was so hot it was impossible to know what time of year it was, and then her time in Mesopotamia, when again, the heat was searingly hot. As much as she could focus on her increasingly fragmented thought process, she just couldn't recall a scenario like this before. The only thing that was stable was her being in the secret walled garden and even that looked different.

'Hang on a minute,' she mumbled, 'it is different.' She then stood there trying to gather her thoughts and get some bearings. Narrow eyed, she remembered Osgyth saying something about a walled garden and although that was just in passing, she now wondered, reasonably so, she thought, if she was back within the grounds of the Priory. If so, the question was why. As far as she knew, the way she'd left things, she'd released Osgyth and the other folk from Jolinga's spell. Importantly, to her mind, Osgyth had decided to stay in that world and help guide those people and that was why she'd moved on. Thinking about it now, Osgyth had never openly, or verbally made that choice and Rebecca now realised it was just an assumption on her part. Trying to unravel her thought process, she heard an unusual sound coming from the far side of the garden, and not being able to work out what it was kind of caught her off-guard.

She headed over and soon realised it was the sound of water cascading from some granite-like rocks into a clear, almost dreamlike pool. She stood there for a few seconds trying to work out what was going on. It was weird because although the fountain of water was crashing into the middle of the pool, there were no ripples. It was as if the fountain of falling water was hitting the pool surface and just continuing on its way. She leaned over and stared into the pool, which seemed bottomless in some bizarre way. It was the weirdest thing she'd ever experienced and she wasn't at all sure how it was making her feel. Part of her was a tad uneasy, whereas there was this strange feeling of anticipation. It was as if she could feel something was going to happen, but she didn't know if it was good, bad, or indifferent. Whenever she'd felt this kind of anticipation before, she'd always had some kind of notion as to where it was leading her.

She knelt down and became mesmerised by the falling water. Then she caught site of something in the pool and for a second thought, it may have been a fish of some sort. Just as quick, whatever it was, vanished. She leaned forward peering into the pool, and as she did, she thought she saw a face appear in the water. It was weird though because whatever it was, was neither on the surface nor beneath. She sat back, rubbed her eyes, and leaned forward again. This time, the face appeared again with a small shard of focus. Instantly, she knew it was Osgyth's face and she was mouthing some kind of message. Then for what felt like a second, her face focussed and inexplicably she could hear her speak even though there was no sound.

'Save me from the cavern.'

In a breath, she was gone and Rebecca knew exactly what she needed to do. She sat there for a moment, mesmerised by the cascading water, now crashing onto the surface of what appeared to be just a normal shallow pool. She stood up and although soaking wet and freezing cold, the rain had stopped and with her newly found focus, she shook herself down and headed for a large wooden door at the far side of the garden. Although initially, this place had felt like her garden back home, as she made her way towards the exit, she realised it wasn't even similar. She stood by the door and looked back wondering how she could have been so mistaken. Then it occurred to her that perhaps her first steps were indeed in her own garden and at some point, she'd moved seamlessly to this place. A tad unsettled by this weird notion, she was nonetheless focused, her only minor concern was what she'd find behind the garden door.

Okay, she thought, *only one way to find out,* gripped the large brass latch and eased the door open. Although the door opened easily, it made a weird sound, almost as if it was speaking to her. She paused for a moment considering this surreal, almost nonsensical notion, but to her, it oddly fitted with the mindset she'd always had. In the past, she'd been aware people might laugh at her saying hello to doors, shrubs, and anything else she thought would listen. She'd carried on regardless and today was no different. Twice more, she opened and closed the door and both times got the same inkling. *Once more*, she thought. This time, she was as sure as she could be the door was saying, "free Osgyth." It wasn't clear, and certainly didn't make any sense, but it most certainly focused her mindset and fitted perfectly with her beliefs.

As she made her way across a large, formal-looking courtyard, it was strangely quiet. It wasn't simply because there were no people, there was no sound. No birds tweeting, no sound of wind rustling the trees, nothing. It was almost as if she was there, but not there. Then at the far side of the courtyard, she spotted a door open in one of the smaller buildings. She then watched as four rather imposing, almost stately looking people entered the yard.

Rebecca stood frozen to the spot and watched as the four people walked directly toward her. Bizarrely, there was still no sound, even though they were walking on loose gravel, talking openly. It was one thing her being in a situation like this as an onlooker, she'd found herself in this scenario many times before, but never like this. It was as though she was watching a film with no sound, and it actually made her feel rather peculiar. It was clear the people, who were now standing just a few feet away chatting, were unaware of her presence. As she stood there trying to lip-read one of the women facing her, an odd idea came to her. She dragged her foot across the gravel to see if she could hear her own sound. There was nothing, but it did make one of the men turn and look at the ground exactly where she was standing. She did it again, and this time two of them reacted, with one of them pointing at the ground, appearing a little alarmed. All four then started speaking at once, with two of them pointing.

By her foot, Rebecca could see a piece of flint that was maybe two or so inches. She bent down and picked it up with the idea of dropping it on one of these people's foot. However, as she stood up, she wasn't sure if this was either a good idea or fair. For sure, it would get a reaction, but for what purpose. She was certain she was here to observe, and it was clearly evident she was invisible to these people. If she was actually only here as an onlooker, what good would it do dropping a stone on their foot, other than spooking these people any further?

She stood there for a couple of moments, and eventually, the people started speaking normally again. Once more, she tried to lip read, unsuccessfully. She reckoned if she tried to move away, she would again disturb these folk. Without moving, she watched their body language and mouths move, trying to read the mood. Then, just as one of them started heading away, she could hear one of them speak. Holding her breath, Rebecca listened to the slightly muffled voice.

"With the King now dead, you would think Osgyth would have returned to her home."

As the four moved away, Rebecca breathed deeply, aware she'd been holding her breath for at least a minute. She once more found herself alone and in silence, which was a really quiet unnerving feeling. Gathering her thoughts, she had a good idea why Osgyth hadn't returned and so headed across the yard in what she believed was the direction of the cave entrance.

Chapter 27 – The Cave

Leaving the buildings behind, Rebecca made her way across the slightly boggy, open farmland in the direction of a wooded area. To her mind, it looked like the wood where she and Osgyth first hid. Ever since she had arrived in this place this time around, especially with all the weird goings-on, she'd found it a little difficult to focus. With the sun now shining, her clothes drying out a little, and a clear mission, she was able to concentrate her attention a little better.

As she passed a fenced-off area, she noticed some rope laying on the ground. Without thinking, she headed over, and in spite of it being soggy and muddy, she picked it up, looping it over her shoulder. As she continued towards the wood, she wasn't sure why she'd felt such a strong need to commandeer this rope, something just told her to grab it, and as always, she was following her intuition.

Clambering through the wood, she soon arrived by the lake edge and quickly found the large willow covering the cave entrance. Now kneeling directly in front of a narrow gap in the rock, she knew there was no way she was going to fit through. Of course, she tried but knew it was a waste of time. She then tried calling through the gap, but that too wasn't going anywhere. There wasn't even an echo. To her, it looked like a mere gap in the rock, rather than a cave entrance. She could clearly recall Osgyth telling her the cave only opened for certain people and to her mind, she'd got the impression that this was being controlled by Jolinga. The thing was, she believed Jolinga was no more, so this idea was a little unnerving. She considered this notion for a moment and decided she was better equipped knowing Jolinga might still be on the scene.

She stood back for a moment considering her options. Glancing back and forth between the cave and the rope, an idea came to her as she remembered the shard of light, she and Osgyth had passed while in the cave. *That's what the rope is for*, she thought, reckoning it might help her climb down into the cave. The only problem she was now facing, was where the shard of light entered the cavern. She sat there for a moment and with a stick tried to draw a map in the mud. She looked back towards the wood and then started heading up a slight incline.

Now at the top of the slope, she closed her eyes and tried to map the area in her head once more. Off to her left, she could see a few shrubs clumped together and reckoned it was worth investigating. As she came closer, she could see a slight rocky outcrop just behind the shrubs. Pushing her way through some thorny yellow-flowered bracken, she could hear an odd sound coming from the rocks. The problem was, that the sound seemed to be coming from beneath those same rocks. She walked around looking for some kind of way in. There was one possible entrance point but this seemed to be blocked by a large flat granite-like rock that oddly appeared as if it had been placed there. Although to her mind it was way too big for her to move, she gave it a shove anyway. To her surprise, it moved easily in spite of its size. She climbed up on one of the supporting rocks and pushed at the flat rock with her foot, which slid away revealing what looked like an entrance. She knelt down and peered through the hole. She could not only hear voices she could actually see the same folk she'd met previously moving around. They were completely oblivious to her peering down on them and she wasn't at all sure how this made her feel. If nothing else, she could perhaps enter this labyrinth unnoticed. Considering her next steps, she knew she had to find a way in but there was an issue standing in her way. The drop to the ground was straight down with no obvious points to help her clamber to the bottom.

Seeing a sturdy tree nearby, she headed over and tied the rope firmly around the tree. She then measured out the rope, uncertain if it would reach the bottom. She looked around and on the other side of the rocks could see another tree, albeit considerably slimmer. She headed over and after pulling at it with all her mite, felt sure it would support her weight. She then tied the robe to this tree and again measured it out. To her mind it was a little short, but not so short she couldn't drop the last few feet. Her only concern was her being able to reach the rope to climb back out. As she sat there considering her options, she heard a familiar voice behind her.

'You will need this. Mix it with water and use it as a repellent.'

It was Ethernal and for some reason, she just knew he'd gone after his last word. She turned around and could see a tiny bronze container, sealed with a cork, sitting on the ground. Picking it up, she wasn't at all sure what this was, or what he'd meant. *Use it as a repellent,* she thought. To her mind, her only need for this would be if somehow Jolinga was back in control and this was some kind of potion that would have an adverse effect on her. She thought about this for a moment longer and this could be the only answer, reckoning if it was any more complicated than that, Ethernal would have said so. She considered opening the container, but something was telling her not to. She checked to make sure the cork was tight, and then placed it in her pocket. Gathering the rope, she climbed back on the rock and peered down. The sound and those making it seemed to have gone. Reckoning this was her best chance of lowering herself down unnoticed, she pulled on the rope, making sure it was tied tightly, then dropped it through the hole.

As she expected, it appeared to be a few feet short but didn't look to be anything she couldn't handle. Checking her pocket for the container, she started to ease herself into the hole. Fortunately, in the gym at school, climbing ropes was something she'd curiously liked and found easy. She flicked her eyebrows, reckoning this was why, which made her grin, easing any concerns she might have had. As she climbed her way down the rope, she started to hear voices again. As

241

quickly and quietly as possible, she lowered herself down and dropped the last couple of feet to the floor. Fortunately, she could still reach the rope, and spotting a spindly shrub to her left, she tied the rope to it, kind of concealing it.

With the voices getting closer, she looked for somewhere to hide. Before she had time to move, she heard Osgyth's voice and it sounded like she was speaking with Jolinga. To her left, there appeared to be an outcrop of rock that might serve as a place to hide. She quickly and quietly made her way over, and kneeling down behind the rock, reckoned she was out of sight. Just behind her was a tiny trickle of water, and when the time was right, she reckoned this would serve to kindle the potion.

Aware she was holding her breath, she breathed out through her nose as quietly as possible. Watching Jolinga forcibly holding Osgyth's arm, while pointing upwards, Rebecca listened closely.

'You are never going back. Ask once more and I will treat you as an enemy, not a friend.'

The aggressive expression on Jolinga's face combined with Osgyth's almost pitiful appearance was all she needed to know. She took the container from her pocket and removed the lid, letting out an awful smell, not dissimilar to rotting eggs. As she started to fill the casket with water, the smell intensified. This seemed to get the attention of Jolinga.

Appearing somewhat alarmed, Jolinga headed towards Rebecca's hiding place. With the container full, Rebecca swished it around a little and prepared herself to throw it over the oncoming Jolinga. Halfway, Jolinga paused, sniffed the air, and stood still. The look on her face showed an obvious concern.

Rebecca wasn't at all sure what she should do next. One half of her brain was telling her to stay hidden and await a possible better opportunity. The other, valiant half was telling her to go for it, meet Jolinga halfway and use the potion. The problem was, although she trusted Ethernal, he'd never actually said the potion would stop Jolinga. Common sense kicked in and told her to wait it out and see what happens next. Clearly, Jolinga was concerned, so maybe this was actually a sign of vulnerability. As she was weighing up her options again, Jolinga started speaking.

'Ethernal, can I smell your horrid poison again.' Her tone then became aggressive and pulling a long pointed bladed object from a sleeve affair hanging around her waist, she hollered, 'Be off with you, or I will end your existence.'

Just then a character appeared behind Jolinga, and somehow Rebecca just knew this was Ethernal, even though she'd never seen him before. 'It is not I that you need to concern yourself with.'

As he finished speaking, three more characters appeared spaced in a semi-circle around Jolinga. To Rebecca's utter astonishment, one was Matilda, another Rebekah and the third a female she didn't know, but going by her attire, she was able to place her sometime in the 15th-century.

As Jolinga turned to face them, Rebecca got a glimpse of her face. Her expression was a strange mix of exasperation and aggression.

Jolinga stood there for a few seconds, possibly considering her next move.

'Lost for words, are you?' Ethernal asked.

Rebecca could see Jolinga's head, almost swivel like, turning between each of the four.

Rebekah took a small step forward. 'As Ethernal suggested, it is not he, or indeed us,' she said and glanced at the others, 'whom you need to concern yourself with.'

Still hiding, Rebecca reckoned both Ethernal and Rebekah may have been referring to her. This notion was compounded by the fact that all four were now looking, almost scrutinising the rocks where she was hiding. To her mind, it was as if they were summoning her, which made her feel rather odd. She never felt intimidated before by any situation she'd found herself in, or by the people she'd met along the way. Today was slightly different and she wasn't at all sure why. She looked at the container, weighing up her options. She glanced up and was aware the four were narrowing the circle towards Jolinga. To her surprise, Jolinga was backing away a little. Importantly, she was backing in her direction. To her mind, there was a clear plan unfolding here and she knew to wait for the right moment. She wasn't sure exactly what she was waiting for, other than her gut to know it was the right time for her to make a move.

'You appear concerned and so you should,' Matilda said forcibly, as she took a small step in Jolinga's direction. This jolted Rebecca's memory and seeing Matilda act in this intrepidly fearless way, was exactly how she remembered her. This alone, eased her anxiety a little, and this was helped more so when Rebekha started speaking again while stepping toward Jolinga.

Jolinga took another small step backwards and glanced over her shoulder as she did. She then sniffed the air again even though she was clearly preoccupied with the four protagonists standing in front of her.

Tight-lipped, Rebecca quickly put the cork back in the container, realising she should have done this when Jolinga first sniffed the air. She'd initially thought the concoction was to be splashed over Jolinga. Although this was still the way she saw it working, she was now a little uncertain. Considering this, she reckoned she felt hesitant because she didn't know what would happen when she did use the liquid in this way. For her, this was causing a conundrum, which kind of reminded her of how she felt when her malevolent counterpart was imprisoned in Scone Priory. The idea of causing harm to anyone or anything had been something Rebecca had habitually steered

244

away from. This though, was a different scenario and without her intervention, Osgyth's life would be doomed, or so it would seem. Clearly, the more she thought about this, the more she realised, especially with these four key central characters being here, undoubtedly supporting her, it was a bridge she needed to cross.

Glancing up, and now seeing Jolinga only a few feet in front of the rock, her intuition was shouting for her to act now. She took a deep breath, the sound causing a slight twitch from Jolinga, who turned in Rebecca's direction, taking a couple of steps forward. She again sniffed the air, then turned back to the others. With her heart beating through her chest, Rebecca removed the cork from the container and holding her breath, stood up as quietly as she could. With Jolinga just a couple of feet in front of her, she leant forward and splashed as much of the liquid as possible over Jolinga.

She wasn't sure what she was expecting but watching Jolinga evaporate into the air caught her a little off guard. Mysteriously, although it was a weird experience and unlike anything she'd witnessed before, it didn't surprise her. Even so, the way this malicious counterpart seemingly dissolved in front of her was nonetheless rather unnerving. For all her mixed emotions, watching Ethernal, and the other's clearly positive facial reactions offered her some kind of reassuring support. She was in no doubt she'd done what she was here to do, even so, there was a little part of her that felt an odd amount of compassion for Jolinga. She hadn't chosen this life of malevolence it was her destiny and no more. Considering her actions, she watched as Osgyth appeared from one side of the cavern. Almost as if she had been watching from afar, her delight was all too evident. This again offered her a little reassurance.

Then the weirdest sensation passed over her, the likes of which she hadn't experienced before. When she first splashed the liquid over Jolinga, it was clear Ethernal in particular was looking directly at her. Now, it was as if she wasn't there. Just as she was trying to comprehend the way she felt, Rebekah started speaking to Osgyth.

'Osgyth, Jolinga has been expelled from this world, back to her iniquitous' lateral. You are now free to return to the above. You will not be pursued by the King who was Jolinga's unrighteous equerry.'

As Rebekah was speaking, Rebecca noticed Ethernal had gone. Although this caught her unawares, she wasn't surprised. What did surprise her was she now had no idea what Ethernal looked like. Before she had time to consider this, Osgyth started speaking.

'Did Rebecca play some part in the riddance of Jolinga?' Osgyth asked, looking around as if she was looking for her.

The fact that Osgyth looked directly in her direction without any reaction, confirmed Rebecca was once more there as an observer.

'Rebecca, our strongest yet, was the key to ridding this world of Jolinga. Her morality and inner standard were the catalysts. The potion she used to rid this world of Jolinga would only work if used by an individual who carries the same virtuous qualities Rebecca was born with.'

Rebecca wasn't at all sure how this made her feel, but before she had time to consider her emotions, she watched as Osgyth went through the weirdest state. At first, she seemed to hover above the ground, then move towards the top of the cavern, and as she got closer to the entrance by which Rebecca had entered this place, she melted into the air.

Matilda looked in Rebecca's direction. 'I see you not, although I, like us all, feel your presence. Osgyth's history has returned to its rightful outcome. You are…'

Before Matilda finished speaking, Rebecca found herself back in the secret garden. This time, she felt she was home, could feel it was her time and this settled her slightly unhinged emotions. She sat down on the wooden bench, considering how she actually felt and was a little surprised at how relaxed she was. Any thoughts of her censorious, ridding actions towards Jolinga now seemed like a distant memory. The more she thought about what had just occurred, the further it was from her consciousness. It wasn't like a faded dream, more like she read a book chapter, nodded off and woken with splintered chronicles.

She sat there for a few minutes trying to capture this moment. She felt if she could, it would answer the myriad of fragmented memories that kept nudging at her awareness. Over the last couple of days, in particular, she'd experienced many strange, almost tactile, sentiments, all just beyond her reach.

Mentally capturing how she felt, she was suddenly aware it had started spitting with rain. Without a thought that she might be anywhere other than home, she headed for the small doorway back to the kitchen courtyard.

Chapter 28 – Penny Black

As she stepped through the door into her own world, she felt a rather pleasing awareness. It wasn't just the feeling of being home, there was something else in the air. For the life of her, she couldn't put her finger on what she was feeling, she just knew it was good. Extraordinarily though, she still had this urgency nudging her inner thoughts, almost as if she was still on a journey of sorts. This notion was in complete contrast to her conscious feelings of being home. Before she had time to consider her emotions, her father opened the back door.

'Here she is, Liz, our intrepid explorer. Come in Bex, something arrived just a moment ago from Royal Mail.' He then waved her towards the kitchen.

As she entered the kitchen, her mum took one look at her and exclaimed, 'where this time?'

Rebecca shook her head inwardly. 'Is it really that obvious?'

Her mum raised her eyebrows, glanced at James, and said, 'well, for me, I can see it all over your face.'

'Same here,' her father said, 'You get this look on your face, which is difficult to explain.'

Tommy then stuck his head around the kitchen door. 'She looks like she's opened a Christmas present three days early.'

'Perfectly said, Tommy, and don't be nosey, it might be a private conversation,' her father said, kind of smiling, but clearly, he was serious.

'Nout private in this 'ousehold.' He then laughed, a little cynically, and headed off, slamming the door as he went.

'Tommy, don't slam the door,' James said in a firm, but again, slightly grinning voice. He then turned to Rebecca. 'To be fair, he is right with his analogy.'

'Cat with the cream, you'd say, Sweetie,' Elizabeth said, chuckling.

Rebecca shook her head. 'No good me playing poker then, I guess,' she said and chuckled with a smidge of embarrassment. 'So, what turned up from Royal Mail, a present from Queen Matilda?' she asked jokingly, but wouldn't have been surprised if it was.

Her father put a hexagonal-shaped package down on the table. 'Well, this is all a bit odd. The Postman was actually one of the senior Royal Mail quality managers. Evidently, they were rebuilding an early Victorian delivery office in East London and found this behind one of the sorting bays. A bit big to fall behind a bay if you ask me, and that was what he said.' Her father shook his head, 'anyway, he, Steve Davison, gave us this parcel addressed to you.' He then turned the parcel towards Rebecca and pointed. 'Three "Penny Blacks." The rarest stamps known to man. Worth a small fortune by all accounts. Shall we look inside?' he said, pointing at the package.

Rebecca glanced back and forth between the odd-shaped package and her parents. Being mindful of the stamps, she opened the parcel carefully. A little unsure what she would find inside, she definitely wasn't expecting to uncover a very old looking book. Looking at the elaborate, leather-bound volume triggered a clear memory, reminding her of the kind of thing the bookkeeper had shown her in the past. To compound this, there was a yellow rigid card serving as a book mark, exactly the same as the bookkeeper used. Once more, Rebecca glanced at her parents, feeling unusually hesitant. She wasn't at all sure why she felt like this, because normally this kind of thing would excite her.

'What are you waiting for, Rebecca? You appear very deep in thought.' Her father then walked around the table and glanced at the book over Rebecca's shoulder. 'It looks extremely old. The kind of thing you'd see under glass in a museum.'

'I don't know what I am waiting for.' She considered her feelings for a moment. 'I guess I wasn't expecting to find a book inside. I have come across books like this before but every time they were handed to me by the Bookkeeper.'

'Bookkeeper,' her father exclaimed, 'which bookkeeper?'

Rebecca glanced at her mum, knowing she'd taken her to the book shop in town that first time. To her mind, that was years ago, but she knew that was perhaps only a few days previous, certainly the way things had been panning out of late. 'Mum, you know the bookkeeper. You took me to the book shop in town, the one that disappeared after we visited it.'

Elizabeth looked at Rebecca with a blank expression. 'I don't know what you mean, Rebecca.'

'You remember, Mum. The old guy with the wispy beard and the dust-covered books.' She thought for a moment unable to know what to make of her mother's lack of knowledge relating to the book shop. 'He gave me a big old book that I brought home with me. It's still in my bedroom. Dad, you read it with me. You remember, the disappearing pages.' She paused for a moment, hearing her own words. Looking at the slightly bewildered expression on her parent's faces, she realised how ludicrous this must all sound if they had no recollection. She now found herself wondering how this could all be because it wasn't making any sense. For sure, to her mind, meeting the bookkeeper felt like a clear, but distant memory. In spite of this, she knew her journey had only started 4-weeks ago. The more she thought about it, the more confused she felt. The thing that was dominating her thoughts was knowing her mother had taken her to the book shop, and there was no doubting that. This whole episode was starting to play on her mind. For sure, she felt the moment she entered the secret garden that she was back home where she belonged. Indeed, everything that had happened since had enforced that emotion. Now though, things were a little unhinged and she wasn't sure why, or how it was making her feel.

'Go have a look for this book in your bedroom, Rebecca. As intriguing as this one is,' her mum said, pointing at the book on the table, 'I am more curious about this book with disappearing pages, from a disappearing book shop. And, I am at a loss what to think. You seem so sure I took you to this book shop, one that I have no knowledge of.'

Although her mother's words could appear a little condescending, they were anything but. Her mother's, and indeed, her father's curiosity was all too evident. Besides, Rebecca knew her parents were open to any of her suggestions. She knew her mother's tone was only reflecting how she felt, having no memory of this book shop. 'Right, I'll go fetch the book from my room.'

On the way upstairs, she started thinking about having years of memories and yet, according to her parents, everything had happened in just four weeks. None of this made any sense and just wasn't stacking up right in her thoughts. To compound her emotions, her mother having no knowledge of the book shop was just adding to her feeling something wasn't quite right. Now standing outside her bedroom door, something was odd, but for the life of her, she couldn't put her finger on anything specific. Glancing around, every tiny detail was exactly as it should be. She stood gripping the door handle to her bedroom. Something was most definitely stirring in her head and strangely, it was reminiscent of how she'd felt while living with Meredith. As she entered her bedroom, everything was just so, apart from one aspect, her bed. It was her bed for sure, complete with her new bed cover, but didn't look like it had been slept in. She'd had an agreement with her mother since she was ten or eleven that she would make her own bed, which she'd always done. Never, ever, did she do hospital corners and for all her efforts, she'd never made it this tidy. She walked around and both pillowcases still had their price tags on. As if this wasn't weird enough, they were in Euros, not UK pounds. She stood back trying to fathom out what was occurring. She turned the label over and seeing it wasn't bought at the Fenwick store totally tipped her balance. She knew for sure she'd bought the bed set while visiting Newcastle with her mum, Amanda, and Ruth. And, most definitely hadn't paid for it in euros. The weird thing was, this memory was a recent one and seemed to relate to her being 15-years-old. Other aspects of her recollections, mostly, related to her being older, as in, from another life. It was all making her feel very peculiar.

She looked at the label again, pulled it from the pillar case and headed downstairs to quiz her mother. On her way, she realised she'd completely forgotten about the book she had gone up for. She paused on the stairs for a moment and as she was nearer the bottom, reckoned she could ask her mum about the bedding, then go back for the book.

She placed the labels on the kitchen table, her curiosity at its limits. 'Mum, my new bedding.'

'What about it, Rebecca?' her mum asked, narrow-eyed.

She lifted the label and pointing, showed it to her mother. 'I thought we bought this while we were in Newcastle. The label is from a shop I don't know, Maison-Du-Monde. And, it's in Euros.' Something now nagging at the back of her thoughts was her mother calling her Rebecca twice in quick succession. Never did her mother call her Rebecca, it was always sweetie or hunny. To compound this, her father referred to her as Bex, something he'd never done before. Before she had time to consider how or what she was feeling, she could feel her mum looking at her.

Still narrow-eyed, her mum looked back and forth between the label and Rebecca. 'We went to France two days ago and bought your bedding while we were there. You must remember, we were with Jane and Rosemary, my best friends.'

Who are Jane and Rosemary, Rebecca thought? Her mind was now going in circles trying to work out what was going on.

'Did you find the book?' her father asked.

'I got distracted, sorry. I'll go back and get it now,' she said but was finding it difficult to focus her thoughts. Something was telling her to look at the book on the table first. 'In fact, I want to look at this book first,' she said, pointing to the table. She then sat down and opened the book on the first page, which read Osgyth's Story, and the year 905. If her memory served her right, something that it hadn't of late, she met Osgyth in 903. *Hmm*, she thought and opened the book on the page marked by the bookmark. She glanced at her father and started reading.

Precious Rebecca,

If this book falls to you in your world, I want to thank you for my freedom. Your actions altered my life for the good. Prior to your engagement in my time, my destiny was predestined towards a hopeless existence. I wrote this book two years after our paths crossed. I left this page blank to be completed at a later date. That day is today, the day of my wedding to the crowned Prince of York, I finished this page in this book left for you to read. I am happy. Rebecca, thank you for your fearless, earnest, and selfless actions. You will forever be in my thoughts. Your dear friend from afar, Osgyth.

She turned to her father and mother. 'Right, I am going to get the other book. Perhaps you can read this while I am looking.' She then turned the book around to face them. As she'd read the last word, something was shouting at her to return to her bedroom.

'You normally read it for us.' Her mum said, glancing back and forth between Rebecca and the book. 'This is written in an unrecognisable language. I'm not sure how you have been able to read it, and it is most definitely beyond your father's and my capability.' She then glanced at James, who nodded, appearing a little confused.

Although Rebecca wanted to explain how she could read these words, she couldn't ignore this voice in her head, compelling her to head upstairs. 'Sorry, you know what it is like when I am on a mission. I will explain all when I come back. On her way upstairs, although her thoughts should have been all over the place, what with her mum's friends who she'd never heard of, she was actually focused. In fact, the moment she heard her mum refer to Jane and whatever the other one's name was, she knew why she'd felt something was amiss. It was exactly how she'd felt when she was here when her father had died. It was just wrong. She stood at the top of the stairs looking around. Everything was right, but at the same time wrong. She knew, rather than suspected, she'd somehow returned to a life, or existence that wasn't hers. As she walked toward her room, she started wondering how many parallel lives she could have. She shook her head, and muttered, 'one true life.' The question now at the front of her thoughts was how she'd find her way back to her true world.

She entered her room and sat on the edge of the bed, unsure how she felt. Two notions were simmering in her thoughts. One was telling her to go to the summerhouse, but she was sure that was just because that was what she'd always done whenever she was lost. The other was telling her to look for the book. 'Maybe that is it,' she muttered.

'It is, page ninety-seven,' an unfamiliar young female voice said from behind her.

Rebecca felt a shiver of cold air pass over her, and slowly she turned not knowing who or what she was expecting to see.

Standing in the doorway, on the other side of her room, was a beautiful young girl, dressed in a white lace, ankle-length dress. Rebecca instantly knew this as Meredith's era. Mysteriously, the girl's image seemed to be almost floating, drifting in and out of view. Her image never disappeared, just went in and out of focus.

'I am unable to stay long in this world and am finding it hard to focus on you. I am Rebekha's daughter. I lost my battle for life after being infected with yellow fever. I was thirteen in the year, eighteen-fifty-four. I am now lost in this oblivion, floating hopelessly. Turn to page ninety-seven.' She then vanished.

Yellow fever, Rebecca thought. She'd read something only recently about the first natural cure being discovered in Venezuela. It was a plant called Verbena and she knew for sure there was some growing in the secret garden. She'd loved the delightful lilac flowers and beautiful smell since her teacher at school had brought some into class. Now on a mission in her head, she got up to head back to the secret garden. She hesitated, reckoning she had to read page 97 first. The issue was, where was the book.

Chapter 29 – Back to the Garden

She didn't need to look for long, it was in the corner, on an open bureau, one that most definitely wasn't hers. Shaking her head, she sat down at the bureau and turned the book to page 97 and started reading.

"TAKE THE VERBENA FLOWERS AND CRUSH. ADD LEMON AND WARM WATER.

THIS WILL STIMULATE EXTREME SWEATING ONCE TAKEN ORALLY, A CUP A DAY. INITIALLY, THE PATIENT WILL BECOME DISTRESSED. THIS DISTRESS, WITHIN HOURS, WILL EASE.

THE FEVERED PATIENT WILL NOT DIE."

Rebecca re-read it once more, knowing exactly where she was heading. Importantly, she knew her journey had to start in the secret garden.

She sat there for a moment considering her options. *First thing*, she thought, *get something to carry some flower heads in.* She thought about lemons but was confident, Meredith, if that was where she ended up would have lemons, but just in case would take some.

Now on a mission, she headed downstairs into the kitchen, grabbed 3 lemons, and made her way to the back door.

'Rebecca, those are my lemons for my G & T. And, no words, no book, nothing. Are we invisible?'

'Sorry, Mum, Dad, on a mission. The book is on my bureau. Really sorry, must dash.' As she opened the back door, if she'd had any doubts, she knew this wasn't her real world, her mum never drank gin and tonic. She headed around the wall and without slowing, opened the small door and entered the garden.

As soon as she stepped into the garden, she instantly smelt the verbena flowers. Seeing a large swathe of these plants in full bloom, she knew she was on the right track. She considered this emotion for a moment, and it was clear to her mind something inside was telling her she was on a path that would take her home, finally. For sure, she'd felt she was home a number of times, and this included her time with Meredith, but she'd never felt she was actually on her way home before. She considered this for a moment and once more wondered if her real world was with Meredith. She shook her head, knowing Meredith was a part of her journey and although beloved, was not her actual life.

She crammed as many flower heads into her bag, and with her hands feeling sticky from sap, she stood there looking around. As she glanced towards the rope swing in the corner, she suddenly realised the rope swing hadn't been there the last couple of times she'd been here. As she considered this, she heard an all too familiar voice.

'Rebecca, what are you doing in the garden. You were sent to stay with Millicent, while we nurse Rebekha's daughter, Lottie. She has a contagious virus.'

'Meredith,' she said and turned.

'Oh, it is you, the other Rebecca from the future.'

'I know about Lottie and have something that will help her illness.' In the back of her head, she was thinking, *Millicent, two birds with one stone.*

'It is the dreaded yellow fever and there is no cure,' she said, her eyes narrowed a little. 'Unless...' She again narrowed her eyes.

'Yes, is the answer, I have something from the future. It is a herbal remedy.'

Come, you best join us inside then. You can explain along the way.'

As Rebecca walked toward Meredith, Meredith opened her arms for a cuddle. Instantly, Rebecca knew this was the woman she knew, the woman she'd first met all those years before. Just this thought alone made her realise the world she'd just come from as a 15-year-old wasn't her true life. Her memory of meeting Meredith for the first time, although clear, to her mind, was from twenty-plus years before.

She cuddled Meredith and said, 'it is good to see you once more.'

'It feels like a lifetime ago since we first crossed paths. You are older now.'

Older, Rebecca thought and glanced at the skin on her arm. She knew there and then she was on the right path, one that was taking her back to where she belonged.

On the way inside, she explained how the remedy worked. 'So, I need a canister of warm water, a rolling pin and a flat, clean board.'

'What, may I ask, is a rolling pin?'

Rebecca then explained as best she could, and again reiterated the need for everything to be crystal clean.

'Right, follow me to the kitchen, the matron will have everything you need.'

Entering and seeing the matron stimulated Rebecca's emotions. This was a woman she hadn't seen since she first met with Meredith. Once more, she knew she was on a clear path, one that was taking her home. Now, for the first time, having noticed her reflection in the mirror and realising she was once more in her forties, had a good idea of where she might end up, and with whom. That thought though, needed to be brushed to one side for now, because she had two important issues in front of her. One was helping Lottie, and the second, hopefully having the opportunity to amend the date on the bill of reform. Although she didn't know if she was in the right year to be able to correct the mistake, she just knew inside, she was. She didn't know why, she just did. Even this emotion, for the first time for what felt like eons, felt like her own, living emotion. It was clear, almost tactile and felt right, something she hadn't felt for an age.

After a quick chat with the matron, she emptied her bag on the table.

'What a delightful smell. I know not of these flowers,' Meredith said.

'They originate from the Americas, in particular, a country called Venezuela. In my time, they grow freely in England.'

'I know not of this country you speak, however...' Meredith said and pointed to the table. She then seemed to notice the expression on the matron's face. 'Philipa, I will explain it all later. Worry not about our choice of conversation.'

Matron shook her head and smiled delightfully, although Rebecca could see she was a little at sea. She then cut two lemons in half and squeezed them into a rather elaborate glass container. Then, with a brass rolling pin, she crushed the flower heads and with a knife scraped this into the vessel. Lastly, she added the warm water and stirred the contents together. The aroma was delightful, filling the room with a spring-like odour, causing a charming reaction from both Meredith and Matron.

Rebecca turned to Meredith and explained how the potion would work, emphasising the fact that Lottie might appear to be getting worse. 'Lottie will start sweating profusely. Although this may appear alarming, she needs to sweat out the virus. She will be very poorly for some time, but then start to recover. Without this, she will lose her battle and this virus will take her life.'

'To my mind, I understand this concept. Let us go make a start,' she said and indicated towards the door.

Rebecca followed her upstairs and although she should have been surprised to find Lottie was being nursed in the room that served as her own bedroom, this actually fitted.

Upon entering the room, although appearing very poorly, Rebecca instantly recognised her as the ghostly girl who came to her. At no point had she doubted she was on the right track, this just confirmed everything was as it should be. Thinking about the way today's events had unfolded, she realised this was the first time for what felt like an age that she truly believed confidently she was heading in the right direction. Ever since she'd found herself in the secret garden, apparently as the daughter of Meredith, there had always been something amiss. It was nothing she could put her finger on, just her intuition kept throwing up questions, ones she didn't have answers for.

She glanced towards Meredith unsure who should administer the potion. 'We need to wake Lottie if we can. Perhaps it might be best if you woke her, Meredith. Especially with me being a stranger.'

'I agree,' she said and with a damp flannel, gently bathed Lottie's forehead. 'Lottie dear, you need to try and sit up. We have something that will make you better.'

Wearily, Lottie opened her eyes and turned directly to Rebecca. Lifting her hand slightly and pointing in Rebecca's direction, she whimpered, her voice weak, 'I dreamt of you.' She then closed her eyes for a second and uttered quietly, 'I was dead in my dream.'

Trying to offer some kind of reassurance, Rebecca leaned forward and whispered, 'I too had a dream about you and am here to help you get better.' As she spoke, her mind was going in circles, wondering how this girl could have seen herself as a ghost when she was still alive.

Carefully, Meredith and the matron tried to help Lottie sit up in bed.

Seconds later, Rebekha entered the room appearing alarmed. 'Lottie,' she said softly, 'how are you feeling?' She then touched her gently on the forehead.

'Mother,' she whimpered, 'I feel lost. She,' she said and pointed at Rebecca, 'came to me in a dream, and she is now with us to help me fight.'

Rebekha turned, and as if she hadn't noticed Rebecca, wide-eyed, exclaimed, 'you are back with us. I do not need to ask why you are here. You only arrive in our world when you are needed.'

'I have brought a potion from the future that will help Lottie.' Rebecca then again explained that Lottie would appear very ill before she starts to recover. She also stressed that without this remedy, Lottie would lose her battle. 'I think it best if you give her this medical drink, Rebekha.'

After a few attempts, eventually, Lottie managed to drink a full cup. She slumped back in the pillow, glanced towards Rebecca, and mouthed, 'thank you.'

Rebekha suggested she would sit quietly with Lottie and for the others to head back downstairs.

On the way, Rebecca had questions that needed answers, the issue was, only time could answer these questions. At the front of her thoughts was how long it would take Lottie to get better. This question alone caused an odd reaction and made her wonder how she could be so certain she would get better. Like everything else on this day, it was just something she knew was right. The other issue nagging at the back of her thoughts and needing an answer was when she should try to make contact with Millicent.

As she entered the kitchen, she could see Millicent and Henry in the kitchen garden chatting with two gentlemen. The way the four were dressed, to Rebecca's mind, looked like they were on their way to some kind of formal event. She turned to Meredith and asked, 'Why is Millicent here?'

'I am not sure, I thought Millicent and Henry were heading to London today on some kind of business trip, bit cloak and dagger. Let us go find out.' She then indicated toward the garden.

As Rebecca followed Meredith outside, Millicent turned and smiled. But it wasn't just a smile, she appeared delighted.

'I told you Rebecca would be here today, Henry.' She then turned to Rebecca. 'Something told me I needed to come here today before heading to London and Parliament. I do not understand why I knew you would be here, however, I did. As is so often the scenario with you my dear friend, there never is a rational explanation. Somewhere in my thoughts, I knew you would be here with a message for me.'

Once again, the events of today were panning out in a perfect manner. 'I do indeed have a message for you,' she said, briefly wondering how far her reach was, what with Lottie dreaming of her, and now Millicent somehow getting a message to be here. 'I know, and I do not fully understand why I know, you are heading to London with your bill of reform to get votes for women.'

'How you could know this is beyond me,' Henry said. 'Only us four know why we are going to London. I trust Millicent's intuition and once more, it has proved right. How this can be, well…' He glanced at Millicent and the other two men. 'So, what is your message for us?'

'Would you mind showing me the bill? I believe, no, actually, I know there is a discrepancy with the dates.'

Narrow eyed, Henry took the papers from his bag, glanced once at the top sheet, and then handed them to Rebecca. The look on his face was a mixture of reserved curiosity and bewilderment.

Rebecca took the papers. She then checked the date on the first page. 'Is today's date the twelfth of May, eighteen-fifty-four?

Henry glanced at Millicent, his curiosity all too evident. 'That date is in four days when we present our petition to Parliament. The four days allow us enough time to reach London.' Again, narrow-eyed, he glanced at the others.

By his expression, it was clear to Rebecca he was finding this all a little baffling. She then judiciously checked each page of the bill, searching for any dates. Unable to find anything, she looked up and asked, 'is there another date within this paperwork?'

'Yes, on page seven and the last page.' He then half grinned, 'You only checked the front of each page. I am not sure how you use paper in the place you live, but we use both sides.'

Rebecca then checked the back of page seven and the date matched. She then turned over the last page and sure enough, the year was incorrect. Pointing and handing the paper to Henry, she said, 'you see, the year is incorrect.'

Wide-eyed, Henry shook his head. 'We checked this many times.' He then turned to Millicent. 'How could you know Rebecca would be here to correct our mistake?' He looked down at the floor, then glanced at the others shaking his head. 'Rebecca, Millicent told me about you. To be honest, although I trust her implicitly, her memoirs of you raised a small amount of uncertainty. It would seem you are unlike us mortals.

With the two other men now staring at Rebecca, one with his mouth open a little, she wasn't at all sure if she should say anything or just smile. 'I suggest Millicent can explain while you travel to London.' To try and explain to her mother and father that she can travel through time was one thing, but she felt no need to explain her ability to two strangers. Besides, it would take too long and she just didn't feel the need. 'So, you said, you use both sides of the paper. Is there a reason for this?' she asked, both curious and trying to deflect the conversation.

'For every sheet of paper, we use both sides. If not, that is another tree that needs to be felled. Trees help the ecosystem and without them, the planet will suffocate.'

What, Rebecca thought, *they knew about this one-hundred and fifty years ago and still we let our planet burn.* 'That is true and, in the future, well, we may not have a future.'

'I would love to sit and speak with you about such things. However, we need to head to London. Perhaps upon our return.'

Millicent touched Rebecca on her shoulder gently. 'I suspect Rebecca needs to head home soon. Perhaps, when we are back, Henry, you may have an opportunity to chat.'

Hearing Millicent say she needed to head home rang a loud bell in Rebecca's head. Following a clear pattern all through this day, once more everything was indicating she was on her way home. Her only questions were where home was, how old she would be and with whom.

Chapter 30 – Back to

After they had left, Meredith suggested a cup of tea and perhaps some cake. It was a delightful late spring afternoon and so they decided to sit outside chatting.

'I could see the predicament you were in earlier. It must be difficult in such situations. How do you explain to people such as Henry's colleagues, you have travelled here from a couple of hundred years into the future?' She then chuckled, 'to use one of your delightful expressions... Really.'

'That was exactly what I thought. Besides, I could explain until I am blue in the face, but if I couldn't prove it, they would be like, lock her up.' She then thought for a moment. 'During my time with you, I have seen and experienced many different scenarios. Without going into detail, I am delighted your aunt Rebekha is with you, is well, and has a daughter.'

Meredith narrowed her eyes. 'That is most peculiar you should say this. Often, I have had this recurring dream whereby Rebekha is sent to the Americas, deemed a fool.' She pursed her lips. 'I suspect my dream may have an explanation.'

'It does indeed. It would seem to me we have many varied paths set out in front of our life. One small change can alter our very existence. I believe, my destiny is to make sure life continues down a good and even route. I am only now beginning to understand, or even comprehend my role in all of this. It would seem for every one of my kind, there is a malevolent counterpart. Their mission is to derail our life's patterns. My being and reality are to maintain humankind's equilibrium. Yeah, for sure we often chat about why I am here, and as Millicent said a moment ago, "I turn up when I am needed. For me, in the last few days, spread over many, many years, I have gained an insight into my role in all of this. Simply put, I keep the path of our life on an even keel.'

'Crumbs, that is a huge selfless burden you carry,' Meredith said, leaning forward and squeezing Rebecca's hand.

'I learn every day how far-reaching my destiny is. For example, Lottie dreamt of me. The thing is, she dreamt of me two hundred years into the future. What complicates matters, she was a lost, ghost-like soul when we spoke in my time. How can that be when she is still alive today? It strikes me she dreamt of her possible death and somehow found her way to me, perhaps knowing I could alter her path.' Rebecca then thought for a moment. 'Although it is very complex, I've learnt to accept things for what they are. I try not to analyse my path too much because that can cause my anxiety levels to heighten, and that damned anxiety can and will tell you lies. For me, the only answer, as I said just now, is we have many routes our life can follow. Some are good, some not so, it is how we deal with them. For example, Millicent felt an overwhelming need to come here today. Supposedly she listened to a quiet voice and acted upon her intuition and was right to do so. Had she ignored that little voice, she would have gone to London and ultimately their bill would have failed.'

'I must add, both situations raised many questions in my head. I wondered what had led you here today with a remedy for Lottie, and seemingly by coincidence, Millicent turns up at the right time. Clearly, going on what you have suggested, it was not a coincidence at all, it was a kind of destiny if that is the right word. If I find it complex, it must be doubly intricate and byzantine for you.'

Rebecca nodded. 'Destiny is exactly what it is and I have learnt to accept things for what they are. For sure, there are times I question my direction but have always trusted my intuition and cast aside any lies from my anxiety. Overall, I am just fine with it all,' she said and glanced down, 'however…'

'However?'

'Well, for what has felt like an age, I have been in a kind of mental limbo. One day, I am fifteen years old and your

266

daughter, then the next moment, I am still fifteen, just my mother is my mother, Elizabeth.' Just hearing her own words jolted at Rebecca's inner thoughts. 'What complicates my world of late, is having another memory of being in my forties, in the future, where I am married, with two delightful daughters, Faith and Gabrielle.'

'How do you handle these inexplicably multifaceted sets of hugely different memories? It appears you do not actually know where you belong.'

'I do not know. I do, however, for the first time, for what feels like an age, sense I am finally on a path that is leading me home.' Rebecca again considered her words. 'Wherever home is. I am trusting my gut to lead me. It has always served me well in the past. Although during the last few chapters of my life's book, I have felt lost and questioned my path. I do know now I am heading home.' She then thought about this for a moment and realised she actually did know she was on her way home. She didn't know why she knew she just did. Earlier in the day, she'd felt she was going home. Now, she was certain. 'I have had this notion all day. Now though, rather than suspect my path is taking me home, I know for certain. Once Millicent headed to London, my emotions stabilised. It is difficult to explain.'

'How do you keep your feet and emotions grounded?'

'I have asked myself this many times. I believe, because my focus is on the mission in front of me, such as helping Lottie, I can cast aside my own issues and pay total attention to what is needed.'

The two continued to chat for a while. A little later, Rebekha joined them.

'Lottie is sleeping now. She had a period of sweating profusely, whereby we had to change the bed linen three times. She is still very warm, but it would seem she is on the mend a little. This is the first time she has slept properly since she became ill.

As Rebecca sat there chatting with Meredith and Rebekha, her mind kept wondering why she was still here and if there was perhaps another twist or something else waiting for her. To her mind, it would seem Lottie was on the mend, and she'd sorted the date issue with the bill of reform. In the past, she'd always moved on once everything was complete. There were many times when she had wanted to stay and see the fallout from her intervention but realised, she was there just to make sure the various people's lives stayed on a just and virtuous path. To her mind, today was no different, so her still being there meant there must be something else.

Meredith turned to Rebecca and again squeezed her hand. 'You mentioned earlier of a time when you were here as my daughter. I have that memory somewhere in the recesses of my thoughts and can recall feeling you were my daughter. For some reason though within my distant recollections, I recall the episode felt imagined. Earlier, you said, "my mother is my mother." Those few words again stirred something and for the first time in an age, I looked at you as the girl from the future.'

'Those words had an impact on me also. I knew there and then, as much as I loved being your daughter, my mother is Elizabeth and that is where I belong. The only aspect I am unsure of is how old I am meant to be.'

'I suspect, seeing you here today as a grown woman if you are on your way home, it will be as a woman, not a girl.'

Just then matron joined them in the garden. 'Lottie is up and awake. She is asking for food.'

The last vision Rebecca was left with was the delight on everyone's faces. She was now sitting in the secret garden on her own. Before she had time to take a breath, she heard two delightfully familiar voices, calling, "Mum, where are you."

Seconds later, Gabrielle and Faith appeared through the garden door. They hurried towards her. Rebecca got up and with both arms, cuddled them tightly. As involuntary tears filled her eyes, her heart knew she was home, where she belonged.

Suffrage movement 1832 onwards.

Thank you to the British Library for the following timeline.

The article below was written by **British Library Learning.**

From the first petition to the first female MP, follow the key events during the campaign for female suffrage.

1832

August: Mary Smith, from Yorkshire, petitions Henry Hunt MP that she and other spinsters should 'have a voice in the election of Members [of Parliament].' On 3 August 1832, this became the first women's suffrage petition to be presented to Parliament.

1866

7 June: John Stuart Mill MP presents the first mass women's suffrage petition to the House of Commons. It contains over 1500 signatures.

1867

January: Manchester National Society for Women's Suffrage (MNSWS) is formed, alongside many other societies in different cities across Britain.

May: John Stuart Mill makes an unsuccessful amendment to the Second Reform Bill, which would have granted suffrage to women property holders.

1868

April: On 15 April 1868, the MNSWS holds the first-ever public meeting about women's suffrage at the Manchester Free Trade Hall.

1870

December: The Married Women's Property Act gives married women the right to own their own property and money.

1880

November: The Isle of Man grants female suffrage in an amendment to the Manx Election Act of 1875.

1894

December: The Local Government Act is passed, which allows married and single women to vote in elections for county and borough councils.

1897

The National Union of Women's Suffrage Societies (NUWSS) is formed, uniting 17 societies. Later led by Millicent Fawcett, the NUWSS favoured peaceful campaign methods such as petitions.

1902

Women textile workers from Northern England present a petition to Parliament that contains 37,000 signatures demanding votes for women.

1903

October: The Women's Social and Political Union (WSPU) is formed in Manchester at the home of Emmeline Pankhurst.

1905

The WSPU adopts the motto 'Deeds not Words,' resulting in the start of militant action by the suffragettes.

1907

February: The NUWSS organises their first large procession, where 40 suffragist societies and over 3000 women marched from Hyde Park to Exeter Hall in the rain and mud. It later became known as the 'Mud March'.

8 March: The Women's Enfranchisement Bill (the 'Dickinson Bill') is introduced to parliament for its second reading but is talked out.

Dora Thewlis and 75 other suffragettes are arrested when the WSPU attempted to storm the Houses of Parliament.

August: Qualification of Women Act is passed, allowing women to be elected onto borough and county councils and as mayor.

Autumn: 1-in-5 suffragettes leave the WSPU to join the newly-formed Women's Freedom League (WFL).

1908

April: Herbert Henry Asquith, an anti-suffragist Liberal MP, becomes Prime Minister.

June: 'Women's Sunday' demonstration is organised by the WSPU at Hyde Park, London. Attended by 250,000 people from around Britain, it is the largest-ever political rally in London. Ignored by Asquith, suffragettes turn to smashing windows in Downing Street, using stones with written pleas tied to them, and tie themselves to railings.

July: The Women's National Anti-Suffrage League (WASL) is formed by Mrs Humphrey Ward.

1909

July: Marion Wallace Dunlop becomes the first imprisoned suffragette to go on hunger strike. Later that year prisons begin to force-feed inmates on hunger strike.

October: The Women's Tax Resistance League (WTRL) is formed, a direct-action group that refused to pay taxes without political representation. Their founding slogan is 'No vote, no tax.'

1910

August: The WASL merges with the Men's National League for Opposing Women's Suffrage. The League now has a total of 42,000 enrolled members.

November: The Conciliation Bill, which would grant suffrage for one million women who owned property over the value of £10, is passed by the Commons but failed to become law. In retaliation, 300 suffragettes from the WSPU marched on parliament, where they are met with police brutality, assault, and arrests. This day later becomes known as 'Black Friday.'

1911

Emily Wilding Davison avoids the census by hiding in a cupboard in the crypt at the House of Commons.

June: On the eve of King George V's coronation, around 40,000 women from 28 suffrage societies march for female enfranchisement.

November: Asquith announces a manhood suffrage bill, which is seen as a betrayal of the women's suffrage campaign. In protest, the WSPU organises a mass window-smashing campaign throughout London. This heightened militancy continues into 1912, and spirals to include arson attacks.

1912

March: The Parliamentary Franchise (Women) Bill is introduced and defeated by 222 votes to 208.

The Labour Party become the first political party to include female suffrage in their manifesto. This was partly in reaction to the NUWSS's 'Election Fighting Fund,' which was set up to help organise the Labour campaign.

1913

April: The 'Cat and Mouse' Act is introduced (officially titled Prisoners (Temporary Discharge for Ill Health) Act). It allows authorities to temporarily release suffragettes on hunger strike, and then re-arrest them once they have recuperated.

June: Emily Wilding Davison is killed after she steps out in front of the King's horse at Epsom Derby. A member of WSPU, she intended to disrupt the Derby for the suffrage cause, though her exact motives are unknown. Thousands attend her funeral.

18 June - 25 July: 50,000 people from around the UK take part in the NUWSS's 'Pilgrimage for Women's Suffrage', which concludes with a rally in Hyde Park. The NUWSS wanted to display the suffragists' peaceful, law-abiding tactics.

December: As part of her involvement with WTRL, Sophia Duleep Singh is taken to court over her refusal to pay taxes.

The East London Federation of Suffragettes is expelled from the WSPU after Christabel Pankhurst claims that they are too concerned with other causes – such as living and working conditions.

The NUWSS reaches 50,000 members; the WSPU has 5,000 members.

1914

May: The WSPU clash with police outside of the gates to Buckingham Palace, when Emmeline Pankhurst attempts to present a petition to King George V.

July: The outbreak of World War One brings a suspension to the WSPU's and NUWSS's campaigns. Women are urged to support the war effort, and they do, as during this period nearly 5 million women remain or enter into employment.

1916

Asquith makes a declaration of allegiance to women's enfranchisement.

December: David Lloyd George, a Liberal MP, replaces Asquith as Prime Minister.

1918

February: The Representation of the People Bill is passed, allowing women over the age of 30 and men over the age of 21 to vote. Women have to be married to or a member of the Local Government Register.

November: The Parliamentary Qualification of Women Act is passed, enabling women to stand as MPs.

1919

November: Nancy Astor takes her seat in the Houses of Commons, as the first female MP for Britain. In 1918 Constance Markiewicz stands for Sinn Fein and becomes the first woman elected to Westminster, but in line with Sinn Fein politics declines to take the seat.

1928

July: The Representation of the People Act entitles everyone over the age of 21 to vote.

1929

May: Women over the age of 21 vote in their first general election. There is no majority, but Ramsay MacDonald's Labour party take over from the Conservatives.

Thank you to the British Library for the above timeline.

The above was written by **British Library Learning**

The British Library's Digital Learning team welcomes over 10 million learners to their website every year. They provide free learning resources that allow audiences to access thousands of digitised treasures from the British Library's collection and explore a wealth of subjects from children's literature and coastal sounds to medieval history and sacred texts.

The text in the above article is available under the Creative Commons License.

"Rule of Thumb"

In the popular imagination, in England at least, the 'rule of thumb' has been said to derive from the belief that English law allowed a man to beat his wife with a stick so long as it is was no thicker than his thumb.

Legal timelines for women in the UK.

1919 The Sex Discrimination (Removal) Act

Women were now able to become accountants, lawyers, and sit on a jury, or become a magistrate.

1922 The Law of Property Act

Preceding this legislation, women were forced to give up all rights to their property when they got married. This had them on a legal equal ranking to criminals and insane people.

1923 The Matrimonial Causes Act

This act allowed women to petition for divorce if their husbands had been unfaithful. Before the act was passed, only men were allowed to divorce a spouse due to adultery.

In 1937, the act included cruelty, and desertion, as grounds for divorce.

1967 The Abortion Act

This landmark ruling legalised abortions in Great Britain. However, they are still illegal in Northern Ireland.

1967 The NHS (Family Planning) Act

This act made contraception available to all women.

The act also made it legal for local health authorities to give birth control advice to unmarried women.

1970 Women can get their own mortgages

Previous to this, a woman could only secure a mortgage if she had the signature of a male sponsor.

1970 Equal Pay Act

This act made it illegal to pay women less than men for the same amount of work.

1975 The Sex Discrimination Act

This law made it illegal to discriminate against women in work, training, and education.

1975 The Employment Protection Act

This law finally made it illegal to fire women for being pregnant.

1980 Women can apply for credit cards and loans

Inexplicably, it took until 1980 before a woman was allowed to apply for a credit card or loan without first needing a man's signature.

1982 Women can't be refused service in pubs

Unbelievably up until 1982, it was legal to refuse to serve women in British pubs, which were traditionally "male environments".

1990 Independent taxation introduced

This marked women's income as their own. Prior to this, it was deemed as an addition to their husband's earnings.

1991 Rape within marriage becomes a crime

Prior to this date, it was legal for a man to rape his wife because he had "conjugal rights."

1993 Violence against women recognised as a violation

Violence against women was finally established as a violation of their human rights, under the United Nations Declaration on the Elimination of Violence against Women.

2018 Gender pay gap addressed.

Under a new government initiative, all companies employing more than 250 staff must openly declare the salaries of the men and women in their company. The concern must be that this only applies to companies employing more than 250 staff.

Millicent Fawcett

The Legend of St Osyth

The first nunnery was founded for Osyth, daughter of Redwald, the first Christian King of East Anglia and of Wilburga, his wife, daughter of Penda, King of the Mercians.

She was, when very young, entrusted to the care of St. Modwen, at Pollesworth, in Warwickshire. While there she was sent with a book from St. Edith, Alfred's sister, to Modwen, fell off a bridge into a river and was said to be drowned. Happily, she was restored to life by the prayers of St. Modwen.

Osyth's parents, as soon as she returned to them, betrothed her to Sighere, King of Essex; on her wedding day a white hart appeared, which Sighere and the rest of the male

283

party went in chase of, allowing Osyth to escape. This white stag appears on the stained-glass windows in the Chapel and the hart is also seen in other parts of the buildings too.

When Sighere eventually found Osyth she explained that she had vowed herself to Christ, and could not be his wife. Sighere was generous and religious; he accepted her decision, and let her take religious vows. Then he gave her his village of Chich, which became Chich St Osyth, and built a nunnery for her in Nun's Wood, of which she became the Abbess.

Her executioners were astonished when she picked up her head and, holding it at arm's length, walked to the village church, where she knocked several times on the door before slumping to the ground. Legend holds that every October 7th her ghost repeats the miraculous feat, and can be seen in the churchyard at midnight, holding her severed head.

The Priory Chapel, Saint Osyth.   No. 1236

1120 – Monastic Phase – Augustinian Priory Founded

St Osyth Priory is among the most important historic sites in England. The Priory was founded around 1120 and remained a home for the Austin Canons for about 80 years. It was raised to the rank of Abbey and became one of the great Augustinian Abbeys of Europe until it was dissolved in 1537. Surviving remains of the estate's Monastic Phase include parts of the claustral ranges [including the 'chapel'], gatehouses of the 13th and 15th Century and the adjacent 15th Century ranges together with the early 16th Century accommodation which is now subsumed within the present Darcy House [Abbot's or Bishop's Lodging]. It is likely that more monastic fabrics will be recognised over time, such as the 12th Century roof which has recently been discovered over the Bailiff's Cottage.

1123 – Raised to the Rank of Abbey

Raised to the rank of Abbey, it became one of the great
Augustinian Abbeys of Europe until it was dissolved in 1537.
The first Prior of St Osyth Abbey was William de Corbeil, who
was elected archbishop of Canterbury in 1123.

1537 – Reformation and Dissolution

The Abbey was dissolved during Henry VIII's
Reformation. Surviving remains of the Estate's monastic phase
include parts of the claustral ranges including the chapel,
gatehouses of the 13th and 15th Century and the adjacent 15th
Century range together with the early 16th Century
accommodation which is now subsumed within the present
Darcy House (Abbot's or Bishop's Lodging). We may
recognise more monastic fabric over time.

1553 – Dissolution and Darcy

After the Dissolution, the property was granted to Sir
Thomas Darcy, subsequently, the first Lord Darcy, who was

responsible for transforming the monastic remains, between 1553 and his death in 1558, into a substantial country house. Much of his building work re-used existing ranges, and his chequer work masonry is visible today on the Abbot's Tower, the ranges running north and west from it and on the Clock Tower. The third Lord Darcy was created Earl Rivers in 1626, and the estate passed down the line of the river until 1712. In 1671 the Hearth Tax returns recorded 76 hearths at St Osyth Priory, making it the fourth largest house in the county at the time however the physical extent of the house in this period remains unknown. Much of the scheduled ancient monument dates to this period as do the walled gardens south of Darcy's Tower and some of the oaks and sweet chestnuts in the park.

1626 Country House Estate the Rivers Period

The Third Lord Darcy was created Earl Rivers in 1626, and the estate passed down the Rivers line until 1712.

1671 Country House Estate the Rivers Period – The Fourth Largest House in The Country

In 1671 the Hearth Tax returns recorded 76 hearths at St Osyth Priory, making it the fourth largest house in the county. Much of the scheduled ancient monument dates to this period as do the walled gardens south of Darcy's Tower and some of the oaks and sweet chestnuts in the park.

1712 – Earl of Rochford

In 1712 the estate passed to Frederic Zuleistein de Nassau, the 3rd Earl of Rochford, who is regarded as the creator of the fine house that existed at St Osyth in the 18th century. Rochford concentrated his building work on the west wing of the Darcy House and added westward onto the old Bishop's Lodging creating a series of entertaining rooms which continued round to meet the west range of buildings to form a partial quadrangle. There was an oval carriage sweep and lawn to the north of a deep block and wilderness gardens to the west of this on the site of the old monks' cemetery.

The extent of the 18th-century work is considerable and included alterations to the Gatehouse where the second-floor drawing room retains its cornices of this period and to the west range of the Gatehouse which also retains many 18ths century features. The garden and park owe much of their current form to the Rochford period, the 4th Earl being a keen plantsman and au fait with all the current trends. The northern access and lodges, the ha-ha, pleasure grounds and the introduction of the Lombardy poplar into England [c. 1768] all date to the Rochford period. Frederick Nassau, the illegitimate son of the 4th Earl, was responsible for modernising the estate around 1800. It was maintained in this form until the death of his son William in 1857.

1768 – Country House Estate the Rochford Period – Gardens and Park

The garden and park owe much of their current form to the Rochford period, William Henry Nassau de Zuylestein, Fourth Earl of Rochford being a keen plantsman and au fait with all the current trends. The northern access and lodges, the ha-ha, pleasure grounds and the introduction of the Lombardy poplar into England all date to the Rochford period.

1800 – Country House Estate the Rochford Period – Modernisation

Frederick Nassau, the illegitimate son of the Fourth Earl, was responsible for modernising the Estate around 1800.

1857 – Country House Estate – Disrepair and Demolition

Maintaining the estate halts after the death of Fredericks son William Nassau, the Estate fell into disrepair two thirds of Rochford's house was demolished.

1863 – Sir John Johnson

The estate fell into disrepair following the death of William Nassau and two-thirds of Rochford's house was demolished. The estate was finally sold at auction to Sir John Johnson in 1863. He commenced his own building programme, demolishing existing buildings behind Abbot Vintoner's surviving screen wall and creating the sumptuous apartments seen in Darcy House today and extending a range of service accommodation to the east. Johnson undertook the conversion of the monks' dorter into a chapel.

The Japanese garden and lily pond together with the topiary and rose gardens within the Darcy walls are all part of his legacy.

1909 – Country House Estate – Lady Cowley

Sir Johnson died in 1909 and the Estate was maintained by his adoptive daughter, Lady Cowley, until her death in 1920 when it was sold. The Estate fell into disrepair and two-thirds of Rochford's house was demolished.

Post-1945

The Priory was acquired in 1948 by a Friendly Society for use as a convalescent home. It was subsequently purchased by Somerset Struben de Chair in 1954, and he carried out the limited restoration of the Gatehouse and adjacent ranges. Sadly, since the period of Sir John Johnson there has been dwindling investment in the well-being of the estate and maintenance increasingly became a low priority, until it was virtually non-existent. De Chair demolished the North Lodges and Workers' Cottages and sold mineral rights over large tracts of the Estate, resulting in the large areas of gravel workings that remain within the historic parkland today. During his ownership De Chair also sold off large parts of the estate. He married Juliet Wentworth Fitzwilliam, the heiress of the great Wentworth Woodhouse art collection in 1974 and part of this collection was on display at The Priory and helped bring over 20,000 visitors to The Priory when it was open to the public. Even this large influx of visitors sadly did not result in any long-term benefits to the historic estate. Sadly, De Chair died in 1995. His trustees, on several occasions, attempted to sell the estate but despite the undoubted inherent attraction, the estate possesses the enormity of the responsibilities and the scale of the investment required to repair the estate conspired to frustrate the sale process until the Sargeant family purchased it in September 1999.

1948 – Convalescent Home

The Priory was sold to the Loyal and Ancient Order of Shepherds, a Friendly Society, who founded a convalescent home.

1974 – The De Chair Period – Wentworth Woodhouse Art Collection

De Chair marries Juliet Wentworth Fitzwilliam, the heiress of the great Wentworth Woodhouse art collection.

1995 – Decline, Demolition, Sale, and Gravel Works

De Chair demolished the North Lodges and Workers' Cottages and sold mineral rights over large tracts of the Estate, resulting in the large areas of gravel workings that remain within the historic parkland today.

De Chair died in 1995. His trustees, on several occasions, attempted to sell the Estate. Despite the undoubted inherent attraction, the enormity of the responsibilities and the scale of the investment required to repair the Estate conspired to frustrate the sale process

1999 – Present and Future

Purchase by the Sargeant family, owners of City & Country the niche and UK leading award-winning heritage developers. City & Country and the Sargeant family are supported by the St Osyth Priory and Parish Trust and our Patron, George Clarke.

Together, we cherish the heritage of the St Osyth Priory Estate, preserving, restoring, and protecting it for the benefit of future generations to come whilst bringing a new chapter to the life of the Estate with new houses within the idyllic and protected heritage setting and the evolution of the Estate as a Wedding and Events venue.

Thank you to City & Country for allowing me to use the above timeline and photos.

My life within the grounds of St Osyth Priory Estate.

I recently moved, with my wife, to a new home within the grounds of the Priory. This small collection of new homes built by City & Country offered us an opportunity to effectively buy a brand new "200-year-old house.

Our home, appropriately named, "The Bookend."

The developer's attention to detail is exceptional, from real wood sash windows to hand-cast roof stiles and everything in between.

All this, within the beautiful heritage grounds of the Priory, a working, rare-breed, animal farm. Without a doubt, this wonderful environment inspired my writing, with St Osyth (Osgyth as she was originally known) making an appearance in this volume.

For me personally, living within the grounds of the Priory has nurtured my creativity. The town of St Osyth is a wonderful place to live, with the most engaging community. Being a short walking distance from the "Essex Sunshine Coast" is a real bonus. A truly unspoilt Essex town with a feeling of stepping back in time, something Rebecca knows all about. The folk hereabouts don't just say hello, they want to chat and get to know you.

Both my wife and I refer to this place as "the end of our rainbow."

The surroundings are truly inspiring.

Printed in Great Britain
by Amazon

82014538R00169